AFTER THE RAIN

LAILA IBRAHIM

Previously published in 2016 as *Living Right* by Flaming Chalice Press.

Ebook ISBN: 978-1-80508-486-0
Paperback ISBN: 978-1-80508-487-7

Cover design: Debbie Clement
Cover images: Shutterstock

Published by Storm Publishing.
For further information, visit:
www.stormpublishing.co

A strong America must also value the institution of marriage. I believe we should respect individuals as we take a principled stand for one of the most fundamental, enduring institutions of our civilization.

Congress has already taken a stand on this issue by passing the Defense of Marriage Act, signed in 1996 by President Clinton. That statute protects marriage under federal law as the union of a man and a woman, and declares that one state may not redefine marriage for other states.

Activist judges, however, have begun redefining marriage by court order, without regard for the will of the people and their elected representatives. On an issue of such great consequence, the people's voice must be heard. If judges insist on forcing their arbitrary will upon the people, the only alternative left to the people would be the constitutional process. Our nation must defend the sanctity of marriage.

The outcome of this debate is important, and so is the way we conduct it. The same moral tradition that defines marriage also teaches that each individual has dignity and value in God's sight.

President George W. Bush
State of the Union, 2004

ONE

SUNDAY, FEBRUARY 15, 2004

Jenn

The house was quiet when they got home from brunch. *Josh must still be sleeping*, Jenn thought as she threw in a load of laundry. Then she checked the answering machine. Her mom had called to say that her friend Mary had seen Jenn on the news. *Guess this is my fifteen minutes of fame*. Jenn smiled. Then she was immediately ashamed for being arrogant and admonished herself, *I didn't set out today to be on the news but to do the work of the Lord*.

She climbed the beige-carpeted stairs to check on her sick teenager. His was the middle bedroom, adjacent to the kids' bathroom. She tapped quietly. No answer. Opening the door slowly, she peered into the dark room and immediately a foul stench hit her. Her eyes adjusted and she saw the cause: vomit speckled the side of Josh's navy-blue comforter, ending in a puddle on the ground. *Oh, poor honey*, Jenn thought. He'd entirely missed the garbage can she had left in the night. Dead asleep, he likely hadn't even noticed he'd been sick. Fortunately, he was on his side, so she wasn't worried that he'd inhaled his vomit. She went to the bathroom to get washcloths and towels to wipe up the mess. As she approached the bed, she said, "Josh, it's Mom. You threw up while you were sleeping. I'm going to wipe you down."

He didn't stir. She rubbed the damp terry cloth against his slack mouth. No movement.

"Josh," Jenn said a little louder, her pulse speeding up.

She shook him gently and then urgently. "Josh!" He didn't respond.

"*Josh!*" Jenn yelled and shook him hard. His head flopped back and forth. His breathing was shallow. A wave of adrenaline shot through her body, putting every cell of her body on high alert. "Josh, wake up!"

Dear God, help my son. Jenn ran to the wooden banister overlooking the living room and called for her husband. "Steve!" Her voice was ragged and sharp, pushing down the rising force of hysteria.

Without waiting for an answer, she rushed into her bedroom, grabbed the cordless receiver, and dialed 911. *Pick up. Pick up. Pick up!*

"Hello, what is your emergency?" the dispatcher asked.

"My son," Jenn spoke in a rush. "He isn't breathing very well, and he won't wake up."

"What's your address?" the dispatcher asked calmly.

"Forty-four ninety-nine Sparrow Court, Dublin California, 94568," Jenn replied. "Off of Hawk Way."

"How long has he been unresponsive?"

"I don't know. We just got home."

"How old is your son?"

"Sixteen. Please send someone now," Jenn begged. "He needs help. He threw up while we were at church. We left him for just a few hours, and when we got back, he was like this."

The dispatcher asked, "Do you see a bottle near him?"

"What?"

"Has he taken any pills?" the woman asked in a flat voice.

"No!" Jenn was shocked. "My son doesn't do drugs."

"An ambulance is on the way."

"Thank you!" A small measure of relief washed over her. "Thank you so much."

"Keep him on his side in case he vomits again. Otherwise, don't move him."

"We won't," Jenn said. "Thank you. Tell them to hurry, please."

"I'll stay on the line with you until they arrive. Someone will be there soon."

"Thank you."

Jenn rushed to the banister overlooking the living room and screamed down into the large, cathedral-height space, "Steve. Steve!"

"What?" He came from the kitchen and looked up at her, his blue eyes wide with concern.

"Josh won't wake up. I just called an ambulance. Wait for them outside," Jenn commanded. "Wave them down so they know where to come."

"What are you talking about?" He ran to the stairs. "What's going on?"

"I don't know. Please, wait for them. Outside," Jenn begged. Steve hesitated, his eyes on the bedroom door behind her. "Steve, please."

Her husband turned to the front door and Jenn went back into Josh's room. Standing over his bed, she searched his face for some hint that he was about to wake up, but his face was slack, with no hint of awareness or response. Her heart beat so hard her chest hurt. She knelt by her son and brushed back his brown hair. The typically silky strands were stuck against his cold, clammy forehead. Something was terribly wrong.

"**Great physician, Lord Jesus Christ,**" Jenn prayed out loud, "please restore Josh to full health; Lord, if You save him, You'll be glorified through his life."

Steve led two tall men into the room, one thin and the other broad, dressed in identical blue shirts. Jenn scrambled away from the bed to give them space to work.

"Hello? Hello?"

Jenn startled at the voice coming from her hand—the 911 dispatcher on the phone.

"They're here," Jenn rushed to say into the receiver.

"Okay. Best wishes to all of you," came the steady voice.

"Thank you," Jenn replied automatically and then hung up.

Jenn grabbed onto Steve's arm, desperate for his strength, as the paramedics dealt with their Josh, working calmly and efficiently. The thin one tipped back his head and leaned over their son's face. The other searched for a vein in his arm and then inserted an IV needle. He attached wires to Josh's body and connected them to a machine. Numbers came up on a monitor: 110, 93, 73/41.

"What does that mean?" Jenn whispered to Steve without taking her eyes off the bed.

"I'm pretty sure one hundred ten is his heart rate, which is high. Ninety-three is the oxygen level in his blood. That's low. And the seventy-three over forty-one is his blood pressure—way too low. Oh, Jenn. Praise God you found him." She could feel Steve trembling.

"I didn't give him a hug," Jenn whispered. She blinked back tears.

"What?"

"I wouldn't hug him. Last night when he threw up. I was afraid I'd get sick. I could have... hugged him—" Her voice broke. "And I didn't."

"Oh, Jenn. He knows you love him," Steve reassured her. "That single lost hug won't matter."

Jenn shook her head slowly. "Of course it matters. What if

he...?" Her voice broke. Her mind flashed to a brain tumor. She'd recently read about a teenager who fell into a coma in the night and never woke up. What if her Josh was gone just like that?

An EMT interrupted her thoughts. "We'll take him to Eden. One of you can come in the ambulance."

"What's wrong with him?" Jenn asked, desperate for a reassuring answer.

"I don't know, ma'am," the paramedic said. "But he's stable enough for transport."

The other EMT squeezed a gurney into the room. Obviously experienced, they were well synchronized as they transferred Josh's floppy body out of his bed. Jenn noticed the stain on the navy-blue comforter. The matching washcloths and towels were in a heap on the sage Berber carpet. Just a minute ago, she was going to clean it up, and now that didn't matter at all.

Steve pulled gently on her arm, leading her out of the way. Rachel was hovering by his door in the hallway, her blue eyes wide, and her white skin pale.

"Mom, what's wrong with Josh?" Her voice was high and tight. "What happened?"

Jenn shook her head. "We don't know what happened. He's unconscious and being taken to the hospital. We'll find out more when we are there." She hugged her daughter and talked to her husband over Rachel's shoulder. "Who should be in the ambulance with him?"

"You go," he replied. "Rachel and I will drive. Should I call Pastor James before we leave?"

Jenn nodded. "Sara, too—she can start a prayer chain. And let Lindsay and Mark know we won't be there for dinner tonight. I can't believe this is happening."

Jenn followed the EMTs down the curved stairs; her hands trembled as she grabbed her purse and cell phone. The para-

medics loaded Josh into the ambulance and stared at the moni-
tors. The big one whispered something to his partner. The thin
one nodded and took out a long plastic straw. He tipped Josh's
head back a bit and shoved the tube down her baby's throat.

Steve sucked in his breath "They're intubating him," he
muttered. "That's not good."

Her stomach dropped.

The bigger EMT climbed out of the ambulance after stabi-
lizing Josh and pointed to a seat for her. Steve squeezed Jenn's
hand goodbye.

Jenn's foot slipped on the first attempt to join her son. She
wiped her sweaty hands on her flowered skirt and grabbed the
handle hard. As she moved up and forward, she felt Steve's
steady and supportive hands on her hips. In the back, she
settled into a small jump seat and buckled up. Josh lay still
across from her. The thin EMT sat at his side.

"Ready?" the driver shouted, and then the metal doors
slammed shut with a loud clang.

Jenn looked for Rachel and Steve through the cloudy
window, but they were gone. Scared and alone, she closed her
eyes, took a deep breath, and gazed at her sick son.

He showed no awareness of the violations to his body. His
head flopped a little with every bump. Jenn's throat tightened
in empathy at the tube coming out of his throat. It looked like it
was suffocating him, though she knew it was doing just the
opposite. The hiss of oxygen filled the ambulance. His arms
were belted tight to his side, the black straps contrasting with
the white sheet that covered his body. She wanted to touch
him, to let him feel that he wasn't alone, but he was too far
away.

Jenn heard a steady, too-fast beep from the heart monitor
and glanced at the numbers on the machine. His blood pressure
was a little higher now: eighty-six over fifty-two. His oxygen
read ninety-nine. Her mind flitted through all the possible

causes. She could only think of horrible reasons for him to be like this: meningitis, a seizure, cancer, a stroke.

God is watching over him. I trust in the Lord. God is watching over him. I trust in the Lord, Jenn intoned to herself over and over again on the long ride to Castro Valley.

At the hospital, Josh was pulled out in a rush. No one said anything to Jenn. She was uncertain what she should do but ran after the gurney as it was wheeled through the automatic sliding glass doors and into an ER bay. The paramedics spoke to the medical staff while she stood by.

A person in light-blue scrubs walked up to her with a clipboard in his hand. "You're the mother? Does he have any medical conditions we should be aware of?"

Jenn shook her head silently. Her throat was tight.

He looked up from his clipboard and repeated the question. "Does he have any medical conditions we should be aware of?"

Jenn cleared her throat. "Sorry." Of course he hadn't seen her head shake. "No. Well, last night he threw up in the middle of the night. I heard him once just after midnight. I thought it was just a bug. When we got home from church there was vomit by his bed."

He looked back at his clipboard and wrote something down without saying a word.

"Did you find an empty bottle near him?"

"No." This time she was more prepared for that question.

"Does he have any history of drug or alcohol abuse?"

"No." Jenn was emphatic.

He wrote again. "Is he depressed, or does he have a history of depression?"

"No."

"Has he had a head injury lately? A fall or a blow to his head?"

"Not that I know of. He's on the basketball team at Dublin High."

The man finished writing and turned away. Jenn looked at Josh. He was half hidden behind the doctors and nurses and other medical staff attending to him. She watched, feeling helpless. She wanted to tell them to be careful, to make sure they were doing the right thing, to think before they acted. But she just stood back, because they had done this many times before, while she had no idea what to do for her son except love him. And pray.

She caught snatches of words, some of which passed right by her while others caught in her brain like flies in a spiderweb: CBC, *blood cultures, chest X-ray, head CT.*

Staff came and went, and then suddenly the room cleared except for one middle-aged nurse. Josh looked vulnerable in the bed. The breathing tube taped to his cheek covered the lower part of his face, and wires connected his chest to nearby machines. His basketball camp T-shirt, the one he slept in, was cut down the middle. The yellow sleeves still covered his upper arms, but the rest of the shirt bunched sideways at his ribs. Jenn felt paralyzed. Was she allowed to touch him?

She looked at the nurse with a question in her eyes. The woman gestured to Jenn to come over.

"This side is easier—no IV," the nurse said with a Filipino accent, pointing to Josh's right. "You can touch his hand and the top of his head."

Jenn came to Josh's side and took his hand. It felt moist and flaccid—as if he weren't even there. She bit her lip to prevent herself crying.

"You did good," the nurse said kindly. "It's not easy to be in this situation. A lot of the time we have to take the parents out. He's stable. Now we watch. We'll make adjustments as we need to. He'll be transferred to the ICU soon."

"What's wrong with him? When will he wake up?" Jenn questioned, though her voice was shaky.

Gently the nurse replied, "I don't know. We have tests to run. Dr. Aziz will explain more when your son is settled. He's writing orders now."

The woman's tone terrified Jenn. "Josh is going to be fine, right?"

"Dr. Aziz will tell you more."

"But... what..."

The nurse shook her head. "There's nothing more I can tell you. We don't know what's causing him to be unresponsive, so we can't predict. We'll know more in twenty-four to forty-eight hours. I'm sorry I don't have answers, but I'll take good care of him—I promise. We all will. We're good nurses at this hospital."

Jenn felt light-headed, like she might faint. She grabbed the bed rail, leaned against the bed for support, and prayed, *Lord God, I trust in Your wisdom and love. I give Josh over to You. I know You'll care for him because You love him...*

Jenn was interrupted by the vibration of her cell phone. It was a text from Steve:

Update?

Jenn hated texting, so she dialed his number.

The nurse interrupted. "No calls in the ER, sorry; you'll have to go to the waiting room."

Jenn sighed. She hated texting, but she wasn't going to leave Josh. She slowly pressed the numbers on her keypad—4-4, 3-3, space...—over and over until she typed out:

he is stable. Pray.

And she hit send.

· · ·

The staff sent Jenn away while Josh was being transferred to the intensive care unit. Joining Rachel and Steve in hard plastic chairs in the waiting room, she answered her husband's and daughter's questions as unsatisfactorily as the nurse had answered hers. She'd calmed down a little since she found Josh, but her body was still on alert; the slightest stimulation would get her heart racing again.

Feeling fidgety, she pulled out her phone as a distraction—three missed calls and a new text message. Lindsay had called twice and her mom once. She pressed the button to see the unread text from Lindsay:

> Can I bring u dinner?

That's so sweet, Jenn thought. Lindsay was one of Jenn's greatest blessings. They'd been best friends since Jenn's eldest daughter Sara and Lindsay's child Rebeccah were in the church nursery together. Their kids were like cousins, and their families ate together most Sunday nights.

Jenn said to her husband, "Lin's offering to bring us dinner. What should I say?"

Steve shook his head. "I love them, but I can't handle seeing anyone right now, even them. Tell her thanks. One of us can run out for something later. Or get food from the cafeteria."

Jenn texted Lindsay back, but she wasn't ready to talk to her mom. She would be full of questions Jenn couldn't answer and would want reassurance that she couldn't offer. Instead, she attempted to center herself in prayer, to be an example of faith to her daughter, and to find a place of comfort. But she just ached to be at Josh's side. Her mind kept flitting to images of him: vomit pooled by his mouth in bed, his floppy head jostling as they put him in the ambulance, a tube sliding down his throat. She stood up. Rachel looked up at her, her brow arranged in a question.

"I just have to move," Jenn explained. "I won't go far." She paced in the waiting area while Rachel and Steve flipped through old magazines. She watched the clock intently, but it never seemed to change. Her phone rang—Sara.

"How is he? Do they know what's wrong with him?" their eldest child asked in a rush.

"He's stable enough to be moved to the ICU. We're waiting for test results."

"I want to come to the hospital. I'll take BART to Castro Valley. Dad said to ask you."

"And miss class tomorrow?"

"I don't care about school!" Sara declared. "Part of why I picked Cal was so I could be home for the important things. It matters that I'm there, too."

Jenn was touched by the passion in Sara's voice. "You know he's unconscious. He won't even know you're here."

"I'll know."

Jenn's throat tightened up. She'd be grateful to have Sara here. "Okay," she agreed. "Call us when you get to the station. One of us will come."

"Thanks, Mom. I love you. Tell Josh I love him—even if he's asleep." Jenn heard the emotion in her daughter's voice.

"I will. Love you, too."

She walked over to Steve and Rachel. "Sara's on her way."

Jenn looked at the clock again. It had been forty minutes since she left Josh. They said the transfer would take half an hour. Her anxiety revved up with each passing second and she said to Steve, "This is taking too long. What if something's wrong?"

Steve took her hand and pulled her down to the chair next to him. "Jenn, we're all scared for him, but leaping to conclusions based on nothing is pointless and harmful."

"It's just where my mind keeps going. I feel so much better when I'm with him."

"Let them do their jobs," Steve reminded her.

"Family of Josh Henderson," a nurse called from the desk.

Jenn rushed to the station with Steve and Rachel trailing behind. "We're here."

"Only two at a time in the ICU," the nurse explained. "You can trade off."

Jenn was crushed. "Can we just have a few minutes with him as a family? Just in case, you know..." She couldn't go on. Her eyes welled up and Steve put an arm around her. "I'm sorry..." Jenn began.

"You don't have to apologize," said the nurse. "No one wants to be here."

Jenn gave a shaky nod. The nurse explained, "I'll let the three of you go back. But they'll probably kick one of you out. Be calm and quiet, and you might get ten minutes together."

"God bless you. Thank you," Jenn said.

"He's in bed six," the nurse told them.

"Thank you very much," Steve said as they were buzzed through.

Jenn held Rachel's hand as they walked down a short, bright hallway. She hated to be so emotional in front of her daughter, but it was hard to be a strong and confident mom in this situation. The ICU was an open room with rows of beds separated by curtains. Josh lay in the third bed to the right. His color was better, but he seemed just as small and vulnerable as he had in the emergency room.

A young white nurse with bleached-blond hair introduced herself. "I'm Jessica. I'll be with Josh until this evening."

"How's he doing?" Steve asked.

"He's stable. So far, so good," the nurse replied. "Were you told he's only supposed to have two people at the bedside in the ICU?"

Jenn took a deep breath to keep herself calm. "We want to

say a family prayer over him," she pleaded. "Then one of us will go."

"Okay." The nurse consented. "Five minutes?"

Jenn nodded. She smiled at Rachel and gave a thumbs-up. Her youngest child's eyes were red and puffy. When had she started crying? Jenn hugged her close and murmured soothing words into her hair. "He's going to be okay. I have faith... in God and in the doctors."

"I'm so scared," Rachel said. "How could this just happen with no warning? What's wrong with him?"

"We don't know, honey," Jenn said, pushing aside her worst thoughts. She wanted to offer some comfort to her daughter, so she explained, "The doctors will know more soon."

Just then a middle-aged man with dark complexion, hair, and eyes walked up. "I'm Dr. Aziz. I'd like to update you." He glanced at Rachel. "Can we speak in private?" Just that question scared Jenn.

The doctor led the parents to the other side of the curtain, giving them a small veneer of privacy.

"What's wrong with Josh?" Steve questioned.

"We don't yet know what's causing your son's condition," Dr. Aziz explained. "But we've stabilized him. We pumped his stomach and took blood. The lab should have results soon. He's getting fluids to increase his blood pressure and keep him hydrated. We'll know more in a few hours. Has he been sick?"

"He threw up last night. That's the first we knew of anything," Jenn replied.

"Does he have a history of drug abuse?"

"No!" Jenn replied. "Why do you people keep asking me that? He's Christian. He does not use drugs."

"I'm sorry, ma'am. We want to rule everything out. Most of the time, with a presentation like this, it's an intentional or unintentional drug overdose," Dr. Aziz said. "I'm not saying that's the situation with your son, but we haven't ruled it out. We're looking into infection, medication, and diseases or disorders. When I have more answers, I'll find you. You don't believe he has a concussion or has had trauma to the head recently?"

Steve shook his head.

"Did you give the nurse your phone number? For updates."

"If you have something to tell us, you can find us in here," Jenn said, more sharply than she meant to. "My husband and I will be by our son's side."

"Thank you, doctor," Steve interjected evenly.

"Yes, thank you." Jenn sighed. "Sorry I'm so upset."

"This is a difficult situation," the doctor said calmly. "I'm on until eight o'clock tonight. Hopefully I'll be back with some results before I leave."

The family gathered around Josh, and Steve spoke a prayer, asking for wisdom for the doctors, healing for his son, and faith for his family. Jenn concentrated intently. Then Steve took Rachel back out to the waiting room.

A nurse put a chair by the hospital bed for Jenn, a very welcome gesture of support. The constant beep of the monitor was oddly comforting. Jenn stared at it as if it were a video game. She prayed for Josh's pulse to slow down and his blood pressure to go up. It wasn't much, but she knew to ask for that. She startled whenever the blood-pressure cuff filled up without warning. In contrast, Josh didn't notice it at all. He lay there oblivious to his surroundings, with an IV in his arm and a tube of oxygen down his throat.

Jenn held Josh's hand and sang quietly into his ear. She started with the lullabies she had sung to him as a baby and then moved on to his favorite church hymns. When she got hoarse from singing, she sat up and studied his face. It had changed so much. All traces of baby fat were gone. His dark lashes and eyebrows were thick and healthy, and stubble covered his skin.

She didn't realize he needed to shave every day. When did that happen? Her thoughts were interrupted by a tap on the shoulder.

Steve stood over her. "We got some dinner when we picked up Sara. Rachel has a burrito for you. You sit with her and eat; Sara can come in when you go out."

"Can you just bring it to me?" Jenn asked.

"Rachel needs a little time with you, and Sara wants to see Josh," Steve countered.

Jenn was so focused on Josh that she was being selfish. She shook her head. "Of course," she said as she stood up. "We're going to get through this, right?"

"Of course we are," Steve replied. "And so is he."

She reached for Steve's arm. "Are you sure? Do you know deep down that God does not want him home yet?"

"I'm sure of it. I feel it in my bones. Josh has something he's called to do on Earth. He hasn't done it yet, so it's not his time to go home."

Steve's words were a balm to her soul. His certainty filled her with confidence. Jenn nodded and gave Steve a long hug. Then she forced herself to break away to find her daughters.

When Jenn walked through the double doors into the waiting room, Sara was standing right there. Her blonde hair was pulled back into a messy ponytail, and she didn't have any makeup on. She looked close to tears. Jenn opened her arms wide, and Sara melted against her body. After a few breaths, Sara broke away.

"How's he doing?" her older daughter asked.

"He doesn't look too bad, if you ignore the tube coming out of his mouth," Jenn explained.

"Okay. I'll just look at his gorgeous hair," Sara joked weakly as she was buzzed through.

Jenn looked around the harshly lit waiting room for her

third child. Rachel sat alone, flipping through a magazine on her lap, unconsciously picking at the skin on her thumb. Jenn felt a welling up of sympathy for her youngest. This situation was hard enough for her to deal with as an adult; it had to be more overwhelming for a fourteen-year-old.

"What'd you get me?" Jenn asked casually as she sat down.

Rachel looked up, startled. "Oh... hi, Mom. Chorizo with everything. We know what you like."

Jenn smiled as she took out the shiny, aluminum-wrapped meal. It was warm and substantial in her hand. She hadn't realized the comfort one could get from a burrito.

"How's Josh?" Rachel asked, hope and fear in her voice.

"Same," Jenn replied. "Stable. Whatcha reading?"

"*National Geographic.*" Rachel turned the magazine so Jenn could see the spread of marine animals. Images of penguins, sperm whales, and dolphins filled the pages. Rachel pointed to a page. "Aren't they adorable?"

Jenn nodded with a smile. "You've loved penguins since that trip to the Monterey Aquarium when you were four."

"What's not to love? They're cute, and they waddle, and they cuddle with each other. They're the best animals ever."

"It's been too long since we've gone to the aquarium... Maybe we could go over Easter break."

Rachel perked up. "Really?"

"No promises, but..."

"Josh'll be fine by then, right?"

Though Jenn had her fears, she didn't share them with her daughter. "There's no reason to think he won't be. He's in the Lord's hands. Just keep on praying for him."

Rachel leaned her head against Jenn and went back to the magazine. Despite the pit in her stomach, Jenn ate the burrito. She wanted to say the perfect words to her daughter, to reassure her that their lives were not turned upside down irrevocably, but she couldn't offer Rachel something she wasn't certain of herself. As hard as she tried, she couldn't imagine an innocuous explanation for Josh's illness. She desperately hoped he could be cured with an antibiotic or some simple medicine, but her mind kept flitting to a brain tumor. She knew it was dramatic, but it was her biggest fear.

After eating most of her dinner, Jenn texted Sara to trade back. When she got to Josh's bedside, Steve's brow was furrowed. Jenn's heart skipped a beat.

"What's going on?" she asked. "What happened?"

"Dr. Aziz stopped by before his shift ended," Steve explained. "None of the tests show anything that would cause this."

"That's bad?" asked Jenn.

Steve replied, "He says this profile is entirely consistent with an overdose of sleeping pills."

"That can't be it—you know that, right?" Jenn insisted. "There's no reason for him to take sleeping pills. Where would he get them?"

"I don't know." Steve changed the subject. "It's late. Rachel needs to get home. Do you want to stay here tonight or be with the girls?"

"I can't bear to leave him. Can I please be the one to stay? I'll call you right away if there's a change," Jenn promised. "Is that okay with you?"

"That's fine." Steve rubbed his head. Jenn felt a rush of gratitude for her husband.

"Rachel asked me if she has to go to school tomorrow. I don't think so. What about you?" Jenn asked.

"No," Steve answered. "It's one day of ninth grade. I doubt she could concentrate anyway."

"I can't believe this is happening."

"Me neither," Steve agreed. "Do you want me to bring you back some other clothes for the night?"

Jenn looked at her church outfit: flowered sheath, hose, and blue flats. She wasn't comfortable, but it didn't matter. She pulled the small gold hoops off her ears and slipped the gold bangles from her wrist. She shook her head. "I'll be fine; just take these."

Steve kissed his son's forehead. Then he gently cupped his head and stared down at him. Tenderness welled up in Jenn. Steve stepped away, his eyes moist, gave her a long hug goodbye, and left.

Once again, she was alone with Josh and the sound of beeping machines. Jenn was finally ready to contact the outside world. Unlike the ER calls were permitted in the ICU. She dialed her childhood number in Orange County. The Southern California suburb she grew up in had no defined urban center except, perhaps, for Disneyland. In sharp contrast to her current home in the San Francisco Bay Area, Orange County was a center of conservative political and religious values. Jenn had made peace with being a conservative in a liberal bastion, and there was a lot she preferred about the Bay Area, including the weather, the food, and the traffic.

On the third ring, her mother picked up. "What's wrong? Sara asked me to pray for Josh, but she didn't say more than that." Her mom sounded as worried as Jenn had expected.

At the sound of her voice, Jenn's eyes welled up. "Oh, Mom. Josh was passed out when we got home from church. I'm at the hospital with him."

"Is he okay?"

"They don't know what it is," Jenn explained. "He's still unconscious."

"Josh is sick? Really sick?"

Jenn nodded even though her mom couldn't see her. "The doctors are running tests. We should have answers in a few hours. I don't want to worry you, but I knew you'd want to start praying for him."

"Oh, honey, of course. I'm so sorry. For you and for our Joshy. The prayer chain has already been started."

Jenn felt a sweet comfort from her mother's words. "Thanks, Mom. That means a lot."

"What's his doctor's name? We'll include him in our prayers."

"Dr. Aziz. At least for now. A new one will come on soon."

"That's not a Christian name, is it?"

"No, Mom. But he seems like a fine doctor." Her mom's not-so-subtle biases always rubbed Jenn the wrong way. Jenn chalked it up to age, but it was hard to hear and even harder to know how to respond.

"We'll pray for the Lord to guide all his doctors to find what's wrong with Josh and for Josh to be strong in mind, body, and spirit. Josh knows the Lord's love so deeply. I know he's being held by Jesus right—"

Jenn's phone beeped. She looked at the screen. It was her home number.

"Mom, I'm getting a call from Steve or one of the girls. I have to go. I'll let you know when we learn more. I love you. And tell Dad I love him."

"Will do, honey. And don't you worry, God's going to fix Josh right up."

Jenn accepted the other call.

Steve's voice came through: "It's me."

"There's no change," Jenn said.

"I searched Josh's bedroom," Steve explained.

"Why did you do that?" Jenn asked, upset though she didn't know why.

"I had to be certain. Are you sitting down? This isn't good."

"You're scaring me."

"I didn't find anything in his room, so I searched all the trash cans. I found an empty bottle of Ambien in the garbage outside."

A hot wave passed through Jenn. "Dear Lord! Where could he have gotten that? What doctor would give a sixteen-year-old Ambien without permission?"

"It wasn't made out to him," Steve explained gently. "It's yours."

Jenn's stomach lurched. "Mine?"

"The bottle was empty. Do you remember how many were left in it?"

Her brain buzzed. It was hard to think. "From our trip to France last summer? For the flight?"

"Jenn," Steve pushed her, "how many pills were in the bottle?"

"Most of them. I only took three: one for each flight and one to sleep the night we got there. How many were in the prescription?"

Steve paused and then replied, "It says thirty."

Adrenaline coursed through her veins, and she started to shake. "Josh took twenty-seven sleeping pills?"

"You have to tell the staff right away," Steve instructed.

"Why would our son do that?" Jenn questioned her husband. "Why would our Josh hurt himself?"

TWO

Jenn

Jenn flipped the channel to Fox News, her morning cooking companion. The news floated in the background as she pulled out ingredients—eggs, bread, OJ, sausage, yogurt, protein powder, and frozen blueberries—and placed them on the beige soapstone countertop. She knew what everyone in her family liked for breakfast and took pride in starting their days off right.

The eggs, sausage, toast, and OJ were for Steve. He preferred his eggs over easy but didn't like to get in a rut, so every few days she scrambled them. Today was a scramble day.

Sara and Josh liked smoothies. This morning would be blueberry-banana but only for Josh, a junior at Dublin High. Sara, a freshman at UC Berkeley, came home only on the weekends, though lately she'd been staying on campus many Friday and Saturday nights, too, coming home only for church on Sundays. Jenn didn't like to use frozen, but her kids preferred berries, and there weren't any fresh this time of year.

Rachel was her picky eater. Youngest kids seemed to go either way: flexible or fussy. Rachel went finicky. She ate white toast with sweet butter and strawberry jam for breakfast. A few times a year, she would get in a Frosted Mini-Wheats phase, but right now she wanted all white bread, all the time. Jenn had hoped that her tastes would expand now that she was in high school, but so far they hadn't.

Jenn thought through her day while she cooked. Thursdays were spacious because she didn't drive carpool. She'd meet Lindsay for their walk in the neighborhood at nine-thirty. After that she'd run her errands: first the dry cleaner's and then Walgreens, Jo-Ann Fabric, and Safeway. She never shopped for groceries anywhere else, out of loyalty to Steve's employer. She might even take herself out to lunch. Something else was on her errand list, but she couldn't remember what it was. She ran through her family in her mind, finally getting to Wynnie, their golden retriever. Then she remembered they needed dog food and added Pet Food Express to her mental list.

"Breakfast!" she yelled up to her family. Josh arrived first. Her middle child took after her, with the Mediterranean look that some people of French descent shared. They had the same brunette hair and dark-brown eyes with olive skin that tanned easily. Before she and Steve had had kids, she'd thought their sons would take after him and their daughters would resemble her. But it went the other way—Josh looked like her, and the girls had Steve's Scandinavian features: golden-blonde hair, blue eyes, and pale skin.

"Do you know what time we have to leave for your game tomorrow?" Jenn asked.

"Coach wants the drivers at three," Josh replied.

"I'll be there."

"Thanks, Mom."

Jenn smiled at her son. "Of course."

Rachel walked in and asked, "Did you sign my paper for the field trip to the Lawrence Hall of Science?"

"There's an envelope by the computer in the study with the

form and a check. Let me know if they need drivers. It didn't ask for them on the permission slip."

"I think they got a bus, but I'll tell Ms. Ahn," Rachel replied as she pulled her long hair into a high ponytail. Then she grabbed her toast and started to leave.

"Sit, Rachel," Jenn commanded. "Your dad will be down in a sec. You have time for a prayer before school."

On cue Steve walked in. Even after nineteen years of marriage, her heart swelled when she saw him. God had chosen well when He put Steve in her path during her junior year of high school. They were true partners in this life, both doing their roles to make their family strong. He'd never disappointed her. They sat down, reached their hands around the table, and formed a precious connection.

Steve prayed, "Dear Lord, thank You for the night's rest You gave us. We accept this new day as a gift from You. May we use it minute by minute to do Your will. Help us to treat everyone kindly, fairly, and thoughtfully and to know that there is nothing we can't handle with You. In Jesus's name we pray. Amen."

"Amen" echoed around the table.

Rachel grabbed her toast, kissed her parents goodbye, and left.

"Did you make a reservation for Saturday?" Josh asked. The kids were insisting that Steve take Jenn out somewhere nice for Valentine's Day... without them.

"Yep," Steve replied. "Seven o'clock at McNamara's Steak House." Steve wiggled his eyebrows. He loved a good steak.

Rachel yelled from the study, "Mom, it's not here! I'm going to be late!"

"What's not where?"

"My permission slip!"

"Look again, Rach. On the right side of the keyboard."

"I can't find it!"

Jenn sighed and went into the study. She spotted the envelope immediately.

Pointing, she said, "Right there, Rach."

"Oops. Sorry, Mom. I thought it would be a big envelope."

"I swear you couldn't find—" Jenn stopped herself. Insulting Rachel's observational skills wouldn't help her daughter to mature.

Rachel shrugged and rushed out.

Josh was asking a question when she sat back down to breakfast. "Can we go to *Catch that Kid* on Saturday?"

"What's it rated?" Jenn asked.

"It's PG, but at youth group Pastor James said it's wholesome."

Steve said, "If he says it's appropriate, then sure. Who are you going with?"

"Just Sara and Rachel. You know... a sister-brother Valentine's thing," he said with a wry smile.

"Sounds fun," Jenn said. "Any requests for dinner? I'm shopping today."

Immediately Josh replied, "Fettuccine Alfredo. And Caesar salad."

"Yum," Jenn agreed. "Pasta it is. With some chicken—protein, you know."

Josh laughed. "Yes, the all-important protein." He cleared his plate, kissed Jenn on the head, and headed out.

"Can you take in my blue suit today?" Steve asked.

"It's already on my list," Jenn replied. "I'm getting ribbon for the welcome team at church. I'll swing by the dry cleaner's on my way."

"You're getting so involved with the welcome team," Steve commented.

Jenn shrugged. "It's creative and helpful to the church. I love knowing I'm guiding new Christians to a deep relationship with Jesus. Pastor James asked me to be the chair next year."

"Are you going to say yes?"

"If you don't mind," Jenn said. "We meet during the day, so it won't affect the family too much."

"Not at all. It's good for you to do things outside the family."

After cleaning the breakfast dishes, Jenn went to her room to pray, with Wynnie following close behind. Jenn got comfortable in her favorite chair in the corner. It was covered in a blue and tan plaid fabric that brought the colors together in the room.

The Bible on the little table next to the seat was a gift from her mother on her wedding day. The holy book had been her grandmother's, given to her on *her* wedding day. Jenn felt God here. She closed her eyes and took in the warmth of the sunlight streaming through the window, like a blessing directly from the Holy Spirit. Her body and mind calmed quickly. Then she spoke silently to her Lord.

"God, thank You for the power of the Holy Spirit. I ask that Your presence fill me with wisdom and revelation so that I may follow You, love You, and serve You entirely. Bind up all distractions and show me Your will for me. In Jesus's name I pray. Amen."

And then she listened. Some days God spoke clearly to her, and other days she didn't hear anything. Some days her mind wandered to her to-do list, and others she could really listen. Today she was focused, and God was quiet. She took that as a sign that her life was on track. Jenn got up, put on her walking shoes, attached Wynnie's leash, and set out to meet her best friend.

Twice a week, on Tuesday and Thursday mornings, Jenn and Lindsay met for a walk, usually in their suburban neighborhood, but sometimes they hiked at Marshall Canyon. Dublin, named for the Irish city, had bright-green rolling hills in the winter and spring. Once it stopped raining, they turned

golden brown, reminding her of the hills of her childhood in
So Cal.

The two women leaned on each other in all things—most
especially in guiding their kids in righteous living. Both women
would have preferred Christian schools, but neither family
could afford that on one salary. They were a team, fending off
the secular influence of public schools.

"How's your dad?" Lindsay asked.

"Much better," Jenn replied. "He's still tired, but the antibi-
otics knocked out the bronchitis."

"Mark's leaving for OC tonight, so he can be there when his
dad gets the stent tomorrow. Guess we're hitting the sandwich
generation time of life."

"Yeah," Jenn agreed. "When did we start worrying about
our parents as well as our kids? I feel like a stereotype
sometimes."

"Me, too!"

"Let me know how I can help when Mark is gone."

"Thanks, honey." Lindsay smiled at her friend.

Jenn switched topics. "I'm getting ribbon for the welcome
board today. Do you think crosses are too much?"

Lindsay shook her head. "As far as I'm concerned, there can
never be too many crosses! Or too much glitter." They both
laughed.

THREE

FRIDAY, FEBRUARY 13, 2004

Josh

Josh sat on his bed cramming in trig homework before dinner. He had to finish so he'd have time to write that essay for AP lit. Fitting in schoolwork, family time and practice was getting harder and harder. Junior year was make or break. He had to hang onto his GPA if he wanted to get into any college next year.

"Steven!" Mom's voice interrupted his concentration. "Steve! Come quickly!"

Josh rushed downstairs. Mom was standing in front of the television, disgust on her face.

"What happened? Are you okay?" Josh asked. He glanced at the screen and saw a mass of people protesting in San Francisco—not anything out of the ordinary. Mom often got worked up by news that didn't really affect her directly, but her concern looked real.

"Get your father," Mom replied without looking at him.

"He's next door—returning something to the Engs. Should I

go get him?" His voice, tight and high, made him sound like a kid.

She looked at him and shook her head. "No, it can wait a few minutes."

"What happened. Another attack?" He pictured the planes on 9/11, but there wasn't anything like that on the screen.

"No, honey, nothing like that. It's bad, but not *that*." She exhaled with a sigh. "I'm sorry to worry you. It's just something on the news. Gavin Newsom is mocking marriage."

"The mayor of San Francisco?" Josh asked.

"Yes. He's giving out marriage licenses to homosexuals," Mom said. "Remember the sermon from a few weeks ago? This is what the pastor was talking about. This is a blatant political attack on family values."

Josh's stomach dropped. He tried to keep his face blank, but he feared he was flushing bright red.

"Honey, you don't need to worry about this. It doesn't affect you," Mom stated.

She hugged him. He squeezed back hoping to seem like this wasn't personal for him. It was, or it might be, but he *never* wanted her to know that.

When she released him, she said, "After dinner, let's register you for the ACT and SAT, okay?"

Josh nodded and mumbled something noncommittal. He'd rather not do it tonight with all the homework he had to finish, but he didn't want to argue or explain. Mom didn't get the pressures in his life. She thought going to college was like when she was young: apply to one school, you get in, you pay for it with a summer job, and you go there. She had no idea how competitive getting into college was... or how much it cost. Just because Sara was accepted to a bunch of great schools didn't mean that he would be. He wasn't Sara, nowhere close.

And now this was on the news. He'd be distracted—wanting to ignore it, but fascinated by it, like the GSA sign in Ms.

Hodder's class or Justin. Thinking of Justin made Josh's heart speed up in the wrong way. He didn't want anyone in this house to be thinking about homosexuality—in any context.

Dad walked in and Mom pointed to the TV. "They're breaking God's law in San Francisco, not to mention state and federal laws, too."

Dad opened his arms, inviting Mom into an embrace. She leaned against his chest, her face turned toward the television. The two of them were such a team. As Christians, Dad was supposed to be their family captain, but it was obvious that she was a co-captain.

Josh was fine with their firm leadership when he was a kid. Some of his friends talked back to their parents. Not in their family. His Mom and Dad were loving, but clear that they expected *complete and immediate obedience*. That was easy when it came to brushing his teeth and doing homework, but when it came to what he felt inside, he was a complete failure at *complete and immediate obedience*. His parents had no idea what a failure he was.

He was supposed to be ready to make his own perfect life. If Josh ever showed any opinions different from hers, Mom rushed in with a solution, so he'd stopped sharing his doubts or insecurity. She didn't want to know that he was scared he might not get into college. Or that his track friends got high on the weekends. Or that there weren't any girls that he liked. She acted like *she* was a failure if he wasn't one hundred percent confident and successful.

He watched the news with his parents all cuddled up. On the TV, a crowd of people were amassed at City Hall in San Francisco. More than three hundred homosexuals had been given marriage licenses during the day. There was a long line of people snaking around the entire block waiting for their turn. City leaders planned to give them out on Friday, too.

A commentator on the TV said, "Marriage is between a

man and a woman for the purpose of creating a family. These people want to destroy the most basic foundations of society. These attacks on our values are going too far."

"It's just wrong, and so close to our home," Mom said. "We need to do something to stop it. Should I call Governor Schwarzenegger?"

Steve shrugged. "Pray on it, Jenn. God will guide you."

They stood watching arm in arm until the next commercial.

Mom turned the TV off. "Josh, tell your sister it's time for dinner."

His trig assignment wasn't done. Once again, he'd have to stay up late, but he just nodded and did as he was told.

After the prayer Rachel launched into a long story about a cat in the cafeteria at lunch. Josh pretended to pay attention, but his mind wandered to what he had seen on the TV and then he pushed it away. He didn't want to care about what was happening in San Francisco.

"Josh." Dad's voice got his attention.

"Sorry, what?" Josh responded.

"Can you help me in the garage?" Dad asked.

"Now?" Josh asked. "For what?"

Mom spoke in that disappointed tone: "Josh, dinner is family time. Please focus on the conversation."

Josh nodded.

Dad explained, "I was saying that the ants are getting into the garage somewhere. I need to pull everything from the back wall to spray and caulk in the corner. Can you help me after dinner?"

"I have trig and AP homework," Josh replied. "Can we do it over the weekend?"

"Josh," Mom chastised, sounding mad and disappointed at the same time, "you can help your dad for ten minutes."

"Ten minutes, Josh. No more," Dad reassured. "Some of it's too heavy for me to move alone."

"Of course," Josh acquiesced.

Dad said, "Want to do your math first—then take a break to help me?"

"Yeah. Thanks, Dad. I'll finish my trig and then find you in the garage."

Mom said, "After dinner I'm going to pray for all those people in San Francisco and for our purpose. It's just like Senior Pastor Williams spoke in that sermon a few weeks ago. Homosexuality is harming good families by leading children astray from God's rules."

God's rules. It was easy to live by them when Josh was young: obey his parents, avoid unholy temptation, pray, love God, and be kind. His parents set the path, and he walked it. But he was listening for God's path on his own now. Which sport? What college? Which friends? A girlfriend? How could he know what was a distraction and what was his purpose?

He prayed to live righteously, but God wasn't taking away his sinful longings.

He finished trig and went to help Dad. Hopefully it would be as quick as promised. The math had taken longer than he wanted.

Dad had already taken all the boxes off the shelves and piled them up in the middle. He was leaning over the work bench peering at the wall behind it.

"I'm here," Josh interrupted.

"Great. Help me move this bench. I can't see where they are coming in. Actually, can you get the flashlight first?"

"Sure, Dad." Josh tried to keep the sigh out of his voice. He actually liked working with Dad on things. When he was a kid, he'd skip playing with friends to do house projects. But skipping homework or practice wasn't an option.

He went into the house and returned with the flashlight.

"Help me pull this away from the wall, just enough so I can

get behind it. And move two shelves—then you can get back to your homework. I know you have a lot to fit in after practice."

"Thanks for understanding, Dad," Josh said. "It's not that I don't want to help." His voice broke. Why was he so emotional. He took a slow breath. "I do want to be part of the family and help out. I just have a lot going on."

"I get it. I remember being sixteen." Dad smiled. "Ready?"

Josh nodded and lifted his side of the workbench. Dad thought he got it, but he didn't, couldn't. If Dad knew what was in his heart, he'd be... shocked? Ashamed? Devastated? All of them?

Josh didn't know what Dad would be, but it wouldn't be good. He never wanted Dad to know that he was struggling for righteousness. His plan was to overcome his sinful nature without ever revealing his struggle to his parents.

Mom rushed into the garage, looking like she'd won a prize at Great America.

She started talking to Dad right away. "Steve, I just prayed. I said to God: You know about the tragedy in San Francisco. You know Massachusetts has already succumbed to the forces of secularization. Show me what You want me to do about it. Help me know what to do to protect my family. Clear as a bell He answered: 'Love my children.'"

Mom teared up, she was so happy. Josh used to have that kind of response from God, and he desperately wanted it now, but He hadn't removed Josh's lust no matter how much he prayed for that.

"He said to *love His children* and then sent an image of Pastor James. It's pretty clear, don't you think?"

"Seems like Pastor James is your next step," Dad said. "Call him up and offer him your hands for this ministry. You've been looking for a little more to fill your time now that Rachel is in high school. I think you're being called."

"You think so?" Mom asked. "To do what?"

Dad shrugged. "I don't know. Write a letter or make phone calls. The pastor will have ideas. You know he saw the news tonight and has a heavy heart, too."

"I bet Lindsay will want to team up with me. In the morning I'll call the church to offer my hands for this ministry." Mom sounded excited. "Thanks, hon."

They made each other so happy. Envy rose in Josh. Would God ever grant him that kind of love?

Every day Josh prayed to feel that way about a girl, but it hadn't ever happened. He wanted to feel lust like his friends. He used to think he'd been especially blessed by God because he was spared from unholy thoughts about girls, but eventually he realized his lust was worse, far, far worse. It had taken him years to see it—he didn't feel that way about girls, but he felt that way about boys. It made him sick to admit it to himself. His struggle for his soul was a secret from everyone he loved. He only wanted to overcome his sinful nature, but he was losing faith that he could.

Mom was waiting in the parking lot after school so she could drive to the game. She waved him over to the Land Cruiser. He left his friends and leaned against the driver-side door.

"My meeting with Pastor James went very well." She spoke in a rush, like Josh had been waiting to hear this information. "He wants us to invite the whole youth group to stand up for our values. We'll invite everyone from the youth group and their parents. Sara's going to meet us at the West Oakland station. Hopefully we'll get at least ten kids to go with us. After the game you and I are going to make signs."

Adrenaline rushed through Josh. His heart raced and his palms were sweating, but he kept his face calm. Going there, to San Francisco, being surrounded by those people? He couldn't do that.

Glad for a legit excuse, he kept his voice matter of fact, "Sorry, Mom. I can't go—game tomorrow."

"You'll have to skip this one," Mom replied. "Sorry."

"You want me to miss a basketball game? No, Mom."

"Josh, you have to pick God over everything else." Mom sounded like she was talking to a four-year-old. She probably meant to be kind, but she was being patronizing.

"Dad won't want me to miss a game," Josh offered.

"I am sure he will agree with me," she told him. "Our family is being called. He has a plan for us. You may not know why this is so important right now, but someday you will."

"Coach doesn't like excuses." Josh tried a different tack. "He might cut me from being a starter."

"Your coach claims to be a Christian. This is his opportunity, and yours, to show faith. It's easy to say you are faithful when you don't have to make a sacrifice. You have to walk the walk if you're a true soldier for Christ."

Then Mom gave him the look. Josh wanted to keep arguing, but instead he hit the car door with the palm of his hand and walked away. This was awful. Missing a game was bad enough, but for this? It was going to be humiliating.

Over dinner that night, Dad said, "Congrats on the win today, Josh. Mom says you played well."

Josh shrugged. He'd been fine when he was actually playing, but he was a mess when he was on the bench, and after the game. Whenever he sat down his leg shook, betraying his anxiety. He had to act like nothing was wrong with him.

"Next year you guys are going be a force. I think your team might go all the way," Dad said.

"Coach says so, too," Josh replied, keeping his voice cool. "That'd be awesome."

"I got some great shots of the game. I'll get them printed out on Monday. What did Coach say when you told him you would miss the game tomorrow?" Mom asked.

"He said he's proud of me. So, you're right," Josh said, "he hates gay people more than he loves basketball."

"Honey, we don't hate homosexuals!" Mom exclaimed. "Don't ever think that. We want to help them find their way back to righteous living."

"But what if they can't?" slipped out of Josh's mouth without thought. He regretted it as soon as he said it.

"They can, if they accept that our Lord Jesus Christ died for their sins," Mom replied. "All we have to do is recognize that and live by His rules. It is very simple. Are you worried about someone who's homosexual?"

Josh shook his head.

"There's a bunch of gay kids at Dublin High," Rachel said with a shrug.

"How do you know?" Mom asked.

Rachel replied, "They wear rainbow pins."

"I don't know why the school encourages these things." Mom shook her head. "It's unfair to those children. Do you talk to them?"

It was like Mom was back in the 1970s. She had no idea how much things had changed in the secular world. His English teacher, Ms. Hodder, had a picture of her partner and children on her desk like it was totally normal. She talked about their weekends together just as the other teachers talked about their families. Ms. Hodder and Mr. Franco had GSA safe space posters on their walls.

"Of course," Rachel said. "They're just kids. I'm not going to call them the F-word or anything."

"The F-word?" Mom asked.

Josh bristled at the naivety in his Mom's question. He blurted out an explanation, "Faggot, Mom. The F-word is

faggot. Kids who are out get called that all the time." Josh swallowed his emotion.

"That's horrible!" Mom exclaimed, shocked. "And exactly
why we're going to San Francisco: to fight for the souls of those
children, every one of them."

Rachel declared, "I think it'll be fun. I love going to San
Francisco—the tall buildings, the shops, the wacky people."

"This isn't about fun, Rachel. This is about witnessing and
standing up for family values," Mom said.

"That doesn't mean I can't have fun while I'm doing it,"
Rachel retorted. "Now can I join Myspace—to tell people about
the witness? A bunch of the youth group uses it. If kids see
other kids are going, they'll jump right in." In her cutest snotty
tone of voice she said, "It's called social media, you know."

Rachel had been begging to join MySpace for ages. She
hadn't yet figured out how to hide things like that from Mom
and Dad. Mom looked at Dad with a question in her eyes. He
raised an eyebrow.

Mom said, "Dad and I will pray on it and let you know. Are you
sure Pastor James thinks it's in keeping with our Christian values?"

"He said so, I promise!" Rachel said. "At youth group he
told us he researched it, prayed about it, and decided it's a great
way for us to"—she mimicked Pastor James's accent—"'stay
connected to each other in Christ.'"

"Tonight I want you two to make phone calls to the youth
group," Jenn said. "I will, too."

"Sure," Rachel replied.

Josh shook his head. "I have to study."

Mom gave Dad her "talk to your son" look. It was their way
of pretending he was the only one in charge of their family.

Dad spoke up. "You can take fifteen minutes from your
night, Josh. Those kids look up to you. Show some leadership."

"It's Friday night," Mom said. "Your studying can wait.

This is the moral issue of our time. I'll use our home phone. Josh, you can use your cell phone, and Rachel can use mine. It's worth the minutes."

He had to act as if this wasn't personal. Josh nodded. "What am I supposed to say?"

"We'd like them to join us as we take a stand for marriage and family values. They can meet us at the Dublin BART station at nine in the morning. Lindsay, Dad, and I will be with the youth group the whole time."

"And Pastor James?" Dad asked.

"No, he has a wedding," Mom said. She looked scared and excited. "He said that he prayed for God to send him a servant to lead a public witness and I called less than five minutes later. He knows I was the answer to his prayers."

"Are you sure you can do this, Mom?" Rachel asked.

"I've never led a public witness, but I went to them all the time when I was in high school and college."

"You did?" Rachel asked.

"Yes," Mom replied. "I had a whole life before you were born, and now that you are growing up, I'll be doing more outside the house, though still Christ centered, of course." She continued, "We have enough adults, but please encourage parents to join us. I'll bring all of the signs we made today, and Lindsay is making sack lunches, but they should bring their own water bottles. Try to get a head count. And, Rachel, we'll let you know about 'my place.' That might be perfect as we continue to organize."

"MySpace! Capital M-y, capital S-p-a-c-e. With no space between the 'My' and the 'Space.'"

Mom laughed. "MySpace. Got it. I stand corrected. Let's do this soon, so we can start our video at eight. Okay?"

Josh nodded. He just wanted to get this over."Who's picking tonight?" Dad asked.

Rachel pointed at him. "Josh, so I guess we're watching something *Star Wars*..."

All eyes turned to Josh. He shook himself out of his thoughts. "Umm," he said while his family waited, "I'm feeling *Empire Strikes Back—ish.*"

"I'll make the popcorn," Mom said.

"Duun, dun. Dun, dun, dun, duuun, duuun," Dad hummed. Darth Vader's foreboding theme song fit Josh's mood.

FOUR

FRIDAY, FEBRUARY 13, 2004

Sara

"Anyone want to go to SF tomorrow?" Maya asked as she put down her tray in the cafeteria. The table was filled with the usual kids from Sara's floor.

"Too much homework," a few people responded.

"I have a game," came another.

Maya looked at Sara.

"To protest gay marriage?" Sara asked her roommate.

"Protest *for* gay marriage, you mean," Maya replied. "Yeah!"

Sara swallowed. She hadn't told her roommate she was Christian. She'd avoided it when they met six months ago, and now it was awkward. Sara didn't want to be the *Christian girl* in college like she was in high school. She wasn't embarrassed to admit it, but she didn't want to be treated like a stereotype.

"I can't either," Sara replied. "Too much to do tomorrow—and my mom wants me home for a family thing." The *family thing* was church on Sunday, but she didn't tell her Cal friends. They wouldn't understand her family weren't the closed-minded bigots that were stereotypical of Christians.

Aisha from down the hall asked, "Why can't they just be happy being domestic partners?"

Sara perked up. That's what she thought, too, but avoided saying so out loud at school.

"Separate, but equal?" Heather challenged. "*Brown vs. The Board of Education* was decided a long time ago."

"Besides, that only gives rights in this state. Are gay people supposed to be confined in California?"

Sara asked, "Like what rights?"

"Like, visitation rights in a hospital," Heather lectured. "If there's a car accident and you are domestic partners in California, you get the right to visit and make medical decisions. But you have that accident on the way to the Grand Canyon and you're queer—you are out of luck! No visitation. You die alone and in pain!"

"Chill out, Heather," Maya spoke up. "Not everyone knows every little detail about gay rights. Give Sara a break. She's trying to educate herself."

"Sorry, Maya, Sara. I just care... a lot," Heather said.

"It's okay," Sara replied.

"Do you want to go tomorrow?" Maya asked Heather.

"Can't," Heather replied. "I have a thing."

Sara's phone buzzed. She looked at the screen and read a text from Mom:

Call me ASAP

Her mom wasn't a nag like many of the other moms. She only called when it was important, *and* she'd learned to text first. *ASAP*. It must be important. Otherwise, she would have said when you can. Sara got up.

"Gotta call my mom," she told her friends. "I'll be back— DON'T clear my tray. I'm not done yet."

She dialed the landline as she walked, and Mom picked up the phone on the first ring.

"Hey, Mom. What's up?"

"Oh, Sara, thanks for calling so quickly. I hate to bother you, but it's important."

Sara's heart raced. "What's happened?"

"You've seen the news about San Francisco?" Mom asked.

"Is everyone okay, Mom? I thought someone was hurt."

"Oh, no. Sorry, dear, everyone is fine. Our *values* are being attacked. Lindsay and I are leading a witness in SF tomorrow. I want you to be there for moral support. Can you come?"

"What? When?"

"You can meet us at West Oakland BART station at nine thirty. Then come home for the rest of the weekend. This is going to be a very important day for our family. We've never witnessed together before. Your Dad and I used to do it ALL the time before you were born. You'll like it."

"Tomorrow?" Sara asked.

"Yes."

Her mind raced for an excuse. "Won't City Hall be closed on a Saturday?"

"The news says they are continuing all weekend unless they get a court order to stop."

Sara hesitated.

"Pray on it, Sara," Mom commanded. "Text me when you decide. I have to get back to my phone calls to the youth group. But I hope God tells you to go."

Sara laughed. Her mother was always telling her what she wanted to hear from God. Mom was a woman of faith, but she had no qualms suggesting to God how to do His job.

"Yogurt Park?" Maya asked when Sara returned to the table. "*After* you finish your dinner."

"Sure," Sara replied.

"Then we're thinking movie, no frat party tonight, unless you REALLY want to," Maya said.

On the contrary, Sara was relieved. "Froyo and movie sounds great to me."

"Everything okay at home?"

"Yeah. Mom wants me home early."

"That's why I picked a college six hours away," Aisha said. "I would not want my mom asking me to come home on a Saturday morning."

Sara nodded like she agreed, but she was glad to be close. Flying home once or twice a year for visits sounded terrible. Her mom could be annoying, but it was all out of love. Sara couldn't imagine going months and months without seeing Dad, Josh, Rachel, and Mom.

Thankfully, Maya was still asleep when she left so there was no need to make up a slanted explanation. She wasn't ashamed of her faith, but she just wasn't ready for the questions and the judgment.

This early on a Saturday morning it was quiet at BART, though there were a few people going to San Francisco this early; their rainbow flags and T-shirts marked them as people on the other side. Sara wasn't against being gay. Unlike the rest of her family, she thought they weren't hurting anyone and should be allowed to just live in peace, but she did wish they would leave traditional marriage alone. Heather's comments made her see that homosexuals needed something like marriage, but not actual marriage. Maybe there could be national domestic partners in the whole country.

She got off at MacArthur to switch trains. Tons of people dressed in rainbow colors carrying signs waited on the platform at this station. She avoided eye contact with any of them and stood by the door after she boarded. At each stop more people got on until the train was crowded for a Saturday. This event was a big deal.

At West Oakland she was the only one who got off. The Dublin-SF train came quickly. She scanned the doors, looking for familiar faces. Her mom stood at the door of the third car. Sara smiled. Her mom was always watching out for her.

"Mom!"

"Hi, honey." Mom looked relieved and hugged her close as the doors slid shut. "Are you okay?"

"I'm fine." Sara gave her mom an incredulous look. "I ride BART all the time."

"Thank you for being here." Mom beamed at her.

Sara nodded. Her mom didn't need to know it was complicated in her heart. Hopefully she wouldn't bump into Maya or anyone else she knew. Maya hadn't found anyone to go with her to SF by the time they went to bed, so Sara thought it was unlikely she'd come at all.

Mom pointed. Their group was crammed together in the back of the train. Sara waved at her dad and Rachel.

"Where's Lindsay?" Sarah asked.

"Abigail threw up last night—and Mark is out of town." She pointed, "Rebeccah and Michael came without her."

"Wow. So you're doing this on your own?"

"Daddy is here, and Mona. And you—" Mom looked so pleased.

Sara smiled back at her mom and went to stand by Josh and Michael. Josh looked terrible.

"You okay?" she asked.

He scowled and shook his head. "I have a headache."

"Want some ibuprofen?"

"Mom gave me some," he replied.

Out of the corner of her eye she saw someone whisper and point at them. Four heads turned to look.

A tall, blonde woman with spiky hair said, "Hell, no!" She leaned forward, looking ready to fight.

Another woman put a hand on her friend. "Don't engage. They aren't going to ruin this day for us. Let's go." She jerked her head sideways and turned away, two of the friends following her lead.

The blonde looked at her friends, then looked back at the teens. Sara's heart raced. Was she going to say something to them? Had anyone else noticed? She looked at her parents. They were oblivious, lost in their own world. When she looked back at the woman, she'd turned her back, too, ignoring their group.

Sara exhaled. This was awful. Was she the only one who felt that way?

She wanted to ask her mom to turn her signs around but didn't. She just stared at her own reflection in the dark window.

Just before the Civic Center Mom told the kids, "This is our stop. Let everyone else get off first, but be ready."

Sara watched the crowd shuffle between the bottleneck of the doors, a stream of people constricting, like water squeezing past large boulders. Mom signaled to their group, and they joined in at the tail end of the crowd moving off the train. Mom straddled the car and the platform, stopping the doors from closing until the last of their crew made it off the train. As soon as she stepped onto the platform in San Francisco, the doors swished closed behind her.

"Go to the wall!" Mom shouted. "We'll stay down here until everyone clears out."

The station was like a party. People in colorful clothes carried flowers, balloons, signs—and even a wedding cake with two brides in white gowns. A little kid sat up high in a back-pack, and another was pushed past in a stroller. Old men holding hands shuffled by.

Mom was here to rain on their parade. Sara suddenly felt ill.

She had no conflict with any of them. Her mom was against gay rights, and she had come to support her mom without thinking about the other side. She was suddenly embarrassed to be here at all.

Her mom spoke to their group. "We're in San Francisco to save souls for Jesus. I'm proud of all of you for giving your time on a Saturday for this holy work. Pastor James is sorry not to be with us today, but he told me to tell you that we're all in his prayers." Mom choked up and cleared her throat. "He instructed us not to speak to the homosexual activists while we're there. If someone tries to speak with you, just look away," she said slowly, emphasizing each word. "Our signs speak for themselves. We're not engaging in arguments. We want to appear calm, confident, and full of faith. No, not appear that way. We want to *be* that way: *be* calm, *be* confident, and *be* filled with Spirit."

Mom asked each of the kids which sign they wanted: "No same-sex marriage—ever"; "Adam and Eve, not Adam and Steve"; or "Save traditional marriage." She handed the signs to Sara to pass out.

"Adam and Eve" was the most popular by far.

"Steve, will you lead us in prayer?" Mom asked.

Sara looked around. She hoped there wouldn't be another train before they finished. She focused and let his words calm her. Dad's prayer was short and effective.

Mom looked at her and Mrs. Harrison. "Sara and Mona, can you bring up the rear? Make sure all the kids are in front of you, okay?"

They nodded. Mom and Dad led the group to the escalator. At the top they looked around; Mom pointed, and Dad led them through the exit gates and down the hallway to a staircase. Mom shook her head and pointed the other way.

"Sorry, guys," Mom explained. "More choices than we realized."

Sara felt like a shepherd, herding all the kids to make sure they stayed behind Mom and Dad. They wandered through the underground maze, searching for the way out. After another wrong turn, they finally got on an escalator.

As she rode up the long escalator, Sara heard loud noises from the street above. She closed her eyes and prayed for peace and strength. She opened her eyes and looked up through the tunnel. A pigeon flew across the white building shining in the sun above her head. She laughed. It wasn't a dove, but sometimes God had to use what was available.

"Come on," Mom said, sliding her hand into Dad's. She was so confident in all that she did. Sara wanted that same confidence but was afraid that what she was learning about in school would cause a rift between her and her mom. Her mom was the best, but she wanted Sara to think and be just like her.

They crossed Hyde Street and made their way through the center of the plaza between leafless gnarled trees and tall flagpoles. White news vans topped with satellite dishes surrounded the plaza. Mom stopped the group directly across the street from the majestic building. Sara had only ever seen it on the news.

A long line snaked out of the front door and around the corner. People moved through the crowd singing, giving out flowers, and generally celebrating. A female couple walked out of the door holding hands. They weren't much older than Sara, dressed in flowing outfits that were identical but in different colors: one bright fuchsia and the other teal blue. They had white flower leis around their necks. At the top of the stairs, they raised their clenched hands high into the air. Huge grins covered their faces. One of them brushed away tears on her cheek. The crowd cheered for the ecstatic couple.

Rachel pulled on Mom's arm and whispered, "They look so happy."

They *did* look happy. The dread Sara felt at BART came rushing back.

The group looked at Mom for direction. She pointed to the ground.

"We will stay right here," she instructed. "Just hold up your signs and please do not speak with anyone. We aren't here to fight."

Sara was glad to stay this far away. She whispered to her mom and dad, "The news didn't show how happy they are. It's a celebration."

"You know that doesn't make it right," Mom said.

"Yes," she replied, but it made it harder to think it was wrong, too.

Couple after couple came out in the same way: hands clenched over their heads to the cheers of the crowd. They were dressed in all sorts of ways: two men in suits, two men in shorts. Two women in wedding gowns. One woman in a wedding gown and one woman in a tuxedo. Two women in shorts. On and on it went. Some had children with them. Some carried signs. Some were old, older than Sara's grandparents. Some looked as if they were barely eighteen.

Sara had expected to see people angry and shouting like on the television. Fox News didn't show these ordinary-looking people so full of emotion.

The kids clustered into little groups, talking with one another, their signs held up. Josh chatted with his friends and Rachel was with hers. It had only been a few months since Sara had 'graduated' from high school youth group, but she didn't belong with them anymore. She stood with her parents, not belonging with them either.

Mom asked them if she should lead a song or a chant.

Sara shook her head. "As you said, we aren't here to fight."

Dad agreed. They got a few glares, and a few people took

their pictures, but no one talked to them. Some of the kids posed for the camera and others turned away.

Mom pulled out her camera, too.

"Really, Mom?" Josh questioned her.

"We'll be glad to have a record of this day. I won't take shots of people across the street. Just us, in our shirts."

He shook his head but didn't challenge her further.

"You okay?" she asked her brother.

He shrugged. "I'd rather be at my game."

She considered telling him how uncomfortable she was feeling. Ms. Hodder was his English teacher this year. They'd never talked about it, but maybe his thinking was changing, too. He was the most devout of the three of them, but also the kindest. He might be as uncomfortable as she was.

"Sara and Josh, go stand with your sister." Mom ended their conversation.

Sara rolled her eyes but did as she was told. Mom took a shot and moved on to other groups. Josh slipped away to join his friends, his back to City Hall, ignoring what was going on behind him. He didn't look torn to be here like she was. Sara took a deep breath to calm herself, asked God for clarity, and then watched her mom take pictures.

Most of the kids were willing subjects. Rachel and Jamie were outright hams. Sara helped Mom corral them all into a group shot before lunch. Half the kids grumbled, but they would clamor to see the pictures when they were developed.

She looked at each of her family members. How would they react if she told them that maybe she didn't think the same as everything they held most dear? She still loved church and believed in God, but she wondered how only a few people got to go to heaven when God was so loving. She wasn't sure she believed Maya was outside the bounds of God's love because she didn't live a biblically based life.

"Sara, can you give out the sandwiches?" Mom asked after she was done with photos.

Each kid had a choice between turkey and Swiss or PB and J. You'd think they were deciding between gourmet meals with their long deliberations. She ended up handing them out and letting them trade to get what they wanted.

The paper bag held a mandarin orange, carrots and two chocolate-chip cookies, courtesy of Lindsay.

"You think of everything!" Mrs. Harrison said to Mom, clearly impressed. Sara had to agree. Her mom was amazing at organizing.

"Not really, but thanks. All those years as a room parent prepared me for this! We wanted today to be a positive, spiritually uplifting experience for all of us. Warriors for Christ need energy for the battle!"

As they were eating, a newsperson approached them: Ken Brown from Channel 4.

"Can I ask one of you a few questions? On camera?" he asked.

Mom looked at Dad. She pantomimed: *You or me?* He pointed to her emphatically. She was the one who'd gotten them into this mess.

"Lord be with me," Mom whispered. She finished chewing her bite of turkey sandwich and wiped her face.

"Do I look okay?" Mom asked Sara.

Sara studied her mom. She wiped at the corner of her mouth even though nothing was there, then nodded. Mom squeezed Sara's hand, pressing the napkin into it.

"How can I help you?" she asked.

The newsman looked over at the cameraperson, waited for a signal, and then began in a formal voice, "As you can see, most people are excited for these couples, but you seem to have a different opinion. Can you tell us why you're out here protesting these marriages today?"

Mom paused. She looked like she was about to panic. She finally stuttered, "Well, Ken, the Bible calls these relationships a sin—an abomination. As President Bush said in his State of the Union, 'A strong America must value the institution of marriage.'"

Mom paused, looked at their group, took in a big breath and added, sounding calm and confident, "Our nation must defend the sanctity of family from homosexual activists. The definition of marriage has not changed in two thousand years. One man and one woman. It's very clear."

"I see you've brought some young people with you today."

Mom smiled. "Yes, these are members of our church youth group in Dublin. We're out here today standing up for the children. It's their future we're fighting for. These teens leapt at the chance to take a stand for their values."

As she spoke, a crowd grew around them. One person started to chant, "We're here. We're queer. We're married. Get used to it!" Other voices joined in until there was a loud chorus yelling at them. The camera panned to the chanting crowd, then turned to scan Mom and the kids from church. Mom grabbed Dad's hand. Sara looked for Rachel and Josh. The chanting continued, louder and louder.

"What do you have to say to this crowd?" Ken Brown shouted the question at Mom.

She stared at him. "God loves them. Salvation is theirs if they live according to His laws."

The reporter signaled to the crew. "That was perfect," he said, back to a casual tone. "Thanks. You'll probably be on the five o'clock news and maybe again at eleven."

The chanters dispersed as quickly as they had gathered.

The sudden quiet was unsettling. The kids, all in one mass, stared at Mom. Various expressions covered their faces. Some looked scared, others excited, one or two looked like they might cry. They needed leadership to break the tension and instill faith.

"Mom, say something comforting," Sara whispered.

"Everyone okay?" Mom asked the group, but then went right on, "Well done. You handled that situation perfectly. I'm so proud of you. We'll stay just a few more minutes and then go home. If we make the news tonight, we will have truly furthered God's message."

The tension visibly left the group. They spread out and clustered back into the small collections of friends. Mom walked from group to group chatting with the kids. Sara headed over to Rachel who was comforting a shaken Jamie.

"Look at this." Rachel pointed to the paper in Jamie's hand.

Sara read:

What if you're condemning your sister, child, cousin, uncle, friend, coworker?
Gay people are four times more likely to attempt suicide and twice as likely to succeed as straight people. Are you sure this is the message you want to send to your loved ones?
PFLAG
Parents, Families, and Friends of Lesbians and Gays

Sara felt her stomach slide around some more.

Mom came to their group. "Where did you get this?" Mom quizzed Rachel.

Rachel pointed to the crowd. "One of them handed it to me."

Mom looked furious.

"Rachel, we are not harming anyone. No one we know is homosexual. They are terribly misguided. Don't let them confuse you. We came out today to save people. Do you understand?" Mom asked.

Rachel nodded. Mom crumpled the paper and dropped it in the recycling.

"I came over to tell you we had a triumphant day. This witness was a great success."

Sara nodded like she agreed, but she just felt horrible. She wished she had the courage to tell her parents, or at least her sister, that she didn't agree with Mom entirely, but she was a coward.

FIVE

SATURDAY, FEBRUARY 14, 2004

Jenn

"I think we furthered the Lord's message," Jenn told Pastor James when he called her by phone that evening. She sat on the family-room couch telling him about the day. The group was tired but proud to have been a voice for Christian values. The kids were bubbling with excitement on BART.

"Channel 4 News even interviewed me! Steve said I did fine, so I don't think I embarrassed us."

"Oh, Jennifer, that's amazing!" Pastor said. "Were you wearing your church T-shirts?"

"Of course!"

"I'm going to launch our phone tree as soon as we hang up. Our congregants will want to see your good work for our Lord."

Jenn's heart soared. Her church was going to learn about what she had done. Lin called a few minutes later.

"How did it go?" Her cheerful voice came through the line.

"It was amazing!" Jenn said. "The kids were strong and faithful."

"Were people hostile toward you?" Lindsay asked.

"It was scariest on BART but not at City Hall. Well, except during the interview."

"What interview?"

"Oh, Channel 4 asked me a few questions." Jenn tried to sound casual. She suddenly felt bad that Lindsay was left out.

"Wow!" Lindsay exclaimed.

"I'm so sorry you missed it," Jenn replied. "I wish we'd done it together."

"Me, too."

"I've got to go. Steve and I are eating out tonight. I haven't left enough time to get ready. See you tomorrow?"

"If we all stay healthy."

"How's Abigail?"

"Better. I think it's a twenty-four-hour thing. She's kept everything down since eleven o'clock."

"I'll pray for the rest of you to stay well," Jenn said and hung up. "Josh!" she called.

"What?" he asked, coming into the family room.

"Do you have time to set the VCR to record the news before you leave for your movie? Nana wants me to send it to her."

Josh started to say something but just nodded and got to work with the remote.

Jenn rushed upstairs, threw on her favorite red dress, and fixed her makeup. She didn't look her best—after the day in San Francisco, she could have used a shower, but she was ready on time for their reservation.

"I'm proud of you." Steve smiled. He sat across the candlelit table, dressed up in Jenn's favorite suit. The steak house was packed with couples for Valentine's Day.

"Thanks!" She grinned. "You know it wasn't just me."

He shrugged. "But you went out on a limb today. *You* spoke to the news. I could feel you living God's purpose."

Jenn's eyes welled up. "Remember that witness I told you about when I was sixteen? The one my parents made me go to and that I resisted, but in the middle of it, as I was taking photos of all the beautiful, faith-filled people, I felt the Holy Spirit so intensely? The moment I decided to dedicate my life to Christ?"

Steve nodded.

"Today was like that. At first, I was embarrassed to be taking this public stand in the face of hostility. But then the Holy Spirit carried me, and I knew God wanted me on this path even though it made me uncomfortable." Jenn gave Steve an embarrassed smile. "Do I sound prideful and arrogant?"

Steve shook his head and smiled. "Proud but not prideful. Sometimes God brings you to the front. You know it's His glory and not yours that matters."

"I do."

Steve pulled out a box wrapped in red foil.

"Oh, Steve!" Jenn exclaimed, even though Steve usually got her something for Valentine's Day.

"Josh helped me pick it out."

Curious, Jenn took the gift. It was heavy. Within the shiny paper was a Nikon D70, a digital SLR.

Jenn's hand covered her mouth. "Oh, my goodness. Steve! Thank you. I can't imagine how you got one already. They were just released."

"I have my ways." He smiled at her. "It has six point one megapixels!"

"I know this was expensive. Are you sure?"

"I noticed you reading the reviews. You deserve it."

"I can't wait to learn all about it!" She leaned across the table to give her husband a kiss.

She teared up at the thought about her favorite uncle who had made her feel so grown up when he gave her a camera for her twelfth birthday. He was such a dear man, warm and kind in a way that her father wasn't. She knew her dad loved her, then and now, but he'd never been one to express his feelings.

"What?" Steve asked, sensing her emotion.

"I miss Uncle Bob," she explained. "The way he lit up when he saw me and had the two of us be a team at family events. We shared a special role in the family: capturing the love and fun. He would have been amazed at this technology—seeing the image right after you snap the photo."

"He gave you a purpose," Steve suggested.

She nodded.

"He sounds like he was a kind man," Steve said.

"You don't remember him?"

Steve shrugged. "I was...19 when he died. I remember how sad you were, but your grandmother's brother was not in the forefront of my mind back then."

"Touche!" Jenn replied. "Uncle Bob was a very dear person. He was sad to never marry, but if he had kids of his own, I may not have gotten so much of his attention."

"God had a different plan for him."

When she got home from dinner, Jenn was shocked and excited to see the number "26" blinking on their answering machine. They'd never had that many calls before. She hit Play. Her brother Tim's voice came out of the speaker. "Jenn, Mom told me you got on the news tonight. Congrats! From all of us. We'll have to catch up soon. It's been too long. Jessie says, 'Hooray for Jenn!'"

Beep. "Hi, everyone. It's Hannah from Valley Preschool. We saw Jenn on the news tonight. You looked and sounded great, Jenn. Thanks for standing up for marriage."

Beep... It took her nearly half an hour to get through them all: lots of people from church, her cousin Jonah, and parents from Dublin schools and soccer left her congratulatory messages. Jenn did not expect or want this kind of attention, but if this was her calling, she would do her best to be a gracious and faithful soldier for the Lord. It was too late to call people back, but she could do that tomorrow. After she listened to her messages, she checked her e-mail, not something she normally did at night. Her inbox was flooded. When the kids came home from their movie, she was still sitting at the computer.

"You're still up?" Rachel asked, surprised.

Jenn rolled her eyes and made a chagrined face. "I'm listening to messages and reading e-mails. How was the movie?"

"Great!" Rachel said.

Jenn looked at her other children.

"I liked it," Sara said. "It was cute."

Josh shrugged. "It was good, I guess. I'm tired. I'm going to bed."

"How's your head?" Jenn asked.

"Fine, I guess. Not great."

"Take ibuprofen or acetaminophen so you can sleep. But be sure to eat something first so you don't throw up from it."

Sara asked, "How long are you gonna stay up?"

"I don't know. Until I get through the e-mails. Goodnight."

Her kids kissed her cheek, and she turned back to the screen.

By the time Jenn got to bed, Steve was snoring quietly. Each time she started to doze off, scenes from San Francisco popped into her mind. Faces of people chanting around her got her heart racing and startled her awake. As she lay in bed with images streaming through her head, Jenn heard the awful sound of retching down the hall. She hurried to the kids' bathroom and turned the handle. The door was locked.

"It's me. Are you okay?" she asked. Which of her kids was sick?

Josh opened the door. He looked pale and clammy.

He croaked, "I just threw up."

"Oh, honey. I'm sorry. Maybe you have the same thing as Abigail. Something's going around. No church for you tomorrow." She bit back asking him if he'd taken pain medicine without food. It was too late to change anything, now. And he would bristle at the "I told you so" if he hadn't.

Josh nodded feebly. She walked him to his room and tucked him back into bed. They had decorated this space together a few years ago, in the summer between sixth and seventh grades. Out went the Buzz Lightyear bedding, and in came a plain navy comforter and matching curtains. Posters of National Parks hung on the walls. She'd heard that boys never cared about their rooms, but Josh went shopping with her when he'd outgrown his childish taste. He had an opinion about how his room should look.

Jenn liked to redecorate each part of the house every five years. It kept things fresh and up to date. Soon it would be time to redo this space again. Time did fly. It was a cliché but so true.

Jenn brought Josh a glass of water and moved the small trash can next to the bed in case he vomited again.

When he was settled back in bed, she prayed over her son.

After she was finished, he said, "Thanks for taking care of me." His eyes welled up.

"Of course, honey. I love you—down to the ground and up to heaven. I'm not going to give you a hug, because I don't want to get sick. If you need anything in the night, come get me." She blew him a kiss.

"I love you, too. You know that, right? Even though I don't say it or show it so much anymore. I still do!"

"I know, Josh. Really, I do," Jenn said. And it was true. It was right for a young man to distance himself from his mother. She didn't *like* it, but she accepted it as God's plan.

· · ·

The next morning, Jenn poked her head in to say goodbye to Josh before they left for church. He was sleeping peacefully, so she didn't disturb him. He looked so sweet and vulnerable. She wrote him a note and left it against the water glass so he would see it as soon as he opened his eyes.

Text if you need *anything*. *I'll have my phone in my pocket so we can come right back.*

Jenn, Steve, Rachel, and Sara climbed into the car. They'd drop Sara off at the BART station on their way to church. She missed a day of studying to witness yesterday, so she was going back early. God would understand. No one succeeded at a top-rated university without a sacrifice.

Understandably, Jenn was proud of Sara's academic achievements. She'd gotten into Williams, Vassar, and Pomona as well as the top UCs. Jenn had encouraged Sara to consider Christian colleges, but she hadn't applied to any. When Sara accepted the offer from UC Berkeley, Jenn was thrilled. She'd encouraged Sara to simply commute from Dublin. Jenn had stayed with her family when she attended BIOLA, the Biblical Institute of Los Angeles. Steve had, too. But unlike Steve, Jenn didn't regret living at home during those years. Her husband wished he'd had the full college experience and wanted that for Sara, Josh, and Rachel. Jenn didn't understand the attraction of being crowded into a small space with other eighteen-year-olds, but she knew she had to start giving her children more leeway to make their own choices.

Steve pointed out that Sara was a great kid and that they could trust her to live out their Christian values wherever she went to school, which she demonstrated with her choice to reside in Freeborn, the substance-free dorm. Jenn was grateful that was an option, even at UC Berkeley.

When they walked into the church sanctuary, the praise

band was already playing. So many people gave her hugs and high fives that it took a while to get settled into their favorite section: close to the front on the right. Congregants waved at her from across the sanctuary. Jenn felt like a celebrity.

"Everyone thinks what we did is so cool, Mom," Rachel said. "Way to go!" She held up her hand for a high five.

Jenn shrugged and slapped her daughter's hand. She was proud but didn't want to be boastful. It was hard to know how to behave. She waved and thanked and hugged people as modestly as possible. She felt bad to be getting all this attention when Lindsay had done as much as she had to get ready for the witness. She reminded people that the kids and Lindsay should be praised, too.

During the pastoral prayer, Jenn was surprised to be called to the front. When Pastor James put his arm around her, she blushed and put her face in her hands. Then she composed herself by taking a deep breath and looked out at the crowd.

"We all say we want to do God's work in the world," Pastor James said to the congregation. "This woman, Jenn, is a shining example for all of us. Yes, she serves on the welcome team for our congregation, but that is not all. On Thursday morning I saw the horrifying images of marriage being mocked in San Francisco. That night I asked God to send me a messenger, and who called first thing the next morning? This woman! She didn't hesitate to put her faith into action. She took time out of her busy life to organize our teens to stand up for our Christian beliefs. We are in the middle of a war for the soul of our country. Each of us must be soldiers for Christ." He faced her and put his hand on her head. "God blesses you, Jenn. He is blessing you for the leadership and gifts you give to our community and to the world. In the name of Jesus, we bless you."

Jenn's eyes filled up. She hadn't expected recognition. She certainly didn't organize the protest for this kind of attention. But it was nice—very nice. For as long as she could remember, she'd wanted to be known as a good Christian. Or rather, to *be* a good Christian. Her primary goal in life, besides being a good mother and wife, was to be a faithful representative of Christ on Earth. And in this moment, she knew she was doing the Lord's work. The Holy Spirit filled her chest and moved inside her. A chill ran down her back as the energy swirled through her body.

As they walked from the sanctuary to the car, Jenn called home to check on Josh.

"He's not answering," she told Steve. "Should we go straight home?"

Steve shook his head. "He can text us if he needs us. That's the beauty of cellular phones. Most likely he's sleeping and will enjoy the quiet a bit longer."

The kids had been raised with pancakes and hot chocolate at Mimi's after church. It was strange to have just one child with them, but Jenn knew she'd better get used to it. Josh was making it clear he didn't want to stay in the area for college. She'd be lucky if he stayed in California—he was exploring East Coast colleges. They decided that if he got a good scholarship, she and Steve were going to let him go that far. In theory she should be glad to have her kids fly the coop, but she'd just as soon have them nearby forever.

SIX

Jenn

Jenn pushed the red call button. Her heart beat fast and hard as adrenaline coursed through her body once again. She shook as she waited. Questions snapped like lightning through her brain: sleeping pills in Josh? Who did that to him? Why him?

"Can I help you?" a young nurse with light-brown skin and highlighted hair asked.

Jenn took a deep breath. "My husband... Josh's father. At home he found an empty bottle of sleeping pills. We suspect Josh may have taken some. Well, a lot."

The nurse nodded slowly. "Okay. Do you know what kind of pills—over-the-counter, prescription?"

"It's Ambien. There were twenty-seven pills in the bottle, and now it's empty." Despite herself, a tear slid down Jenn's cheek.

The nurse patted her shoulder. "I'll get the attending. Dr. Eastman is on right now. This explains his condition."

Jenn was forced to wait for the new doctor to come and speak with her. She stood up and paced by Josh's hospital bed, forcing herself to take deep breaths. *Why? Why? Why?* ran through her head. She reminded herself, *It's best that we know what caused him to be like this...* and then she prayed, God, please remove the Ambien from Josh's bloodstream.

Jenn stopped pacing when the attending doctor stepped past the curtain. Dr. Eastman looked like she was in her mid-forties, with pale skin and brown hair pulled back into a pony-tail. She looked kind enough but didn't bother with any pleas-antries after introducing herself.

"From a medical point of view," the doctor said, "this is good news. Ambien moves through the body fairly quickly, causing very little damage at that dosage. He should start to wake up about fifteen hours after he took it. It's most likely he'll have a complete recovery within twenty-four hours. He'll need to be evaluated by a psychiatrist to ascertain if he is an immediate danger to himself or others before he can be discharged."

"A psychiatrist? Really?"

"With all due respect," the doctor said slowly, "your son attempted suicide today."

That word was like a slap to the face. "You don't know that. Couldn't it have been a mistake?" Jenn asked.

"I'm obliged to have him evaluated before he goes home," Dr. Eastman insisted but with compassion. "The psychiatrist will determine his mental state. I'm sorry. I know this is hard to hear."

Jenn watched the doctor walk away. She was so stunned she could hardly breathe. Her body trembled. Suicide? She forced herself to breathe. She considered what could possibly be both-ering Josh so much... College? Kids felt so much academic pres-sure, but he was a great student. Girl problems? Jenn didn't know about a special girl—boys often kept those feelings from their parents—but that might be it.

Pregnant! The word leaped into Jenn's mind. What if he'd

gotten someone pregnant? That would go against all of their values. He might think his life was ruined.

"Dear Lord Jesus," Jenn whispered, "it's my will to surrender to You everything that I am and everything that I'm striving to be. I offer You my life, mind, body, soul, and spirit and all my hopes, plans, and dreams. I surrender to You my past, present, and future. I offer You the life of my son, Josh. I know he is in Your..."

Jenn started to sob, tears pouring down her face. Fear and sadness and hopelessness overwhelmed her; she couldn't continue her prayer. More than ever, she wanted to feel the Holy Spirit, but she felt empty. This was her punishment. Last night she went to bed full of ego and pride. And tonight her entire life was turned upside down.

Past midnight, Jenn slept in the chair next to Josh. Her head rested on the bed, and she held his hand as they dozed. She woke up when he jerked his hand away. Groggy yet relieved that he was coming around, she was glad for the chance to finally speak to him directly, to find out if her fear was true.

"Josh?" Jenn said quietly.

His eyes were closed, but he reached for the tube coming out of his mouth and pulled on it. Jenn took his hands and said calmly, "Leave it, Josh. It's there to help you breathe. Stay still."

He yanked his hands away from Jenn's grip and clawed at the plastic on his face, his features contorted. Pushing down the panic that rose in her, Jenn blocked him with one hand and pressed the button for the nurse with the other. Then she wrapped her hands around each of his wrists and used all her weight to push his arms into the bed. He fought against her, grunting and thrashing. He twisted from side to side. Jenn resisted the urge to yell for help. Josh stared up at her, his eyes moving between desperation and anger.

Jenn repeated her words, trying to soothe him. "Josh, it's a tube to help you breathe. Leave it. If you stop fighting me, I can let go of you."

Josh glared more intensely and pushed harder against her. It was horrible to see him like that. Panic rose in Jenn. She closed her eyes to hide from the intense anger on his face.

"Can I help you?" A voice broke into the private chamber of her mind. Jenn opened her eyes to see a new nurse. The woman took in the scene and pushed a button on the wall. Suddenly a team of people rushed into the room. One of them pushed Jenn aside to take over restraining Josh. Jenn stood back and watched. Josh yelled and grunted around his breathing tube. "Ugh, uhh. Uhh!" Jenn felt her heart twist in sympathy. When the medical staff stepped back, Josh's arms were tied down at the sides of the bed. He fought against the restraints, but he couldn't get free. He looked at Jenn, panic shining in his eyes.

"Mmma. Ughh." More garbled, desperate sounds.

"This is your treatment?" Jenn challenged the nurse. "You're going to leave him tied like an animal?"

"The tube needs to stay in," the nurse said. "I know he looks like he's awake, but he's not. He's actually having a nightmare right now. Soon he'll drift into a different sleep state and calm down. He won't remember this tomorrow. See... He's starting to leave REM."

Jenn looked at her son. He had stopped jerking against the restraints. Josh's eyes got softer, then they closed. He blinked them open and shut a few times; his grunts turned into murmurs. Soon he looked deeply asleep. Jenn breathed a sigh of relief.

She asked the nurse, "How long does he need to have the tube?"

"We'll remove it when he's been breathing on his own for thirty minutes. We've been stepping down the oxygen. He's responded well so far. By midmorning the tube should be out, if his numbers stay good."

"This is a nightmare—for both of us," Jenn whispered, her voice faltering.

The nurse said kindly, "I'll pray it'll be over soon... for both of your sakes."

"Thank you," Jenn replied. "That means a lot to me. Thank you very much."

Just past two in the morning, Jenn woke with a start. Josh was awake and fighting against the restraints again. Jenn stood by the bed to soothe her terrified, disoriented son. She sang his favorite hymns, prayed out loud, and rubbed his brow. Eventually he drifted off to sleep again.

She inhaled deeply to calm herself. She was nervous and jumpy. *God, give me the strength to get through this night.*

Jenn took her son's hand. It felt warm and dry. He was there, in his body, in a way he hadn't been earlier that day. Relief passed through her. She studied his face, and then her eyes traveled down his long body. He took up the whole bed. In her head she'd known her son would be a man someday, but in her heart it was shocking that Josh was now more of a man than a boy. That little child she used to carry in her arms was in there somewhere, sort of, but he was also gone.

He'd been the cuddliest of her babies. As infants the girls liked to be held, but as soon as they could crawl, they were off. But Josh was happiest in someone's arms until he got to be too big to hold. And she indulged him in that for as long as possible because she enjoyed it, too.

Jenn bent over and kissed Josh's hand, resting her head next to him. Her chest swelled with love.

She considered their options if she was right about a baby. Could he finish at Dublin High? Only if Josh and his new family lived at home. She'd agree to that. Would Steve? In her mind she started rearranging their house. If Josh and his family squeezed into the downstairs study, they'd have some privacy. The desks could be moved into the family room. It would be crowded but manageable. She could be with the baby during the day while the kids finished high school.

Suddenly she had a nauseating thought: what if the girl's family was pressuring her to have an abortion? That would kill Josh. She looked at him again. He would be devastated to know that his lust had led to the destruction of a life.

"God, please let me be wrong. If I'm right, open their spirits so that they may do Your will on Earth. In the name of Your Son, I pray. Amen."

Jenn whispered into Josh's ear, "Whatever you've done, Josh, I forgive you. Daddy will forgive you, too. But most important, God will forgive you. He already has. He gave us His Son so that we could be cleansed of our sins. Open your heart, and you will feel His love." A tear slid down her cheek. She wanted to do so much more, to fix whatever it was that Josh had done. She wanted him to know that he didn't have to carry his burden alone.

But she reminded herself, the best thing to do in this moment was to rest. So she forced herself to put her head down on the bed and use her favorite trick for falling asleep when she was anxious: she counted backward by sevens from one hundred, starting over again whenever she realized she was ruminating. After six restarts she fell asleep.

She dreamed with her cheek resting against their nestled hands. Each time Josh woke up through that long night, she comforted him, trying to believe that this nightmare would be over soon.

At eight, Jenn's buzzing cell phone woke her up. It was Steve, letting her know that they were at the hospital. Exhausted and bleary-eyed, Jenn clumsily texted that she would come out.

When she looked up from her phone, Josh's eyes were open

wide. He started to roll to his side, but the restraints stopped him. Jenn started to soothe him, but he didn't fight. He sank onto his back with a deep sigh. He was awake, for real now. Relieved and tired, Jenn took his hand. She resisted the urge to question him. There'd be time for that later.

"It's been a long night, hon," Jenn explained gently to him. "They tied down your arms because you were pulling out your breathing tube. But you made it through. Things are going to get better from here." Jenn bit her lip to stop herself from tearing up. "Dad wants to see you. Sara and Rachel, too. I'm going to go trade with him. I'll let the nurse know you're awake and you won't tear out the tube. She'll untie you."

She squeezed his hand, kissed his head, and pulled away to leave, but he held on tight. He struggled to speak but only made grunting sounds. He tried a few more times, frustrated and desperate to say something.

"Just a minute—I have a pencil and paper." Jenn dug around in her bag.

She placed a pencil in his hand and held a piece of scrap paper close to the tip. Josh's fingers shook as he scrawled out the letters: S... o... r... r... y. Jenn looked at her son. Tears rolled out of the corners of his eyes, down the sides of his face, and onto the bed.

"Oh, Josh," Jenn said, anguish in her voice. "Me, too! I'm so sorry that you couldn't tell me how desperate you were. I failed you, honey, but we'll get through this. Together. I have faith. And so does Dad. The whole church is praying for you. God will forgive you for whatever you've done."

Josh turned his head away and closed his eyes. Jenn gently wiped his face, since he was restrained from doing it himself.

"I'm so sorry, honey."

The nurse walked up and matter-of-factly said, "Change of shift. No visitors for about fifteen minutes."

Jenn looked at Josh. It was heart-wrenching to leave him

like this. He tried to say something but then returned to the paper when he realized she couldn't understand him. He wrote *Okay* in large, shaky letters.

"We'll talk more. You know, when..." Jenn pointed at his breathing tube.

He gave a slight nod. Then she kissed his head and left.

"You look like you hardly slept," Steve said after they hugged good morning.

"It was a long night. How about you?" Jenn asked while giving first Sara and then Rachel a hug. Her youngest daughter kept her arms wrapped around Jenn.

"I slept okay," Rachel said. "How's Josh?"

"He's awake and calm. His arms were restrained in the night, and the tube is still in, so he can't talk, which is pretty awful. Hopefully the nurse will untie him now and take the tube out soon, because he's breathing fine on his own. I had to leave during change of shift, but I told him you were coming."

"Tied down?" Rachel asked, her face pinched in disgust.

"He kept trying to pull the tube out when he was dreaming," Jenn explained. "It sounds like it'll be there for a few more hours. I'm sure a doctor will tell us more soon."

They chatted for a few more minutes until Josh's nurse came through the double doors. She was heading home, which meant they could be with Josh again.

"Can I see him?" Rachel asked.

Steve looked at Jenn. She raised her eyebrows and gave a quick nod.

"Sure," Steve said to Rachel. "First Rachel and Sara? Then we'll trade out. Jenn, do you want to go home? Take a nap or a shower?"

Jenn shook her head. "I'm not ready to leave him." Her voice cracked. "I'll go grab some food and then wait out here."

After the girls went back, Jenn said to Steve, "I've been racking my brain for why he'd do this, and I've only come up with one reason that feels right. He got someone pregnant... and she wants to get an abortion!"

"What?" Steve exclaimed.

"What else could bother him so much? Obviously, I didn't ask with the tube in his mouth. We'd help him raise the baby, right? They could live with us?"

Steve rubbed his face and took a deep breath. She knew it was a lot to take in. Jenn gave him a minute to think.

"We'll do whatever needs to be done to make this right, whatever *it* is." Steve sighed and shook his head. "Let's wait to talk to him until he gets home, agreed?"

"Agreed," Jenn said. "I need some coffee."

"Do you want company?"

"Only if you want the joy of a hospital cafeteria early in the morning," Jenn teased lamely.

"In that case I'll pass," Steve said. "I'll just wait here until it's my turn to go in."

"We're gonna get through this, right?" Jenn said.

Steve nodded. "We will, but I just wish I knew what *this* really was."

"Agreed," said Jenn. She squeezed Steve's hand and walked away, hoping their faith would see them through this crisis.

It was disorienting to be out here. The hospital felt vast compared with the cocoon she had been in with Josh all night. Jenn walked to the cafeteria though she had no appetite. The food choices overwhelmed, but she was past ready for her morning caffeine. She settled on a banana and coffee. Standing in line, she was acutely aware of the people around her. She wondered if anyone else here was going through what her family was. Her gaze flicked across the array of faces—many ages, races, and sizes.

Some were dressed in business clothes, chatting with their colleagues. A few people were in scrubs. She spied a couple at a table with red-rimmed eyes; they weren't here for work.

God bless them with a full recovery for their loved one, she prayed.

Somehow, she felt better knowing she wasn't the only person in pain.

A text came through while she was paying for her food. She couldn't manage to juggle it all, so she waited until she finished with the cashier, set the food on a table, and pulled out her phone.

Tube coming out! Steve texted.

Joy filled her chest. That was a great sign. She texted back, Thank the Lord.

She walked back to the reception area, where she found Rachel sitting alone.

"How is he?" Jenn asked her daughter.

"Mom, he looks so much better. Just like Josh. Well, maybe like he had the flu or something. But so much better. The nurse said she'd bring him a tray. After he eats and goes to the bathroom, he can leave."

"Really?" Jenn asked.

Rachel shrugged her shoulders. "That's what I heard her say to Dad."

Jenn's stomach unclenched. Soon they would all be home, and this would be behind them.

She flipped through old magazines, including the one with the penguins and sperm whales that Rachel was reading last night.

Ding. A text came from Steve: J sitting up.

Ten minutes later Jenn's phone chimed again.

Trade? Steve texted.

She replied: Y

Jenn left Rachel to join her son and oldest daughter. She felt nervous walking down the shiny corridor. She'd never felt uncertain around Josh, but he'd never been in a situation like this before. He was sitting up with Sara on the bed right next to him. He laughed at something his sister said. He looked better but also so vulnerable, like a little boy.

A sad smile passed over his face when Josh saw her. Jenn leaned past Sara to give him a hug. He wrapped his arms tightly around her and held on for a long time.

"I'm sorry," he whispered in her ear. "I'm so embarrassed."

She pulled back and looked him in the eye, putting her hand on his cheek. "I'm glad you're all right now. We'll talk more at home. Just know that I love you. So much. We'll get through this together, with our Lord's guidance and love."

Josh gave a small nod.

A middle-aged white man in a lab coat walked through the curtain and introduced himself. He told them he was the psychiatrist who would be doing Josh's evaluation. Jenn knew this was coming, but it still felt strange. Dr. Post went through a few questions in front of Jenn and Sara and then asked to speak to Josh in private.

Sara and Jenn went out to the waiting room. Jenn was anxious, thinking about what the doctor was asking and how Josh might be answering. After a long twenty minutes, Dr. Post found Jenn and Steve in the waiting area. They walked to a corner of the room so Rachel and Sara couldn't overhear their conversation.

"Your son is cleared to go home." A wave of relief passed through Jenn. "I've written a prescription for an antidepressant. It can take a few weeks to take full effect. I want to see him next month. Call my office to make an appointment." The psychiatrist handed them two cards. "Here's the name of a therapist.

You may choose your own, of course, but Kyle is excellent in this kind of situation, and I recommend him highly."

Jenn was dazed. Josh on antidepressants? Seeing a therapist?

"Are you sure he's depressed?" she questioned the doctor. "He's a great student. A student athlete. He's responsible and respectful."

"Actually, those are the kinds of teens we see here most often. They deal with enormous stresses, and it becomes too much. Josh talked to me about social pressures, especially the overwhelming demand to get into a good college. He said he's been unhappy for some time."

Jenn asked, "He didn't give you any other reasons he might be upset?"

"No. We didn't have an extensive conversation. This was a screening. The goal is for the antidepressant to give him the floor he needs to handle whatever pressures he is dealing with in a more constructive way than wanting to end his life."

End his life. Those words hit Jenn like bricks to the belly. She looked at her husband with a silent question.

Steve said, "Jenn, we're going to do what the doctors think is best."

"A combination of talk therapy and medication is indicated," the doctor said, "and generally very successful."

"And prayer," Jenn said, recovering her voice. "We'll be praying with and for our son."

The doctor nodded. "Your family is welcome to supplement the recommended treatment however you see fit. I'll see you in my office in four to six weeks. Call if you need anything in the meantime."

SEVEN

Sara

The family filled the Land Cruiser. Mom kept turning and smiling at her, Josh, and Rachel in the back seat. It was creepy and sweet at the same time. Sara rested her head on Josh's shoulder, giving and getting comfort on this strange ride home.

Sara was a jumble of feelings. She now understood the saying "an elephant in the room." They were being smothered by something huge, but none of them was mentioning it.

Rachel stared out of the window, not paying attention to anyone. Sara wracked her mind for something to say.

She spoke quietly into Josh's ear, "Bet you ten dollars Mom suggests a trip."

He barely smiled. She wasn't helping.

Mom said, "Rachel and I think we should have a family trip to Monterey soon. We haven't been to the aquarium in a long time."

Josh looked at Sara, this time barely able to hide his smile.

"You owe me ten bucks," she whispered.

"I never took that bet," he replied.

"Can we go to the Santa Cruz boardwalk, too?" Rachel asked.

"That sounds like fun," Dad said.

Sara loved the boardwalk when she was in middle school. It felt like the epitome of cool, walking around in your shorts and a sweatshirt, going on rides by the ocean and eating fried food and dipping dots.

"Maybe over Easter break?" Mom suggested.

"Mine's not the same as theirs, you know," Sara said.

Mom looked at Sara with a question.

"My break is in March," Sara explained. "Not at Easter; it's the middle of the semester."

Mom looked deflated. "Of course." She nodded. "I guess we can wait until summer."

"No, you go without me," Sara replied, "My schedule may not line up with yours, even over the summer."

"We can go to Monterey without you," Mom said, "but we have to take a family vacation this summer. All of us. Agreed?"

"Sure, I just won't know my schedule for a while. Everyone says I need to take a summer class if I want to get out in four years."

"Let's look at the calendar when we get home."

"I won't know what summer session I get until registration in May." Sara hoped she sounded neutral. "Something will work out, Mom, but we can't plan now."

Mom sat back with a sigh. Why did she have to push everything so far? They sat in silence on the rest of the drive home.

As they parked in the garage, Mom said, "Josh, take a rest before dinner. Do you want company?"

"No, Mom. I want to be by myself," Josh replied. He looked wiped out from the ride.

"Oh, your room..." Mom stopped, pain covering her face. "I forgot. It's a mess."

Dad broke in. "Rachel and I took care of it."

"What's wrong with my room?" Josh asked, his brows knitted in a question.

"The paramedics... and vomit. Your comforter was ruined," Dad said. "I threw it out. There's a blanket on your bed."

Josh looked horrified. "Sorry, Dad."

Dad replied calmly, "It's okay, Josh."

"Let's talk later," Mom suggested. "You rest. I'll get dinner ready."

Sara felt protective of Josh as he walked away. Tall but hunched over, he looked like a kid and a grown-up at the same time. She remembered how overwhelming junior year was—a bunch of kids couldn't take the pressure. Josh didn't seem to be the type to buckle under school pressure, but she was wrong. She felt terrible that he didn't know he could confide in her.

"Mom, can I be with you when you talk to Josh? I don't have to say anything, but you know... it can be intimidating to have a 'talk' with you two."

"Sara, we are going to be very gentle with your brother. You don't have to protect him from us."

Sara shrugged. "I just..."

Dad interrupted. "Sara's right. You just sit by him and be there for moral support. Okay?"

Sara smiled at her dad. "One hundred percent."

After they ate, Sara sat with Josh on one side of their boring beige couch. Mom and Dad were on the other. She was glad she was with him; just being in the living room and not the family room was intimidating.

Josh looked exhausted and frightened. Mom seemed nervous. She couldn't tell how Dad felt.

"Josh, we want to understand what happened," Dad said, sounding measured and thoughtful. "We're confused. Very confused. Can you tell us what you were thinking? Were you trying to end your life?"

"No. I wanted to *stop* thinking... about everything. I just wanted a break."

"A break?" Mom asked. "Twenty-seven sleeping pills for a *break?*"

Josh hung his head and mumbled, "It was stupid, I know. I'm so ashamed. I won't do it again. I promise."

Dad asked, "Is there something you've done that you're ashamed about?"

Sara's heart pounded. She was scared just waiting to hear his answer. Josh grabbed a down pillow and hugged it to his stomach. Sara put a hand on his back. He muttered, "I don't know."

Dad explained, "God can forgive you, whatever your sins. You know that, right? Tell us what's bothering you."

Josh mumbled, "Like I told that doctor, school pressure, college—" He stopped short and didn't say more.

"Josh, there's no taking back suicide. You can't fix it. It's permanent," Dad reminded him. "Your salvation is at stake."

That word, *suicide*, is that what Josh wanted? Sara felt tears push at the back of her eyes. Not wanting to make this about her she blinked them back.

Mom probed, gently this time, "Whatever is bothering you —grades, college, drugs, girls—can be fixed."

"I don't take drugs, I promise!"

"Whatever you might need a break from, they are nothing, absolutely nothing, compared to"—Mom stopped to choose her words carefully—"taking care of your soul. Do you agree?"

Josh nodded without looking up.

Dad asked, "Does the Bible say you need to go to college?"

Josh shook his head.

"Your primary obligation is to take care of your soul. If

school pressures are too much, then we need to dial back," Dad said. "Do you need to quit the team?"

Josh looked up, panic on his face. "No. Not that, please," he begged.

"Do you need to drop your APs?" Mom asked.

"No. I'm not doing too much. I don't want to quit anything. That would only make it worse. I'd feel like more of a loser," he mumbled.

Sara nodded. Everyone in high school felt like they were about to be a loser—or already were one.

Mom exclaimed, "Honey, you aren't a loser! How can you say that?"

"I'm so different from everyone else. I pretend, but it's true."

"Because you're Christian?" Mom asked.

Josh looked between their parents. He gave a small shake of his head. "I... I can't. I don't know." He shrugged.

"Josh, your faith should be a source of pride," Mom chastised.

Dad placed a hand on Mom's knee to chill her out—he could tell she was being too harsh.

Mom spoke more gently, "Josh, I'm sorry. I was just so scared. We love you. More than you can possibly know."

Josh looked at her and nodded, his expression flat.

"I know high school is hard. It will get better, I promise. Can you imagine what might have happened? Your sisters... us. Our lives would have been ruined..." Mom stared at Josh, tears in her eyes.

Josh nodded, tears in his eyes, too.

Sara didn't stop herself from welling up.

Mom said, "Next time you feel like that, come to us. To me. With anything."

Mom let out her breath, looked at Dad, then back at Josh. No one said anything. Josh glanced back and forth between

Mom and Dad and then down at the ground. He seemed dejected.

Finally, Josh asked, "Anything else?" His voice and face were flat.

Dad replied, "You're not giving us anything, Josh, so we're going to follow the doctor's orders: medicine and therapy."

"And we want you to have counseling with Pastor James," Mom added.

Josh hung his head and dug his hand into his hair. He grabbed at his roots. With his head still lowered, he mumbled, "Do I have to?"

"Yeah," Dad said, kind but firm.

Josh gave a single nod. "Can I go to my room now?"

Dad nodded as Mom said, "I suppose."

Josh got up. "I am sorry."

"We'll get through this, together, with our Lord's guidance." Mom stood up to hug him.

Josh was so much taller than Mom that he looked like he was comforting her. Sara hugged him from the other side. Dad wrapped his arms around the three of them.

Dad prayed, "God, help Josh to know that being Your servant is enough. Guide me and Jenn to shepherd him in his time of doubt and fear. Help him to surrender that he may fully know the Grace that comes with Your love. In Jesus's name I pray. Amen."

They stepped apart. Josh's expression was as blank as an avatar.

Mom asked, "Do you want to go to school tomorrow?"

"Can I have one more day?" Josh asked. "Please."

"Sure," Dad replied.

After Josh was out of earshot, Mom asked Dad, "Do you think we got through to him at all?"

Dad replied, "He seems genuinely ashamed and sorry, but he didn't explain much, did he?"

"He's hiding something from us," Mom said. "Did you

notice he didn't deny the girl? I think that might be it. It's frustrating that he's not being honest. I'm sorry I lost my temper. I'm tired and confused, but that's no excuse."

"You had a rough night after a hard day."

"That was the most awful day of my life. I've never been that terrified."

"Me either, Jenn," Dad agreed. "You need sleep. We all do. Hopefully tomorrow will be a reset. You'll be more patient, maybe Josh will be ready to talk to us. Everything might seem more normal."

"Sara, can you talk to him please? I'm afraid he got someone pregnant, and she wants to have an abortion."

"What?!" Was her mom just making this up?

"What else would make him so upset?" Mom said.

That would shake Josh; there was no way he wanted to be a dad right now. But she'd had no hint he had a girlfriend—not that they'd ever talked about it. Josh kept a lot hidden.

"All of us can forgive that. Human impulses are very hard to control when you are sixteen," Mom continued. "We would welcome a baby with open arms. Tell him, okay? That we aren't mad. That we understand. It can seem like the end of your life, but it's just a different one than you imagined. It's hard to be a parent when none of your friends have that responsibility."

Mom sounded so certain. Sara wondered why she didn't bring it up with Josh in the living room. She was curious, but part of her didn't want to know, too.

"Will you talk to him, please?" Mom pleaded. "In the morning, after he's had a good night's sleep, maybe when I take Rachel to school?"

"Sure, Mom, but I don't know that he's going to tell me anything."

"He trusts you, Sara," Dad said.

Sara smiled. She wished her dad was right. She wanted Josh to trust her.

"You don't think he trusts us?" Mom asked.

Sara replied, "Mom, he doesn't want to disappoint you. None of us do. So, telling you when we make mistakes is hard."

"Oh, Sara. I'm sorry."

Mom pulled her into a hug. Sara rested against her mother. She wanted to surrender, to hand over her fear and sadness like when she was a kid. Back then she believed Mom and Dad knew how to fix anything—chase away nightmares, choose a good gift for a friend's birthday, pick out the right outfit for any event, put friend drama in perspective, put a chain back on her bike. They could handle all the things a kid worries about. She missed being certain that her parents could make everything all better.

The next morning Mom popped into her room to tell her she was heading out to drive the carpool.

"This is your chance," Mom reminded her, "to talk to Josh—let him know we are not upset about the baby."

"You may not be right, Mom. You know that, right?"

Mom sighed. "I know. I'll make you smoothies when I get back."

"Thanks, Mom," Sara said.

Mom nodded. She looked scared and confused, not a normal look for her mom.

Josh a dad? That was crazy to think about. Was she going to be an aunt? She'd be all the more relieved to be a few BART stops away.

She got up, did her bathroom things, and then knocked on Josh's door.

"Come in." His voice was clear. He'd been awake for a while.

"Hey Joshy, how was your night?" His bed looked strange without his comforter.

He shrugged.

"Did you sleep?"

He nodded.

"Any dreams?"

He shook his head.

"Can I sit?"

He nodded and welled up. She welled up, too.

"I wish I had magic fairy spray to make you feel better," Sara said as she climbed onto his bed.

"Like when we were kids," he said. "Me, too."

She jumped right in. "Mom thinks you got someone pregnant. She says she's not mad—that she understands it's hard to control your body."

He shook his head, just the tiniest amount. "I wish," he replied. "I know they could forgive that."

Sara's heart pounded hard, so hard that it actually hurt. *God, please help my brother.*

Josh put his face in his hands. He pulled his legs up and curled up in a little ball, like a fetus. Sara stared at him, not knowing what to say or do.

God, please help my brother. God, please help my brother. God, please help my brother.

"I can't say it," he whispered. He reached into his night-stand drawer and pulled out a notebook. His hand shook.

"Josh, I will love you no matter what. God will love you no matter what. Mom and Dad will, too, I know it."

His hand shook as he wrote. She read upside down:

I
AM

He stopped. He looked at her. She put a hand on his leg.

"We will all love you, I promise."

Then he wrote three more letters:

G
A
Y

Sara gasped. She read the whole sentence: I AM GAY

"Are you sure? How do you... oh, dear Lord. Josh."

He looked at her.

"It's terrible, right?" he asked. "I don't think they can love me."

"Josh, you have to tell them!" Sara insisted.

"I can't. They'll hate me," Josh said. "Do you hate me?" he then asked, despair thickening his words.

"Oh, Joshy! Of course not," Sara insisted. "I'm afraid for you. I love you. I could never hate you. But you have to tell Mom and Dad. They won't hate you either. Have you told anyone else?"

"No." He sighed. "I tried telling Pastor James, but I got too scared. You're the first person I've told out loud. How can you not hate me? I feel so unclean... I hate me."

"Special treat!" Mom burst through the door, her voice forced. She carried two smoothies. "You can have breakfast up here today."

Josh shoved the notebook under his covers. Sara looked between Josh and Mom. His eyes were red; it was obvious he'd been crying. Were hers? She didn't think she'd cried, but maybe. They stung, but Mom didn't call attention to it.

She started to set the smoothies down on the nightstand, but Josh stopped her. "We'll come down."

Sara's head was spinning. She stood up and stared at the two of them. How could she keep this secret? Should she hug Josh? Had she said the right thing? She couldn't even remember how she had reacted. Josh—gay?

"What time do you need to leave for BART?" Mom asked. "I can take you. I'll stop by Walgreens on my way home to get the pictures from the game and your prescription filled." She looked at Josh.

Had she heard their conversation? Obviously, she was pretending to be happy.

"I don't want to take any drugs, Mom," Josh said, his voice full of emotion.

Mom replied, "Josh, I'm not happy about it, either, but the doctor was clear: medicine and therapy. Dad says we're following the doctor's orders. I'll call the counselor he suggested when I get home." More gently she said, "You need something, Josh. They're the experts. We have to trust them."

In a flat tone Josh conceded, "All right."

"Let's sign you up for the SAT today, too," Mom said and then took it right back, "Sorry. Never mind. We can do that whenever you're ready. No pressure."

"It's okay, Mom," Josh said. But he didn't look okay.

"When do you want to leave?" Mom looked at Sara.

"Nine forty-five, 'kay?"

Mom said, "Okay. Actually—how about nine thirty? I want to get to the store before it gets too crowded."

Sara was puzzled, but just said, "I'll be ready."

She waited for her mom to leave before giving Josh a giant hug.

"Do you want me to stay?" Sara asked. "I don't have to leave today."

Josh shook his head. "No. You go back to Berkeley."

She stared at him. "I love you. God loves you. Mom and Dad, too, but it might take them a while to get used to this."

"Really?"

She nodded. "I promise."

"Are you sure?"

"Josh, when you go to college you are going to meet all kinds of people who are good and kind and not Christian. Do you know that most of the people in the world aren't Christian?"

Josh stared off for a moment.

"But every religion says it's an abomination." Josh swallowed.

"I don't know, Josh. I've met all kinds of cool people that don't think like us. I haven't been as certain about who God loves and who God doesn't love."

"Really?"

"Cross my heart," she said. "I was really uncomfortable on Saturday. They looked so happy."

Josh pulled in his lips and bit the lower one. Finally he replied, "It was awful."

"You never have to do anything like that ever again."

He nodded. She hugged him hard and tried to pour a little love into him. Had she made things a little better for Josh? She hoped so but couldn't really tell.

"Call me and text me anytime, K?"

He nodded. Then he shooed her with his hands, "Go. I'll be okay."

She smiled a tender smile at him and left to get ready to go back to Berkeley.

Mom didn't talk as they drove. Sara didn't mind the quiet. She was still thinking about what Josh had told her and what she should say or do about it. Somehow it fit, even though she'd never thought that about him before now. She considered texts in her head: love you, Josh; you got this; xoxo; or just :).

Mom sped through the light.

Sara spoke up, "Mom. Mom!"

"What?"

Sara replied, "You missed the turn."

"Oh, sorry." But instead of turning around she pulled to the side of the road.

"What are you doing?" Sara asked.

"Sara," Mom said cautiously, "I heard you and Josh talking in his room this morning."

Sara opened her eyes wide, and she bit her lip. "So you know. Are you okay with it?"

"I don't know... what 'it' is. I heard you say he should tell us something and then I heard him crying," Mom said. "What's Josh keeping from us?"

"I can't tell you." Sara shook her head. "You have to ask Josh."

"Honey, clearly he needs help with his situation."

"He barely trusts me, Mom. I can't go against that, but please ask him. I want you to know. I told him to tell you." Suddenly Sara started sobbing. She put her face in her hands, and her shoulders shook. She cried like a little kid and didn't stop herself. She was scared for Josh and all of them. What would Mom and Dad do if Josh was really gay? It could tear their family apart.

"Sara." Mom put her arm around her daughter. "This is too great a secret for you to bear alone. Please tell me. Daddy and I can handle this. Hand over this burden to us."

Sara shook her head but didn't look up.

Mom stiffened. "Sara, do you understand how serious this is? Your brother attempted suicide. If you know why, you have to tell us."

"I can't," she pushed out from a tight throat.

Mom scolded, "You're taking his side against us?"

"I..." Sara tried to speak. Her voice caught. She took a jerky breath. "I... I'm scared, Mom. So scared."

Mom's eyes welled up, too. "Oh, honey... me, too."

Sara pulled her seatbelt loose and leaned against her mom, crying into her chest. Mom wrapped her arms around Sara.

"I don't understand," Mom spoke softly into her hair. "Why can't you tell me?"

Sara pulled back from her mom's arms. "I... just... he has to be the one to tell you. It has to be him. I want him to trust me, Mom. He has to know he can trust someone... don't you see?"

"He can trust me," Mom replied. "Why doesn't he know that? Is it a baby?" Mom stared at Sara looking for a reaction. Sara kept her face flat, not wanting to give anything away.

"Drugs?" Mom probed. "We'll take him to rehab. There are treatments."

Sara shook her head. Very quietly she said, "I'm not telling you. At least not yet. I told Josh to confide in you. And I begged him not to do anything stupid. I think he got the message."

Mom sat back in her seat and let out her breath. She wiped her eyes and rubbed her face. Sara sat up, too.

"Sara, our life is unraveling. You know why, your brother needs our support, and you won't tell me?" She was mad.

Sara said, "I can't. Trust me, Mom."

Mom sighed, started the car, and drove to the BART station. In the parking lot, Sara said, "Mom, I'm not taking Josh's side *against* you. We all have to be on Josh's side. He needs each of us right now."

Mom spoke sharply. "I never thought you'd keep important secrets from me. Now I don't know what to believe."

"I love you. You can believe that. And so does Josh. He's confused and needs to know you love him."

"I'm confused, too, Sara," Mom said.

Mom didn't say she loved Sara, or Josh. Everything was coming apart.

EIGHT

Jenn

At Walgreens, Jenn acted as if everything were normal. The world went on despite her personal turmoil. She suspected the clerk gave her a knowing look after reading the prescription, but she didn't care. Exhausted, even though it was only ten in the morning, she found the cold, hard chair in the waiting area a welcome break. Her eyes followed the black lines that divided the linoleum squares. The receptionist called Josh's name. Normally, Jenn leapt up the moment a prescription was ready. Today she just sat in the tacky plastic chair, avoiding going home until she had made a plan for what to do next.

She decided to search Josh's room as soon as possible. She'd never rifled through any of her children's belongings, because she'd never felt the need. But Josh's life was at stake. He had a secret, and she needed to know the truth.

When she got home with the medicine and the photos, Josh was in the shower. This was her chance. She rushed to his bedroom, knowing he'd be furious if he caught her, but utterly certain of the need. She rummaged through his desk, going through each drawer, looking for anything that looked like a journal. She found a few notebooks, but they were all for schoolwork. Nothing journal-like was in the drawers of his bureau. She rooted through his nightstand and even under his mattress. Her heart caught at the sight of a LEGO Stormtrooper in his nightstand drawer. She paused for a moment, remembering the little boy who built for hours on end. She cleared her head and searched on but found nothing that revealed his secret. Worried about being caught, she slipped out of his room the instant she heard the shower turn off.

Jenn went to the computer in the family room. She opened Google and typed in "How to monitor your kids on the Internet." She clicked on the first article from *Parenting* magazine. Reading through it, she learned about parental controls, passwords, and search histories.

Listening for Josh, she clicked on "History" and then again on "February 14," the night before Josh took the pills. A list popped down: yahoo.com, myspace.com, and so on. Nothing jumped out. She looked behind her to make sure Josh had not come down quietly. She went back another day and scanned down: Bank of America, Bank of America sign-in, Yahoo, Yahoo sign-in, MySpace, "How many sleeping pills can kill you?"

Jenn's stomach dropped. Her hands got instantly clammy, and her mouth went dry.

The next URL was a gay quiz. After that, another search query: "How do you know if you are gay?"

What?! That wasn't what she was expecting to see. Her heart squeezed so hard it felt like it might burst.

"Mom?" Josh's voice came from behind her.

She jumped and released the mouse. The search history disappeared. She quickly hit the Back button and was at the Google search page again. Jenn felt her heart pounding in her chest. She hoped her face wasn't flushed. She forced a calm expression onto her face. Then she turned around.

She looked at Josh and asked neutrally, "What?"

"I just want to tell you that you're right," he said. "I need to talk with someone—and you were right about the medicine, too. I'm sorry I was being difficult."

"I'm sorry, too, Josh." Jenn kept her voice calm while her head and chest were exploding. "We only want what's best for you. We can't help you if you won't tell us what's wrong. Do you understand that?"

Josh nodded.

"Is there anything you want to tell me?" Jenn pushed. Maybe he would just come out with it. He looked like he wanted to say something. Unconsciously, she held her breath. She wanted his trust.

Josh shook his head.

She exhaled with a sigh. "All right. I'll call the therapist now," she told him.

"Can I use the computer?" he asked.

"What for?" Jenn asked, trying to sound casual.

"A school project. I have an essay on the Civil War due at the end of the week."

"Don't push yourself too hard."

"I won't."

"Let me just finish what I'm doing." Jenn turned back to the computer. Josh walked into the kitchen, and she closed the windows from her search.

Jenn walked up the stairs, breathing deeply to fend off panic. Her world was coming apart more than she could possibly have imagined. Homosexual? Her Josh? It made no sense. She sat on her bed, her mind reeling as she considered what to do. Her whole body shook. Her immediate impulse was to ask Josh about the search.

But she didn't want to face the answer alone.

Jenn's hands shook as she dialed Steve's work number. He didn't pick up. She went to her chair to pray: *Merciful God, by the power of Your command, drive away from my son all forms of sickness and disease. Restore strength to his body and joy to his spirit so that, in his renewed health, he may bless and serve You, now and forevermore. Please, God, help me to understand or at least accept the path You have put us on. In Jesus's name I pray. Amen.*

She felt a little bit better but not normal. Sitting on the edge of the bed, her leg jiggling up and down, Jenn dialed Steve again.

"What's up?" he asked on the other end.

"It's me." Jenn started to cry. "I'm sorry to bother you." Her voice was high and cracking. "I just don't know what to do."

"Did Josh hurt himself again?" Steve asked, panic in his voice.

"No, but I'm afraid he's going to. I overheard him and Sara talking about a secret. He was very upset. I wanted to know why, so I looked up how to spy on him on the computer. Last week he searched on Google about being..." She faltered. "About being *homosexual*"—she whispered the word—"and how to kill himself." Just saying it out loud made her feel ill.

Sounding confused, he asked, "Are you sure?"

"I'm sure I saw that search history," Jenn explained. "I'm afraid he thinks he's homosexual."

"What did you say to him?" Steve asked, his voice tight and controlled.

"Nothing. I'm too upset. I wanted to calm down and talk to you first. What should we do?" The line was silent. "Steve? Are you there?"

"Yes, I'm thinking. You're sure he thinks *he's* the homosexual?"

"I'm not certain of anything." She sounded angry rather than what she felt—overwhelmed.

"Maybe he looked on behalf of a friend?" Steve suggested.

Hope rose in her chest. "You think it might not be him?"

"Let's talk to him together when I get home. Okay?"

"Mom!" Josh yelled up the stairs, startling Jenn. She wondered whether he'd overheard. She felt guilty but reminded herself that she was only helping her son.

"Okay, together, tonight," Jenn told Steve. "Please leave early if you can. It's going to be hard to be with him and not ask him about this. Josh is calling, so I have to go. I love you."

"I love you, too. Stay strong." Then he hung up.

Strong. Jenn did not feel very strong.

She inhaled to calm herself and draw in energy. Keeping her voice light, she yelled down to her son, "Yes?"

"Should I make myself lunch?"

"No. I'll be down in a sec, after I finish a phone call."

"Thanks, Mom."

He sounded just like her Josh, not like a... homosexual. It just didn't make any sense to her. He was devout and kind. Why would he possibly choose to hurt himself and them? Jenn picked up the card on her nightstand and dialed the therapist's number.

She reached his voicemail. A kind, calm voice invited her to leave a message.

Jenn spoke into her phone, her voice shaky and weak. "Hi. My name is Jenn Henderson. I got your name from Dr. Post at Eden. My son... He thinks... My son. My son may have attempted suicide. We hope you can help him." She left her home and cell numbers and hung up.

She couldn't even admit that Josh had hurt himself on purpose. That was a phone call that Jenn had never made before and had never expected to make.

Dear God, give me strength.

In the kitchen, Jenn put on a calm face. She pulled out a can of tomato soup, some Swiss cheese, and sourdough bread. Fox News ran in the background, but she didn't listen to it as she made Josh's lunch. While she was cooking, he came in and set the table without being asked. He was such a thoughtful person —he couldn't be a homosexual.

She slid a golden-brown grilled cheese onto the plate in front of him and then set a bowl of warm red soup next to it.

"You made my favorite. Thanks, Mom." He looked like he was about to cry.

"Of course. You're my favorite son." She smiled, feeling teary herself. This was their long-standing joke. When he was younger, he'd always replied, "Aw, Mom, I'm your only son." He'd stopped saying that some time ago. When did that happen? There were so many little endings in her children's lives that it was impossible to track them all.

Today he just looked at her and shook his head with a small smile. He grabbed half of the sandwich and dipped it in the soup. She watched as he took the first bite. She longed to say more but was at a loss for words. Instead, she put her own lunch out and washed the pan in silence.

When she finished cleaning up, she came up behind Josh and wrapped her arms around his shoulders. He put his hand over hers. She leaned over and kissed the top of his dark-brown hair. She was full of adoration for her son. Could he feel the love she poured into him? She said a silent prayer: *Lord, heal my son in mind, body, and spirit. Help him, and me, to be the best instruments for Your will. Amen.*

Her cell phone rang from the other room. She gave Josh a squeeze and went to answer. It was the therapist.

"Thank you for calling me back," Jenn said.

"Of course," the kind, calm voice came through the phone. "Can you tell me a bit more about what's been happening with your son?"

"Yes. Let me get somewhere private," she whispered.

Jenn walked upstairs to her bedroom, closed the door, and

sat on the edge of her bed. "Well, he... I don't... What do you want to know?"

"You mentioned an attempt at suicide. Is he stable now? Is he home? Tell me about that."

"On Sunday, while we were at church—we're Christians—he took twenty-seven sleeping pills. Ambien. They were mine from a trip last summer. I had no idea he would do that, or I would have thrown them out. We didn't know he was depressed."

"Has his mood changed recently?" he asked.

"He's been quieter, but he's sixteen. We expect him to tell us less, to be more private."

"Do you know what may be bothering him?"

"Well, he told the doctor at the hospital that school pressure was hard," Jenn explained. She started to leave it at that but then went on. It was hard to say out loud. "I also have a small idea that he might be confused... He might think he is homosexual." Jenn choked up a bit. She cleared her throat.

"What makes you think that?"

"On the Internet he did a search for 'How do you know you are homosexual?' You know, on Google. It's probably for a friend. I'm just telling you what I saw."

"Have you talked to him about this?" Kyle sounded curious.

"Not yet. I just found this today. His father and I want to talk to him together. He can't be homosexual. He knows it's a sin."

"I see," Kyle said calmly. "It makes sense why he might be troubled."

"Can you help him?" Jenn asked.

"I believe so."

Jenn felt relieved; her shoulders loosened, and her breath came easier. She was already attached to the idea that this man could fix her son.

Kyle went on, "We need to meet each other so he can

decide if we're a good match. It's a very personal decision, working with a therapist. He needs to feel I'm the right fit for him. I assume you would like an appointment after school. I have time in my schedule on Thursday at four."

"He has basketball practice," Jenn explained. "Sorry to be difficult."

"It's no problem," Kyle replied. "I have morning appointments, and... I have Mondays at seven. Will that work?"

"Yes, thank you. Very much." Jenn's voice was high and tight, and she knew the therapist could tell she was upset.

"You're welcome. This is hard on all of you. It's natural to have strong feelings."

Jenn nodded even though he couldn't see her. She didn't trust her voice.

Kyle gave her his address and other details. By the time she'd collected herself, Josh had finished lunch. She found him in his room.

Jenn leaned on the doorframe. "I just spoke to Kyle Goss, the therapist. You have an appointment with him on Monday at seven." She hoped she sounded calm and normal, though she didn't feel that way.

Josh's eyes widened. "What did you tell him?"

Jenn paused to search for the right words. "I told him you were under stress, that you took a lot of sleeping pills, and that we're Christian. He seemed to think he could be helpful. He sounded nice, Josh. I think you'll like talking with him."

"I guess." Josh shrugged.

"I'll be downstairs if you need anything. Rachel will be home around three-thirty. Lindsay's dropping her off today." She paused to say more, but nothing came. She felt a giant rock wall between her and Josh. She hoped the conversation tonight would tear it down—or let her know that it was never there.

Jenn made another of Josh's favorites for dinner: lasagna. While she cooked, she ruminated over the previous forty-eight hours. She was so distracted that she nearly burned the onions beyond use. *Trust in the Lord. Stay calm*, she reminded herself. She wanted to have dinner in the oven before Steve got home. The sound of the front door opening and closing told her Rachel was back from school.

"I'm in the kitchen," she called to her daughter.

"How's Josh?" Rachel whispered as she got close.

"Better. A lot better. We've had a sweet day." She kept her voice light. She was not about to share her discovery with Rachel. "How was your day?"

"Not good. I was too worried about Josh to pay any attention. I know I'm going to fail my geometry test on Friday."

Jenn crossed to her youngest child and gave her a hug. This was turning her life upside down, too.

Rachel clung to Jenn. "Is he going to be okay? People at school asked. I didn't know what to say."

"Just say he was sick and he's better now. That's all. Did people hear he was in the hospital?"

Rachel nodded. "I guess Michael told his friends, and it spread."

Jenn's stomach churned. "I'm sorry, Rachel. It isn't anyone's business. He'll be at school tomorrow, so they'll see for themselves that he's fine."

"Is he? Really okay?" Rachel asked eagerly.

"I'm not going to lie to you," Jenn replied. "He's struggling with something big. But I have faith that God will heal him. Have you been praying for Josh?"

"I start, but I don't know what to pray."

"I'll give you my favorite. It helps me—a lot. Say it three or four times a day. Whenever you find yourself worrying about him, just say the prayer. Hand over your fear and sadness to the Lord."

Jenn went to the computer in the family room, typed out the prayer, and printed it for her daughter: *"Almighty and merciful God, dear Lord Jesus, by the power of Your command, drive away from my brother all forms of sickness and disease. Restore strength to his body and joy to his spirit so that, in his renewed health, he may bless and serve You, now and forevermore. In Jesus's name we pray. Amen."*

Jenn's phone vibrated. She flipped it open and saw a text message.

Did u talk 2 j?

It was Sara.

Not yet. waiting 4 dad 2 b home.

K ILY.

Jenn looked up from her phone and asked Rachel, "What does this mean?"

"I love you." Rachel laughed. "You're so cute, Mom." Then she disappeared into the kitchen for a snack.

Jenn was proud of herself for texting at all. And now she was supposed to remember what all these letters meant? It was hard to keep up with these new things.

NINE

Josh

Josh sat at his desk, pushing himself to do his schoolwork so he'd be ready for school in the morning. How many kids knew what had happened? Hopefully not many. He wanted to get back to regular life and pretend nothing was wrong. He couldn't believe he'd told Sara his secret.

She looked... disgusted? Afraid? Maybe stricken was the right word. She eventually came round to saying something kind, like she didn't think he was an abomination, but she might be pretending. He shook his head to make himself stop thinking about it. He had to focus on his English assignment—personal essays for college applications.

The assignment was to brainstorm three possibilities. He'd figured out two: what he'd learned about losing by being on the basketball team and when he experienced the presence of God in Yosemite—though he wouldn't call it God in a college essay, he'd use wonder or awe or something secular to explain how he felt in the valley. He had no clue about the third.

A knock was followed by Mom walking in with laundry. She likely just wanted to check on him.

"You okay, honey?" Mom asked with a small smile.

"Fine, Mom," he said. "Thanks for doing my laundry."

Then he looked back at his spiral notebook. She stood there, wanting something, but he ignored her. Eventually he glanced over. Her eyes were closed, and her hand was up in prayer. He closed his eyes and joined her. *God, please take these unhealthy urges out of me.* Maybe tomorrow he would wake up different.

Mom left without a word. He finished his basketball essay outline and then gave up. He was too tired to think. He'd let himself nap and get back to his work after dinner.

Josh was dozing in bed when he heard his door open. He opened his eyes to see who was there: his parents, both of them. This wasn't good. He pulled his blanket over his face.

"Josh, sit up, please," Dad said. "We need to speak with you about something very important."

Josh froze.

"Joshua!" Mom scolded.

They knew. Sara had told them. Hurt that she'd betrayed him and terrified to talk to his parents, he shook his head back and forth. There was no way he could look at them. Anytime he had imagined this moment, he wanted to disappear, not really die, just be gone. That's why he had taken those pills.

"Complete and immediate obedience, Josh." Dad said the line from his childhood. His heart raced, but he didn't sit up.

He whined, "I can't. I can't look at you. I'm so ashamed of myself. I just want to die."

Mom hugged him over the covers. He tried to push her arms off him with a shrug.

"If you really knew me, you would hate me," Josh mumbled from under the blankets.

"Josh, we can never hate you." Mom sounded like she meant it.

"We're going to help you, son," Dad said, his voice full of emotion. "I've been doing research. There are cures."

Josh asked, "Cures for what?"

Very quietly Dad said, "Same-sex attraction. Homosexuality."

The word pierced Josh. He moaned, turning to his side and curling up as tight as he could.

"Sara told you?" Josh had to know.

"No," Mom practically whispered. "I heard you telling Sara that we would hate you if we knew your secret. I begged Sara to tell me, but she wouldn't. I saw your Google search in the history on our computer."

Josh's heart beat so hard it hurt.

Josh felt ill. "Who have you told?"

"No one, Josh. Just Daddy. I haven't told anyone else," Mom said.

"Don't tell anyone," Josh begged. "I'm so ashamed."

"We should speak with Pastor James," Dad said. "He loves you, Josh. He can be our guide for treatment. There are good cures. I have great faith you won't have to live with this for your whole life."

Josh was doubtful. "Are you sure?"

"I looked into it after Mom called me," Dad explained. "It'll be hard work, and you have to be committed to a cure, but the websites are very clear that treatment is one hundred percent effective."

"*One hundred percent effective?*" A chill passed through Josh. Was that the Holy Spirit? "I'm committed. You know I am, right? I've been praying to be cured since sixth grade."

"Sixth grade?" Mom sounded stunned. "Since you were eleven?"

He nodded.

"Oh, honey." Mom sounded like she was crying. "Five years! You've been living alone with this for that long? I'm so sorry." She bent and kissed the blankets over his head. It was comforting. Dad placed an arm on him, too.

His parents didn't hate him. Josh felt a sob well up in him. His parents still loved him. He was so relieved. They cried and rocked with him.

Then Dad said in his strong, firm voice, "God, in Your name I pray. Lord Jesus Christ, I put my son's life in Your hands, where it has always been. Please heal my dear son Josh of the affliction in his soul. Take away impure longings. Make him strong in mind, body, and spirit that he may live Your will on Earth and in the hereafter. Amen."

Josh felt the Holy Spirit come into his body with each breath. A calm silence filled the room when the prayer was over.

"Pastor James can know," Josh said, still hiding under the blanket.

"Oh, Josh. That's a very wise and mature decision," Mom said. "Would you like to tell him, or should I?"

"You."

"He'll want us all to come in for pastoral counseling. You'll speak with him?"

"Yes."

"That's great, son. You're showing your dedication," Dad said. "I know it's hard. I'm proud of you."

Josh sniffled.

"Do you want to come, too?"

Mom must be asking Dad.

"Of course. First or last part of the day is best, but I'll make anything work."

"You already missed work on Monday," Josh said. "You can't miss more because... of me."

"Josh, your well-being is more important than work." Dad was firm.

Josh pulled the covers back. Mom and Dad's faces were

blotchy and red. His heart twisted. He must look that pathetic, too. He sat up and leaned back against his headboard.

"Are you sure?" he sighed. "I'm sorry to be such a problem."

"I'm absolutely sure," Dad said. "Nothing is more important than my children's souls."

Josh looked back and forth between his parents. "You don't hate me?" He sounded like a whiny kid, but he was desperate.

They both shook their heads.

"We love you, Josh," Dad said, "and only want what's best for you. As a family, we're going to do everything to find a cure. Absolutely everything."

Mom said, "Josh, we're going to work on this together. We'll come through this knowing God's love and Jesus's power more than ever."

Josh leaned forward. Mom wrapped her arms around him, and Dad embraced them both. He didn't pull away for a long time. He felt safe for the first time in so long. His parents knew his secret, they didn't hate him, and they knew a cure.

Thank you, God. I'm sorry I didn't trust in You and them sooner.

Josh was beyond nervous as they pulled into the church parking lot the next morning. He didn't know his heart could pound that hard when he wasn't running. Pastor James had cleared his calendar for this meeting because it was so important.

The tension was thick as they walked on the straight cement path to the church offices. Josh saw a small, yellow crocus poking up from the bare earth of the flower beds along-side the path. It seemed a taunt, way too cheery for what he was about to face.

Josh was twelve when Pastor James came to their church. He still missed the old associate minister, Reverend Gilbert, who'd been there since Josh was born. Pastor James was fine, but not kind, more certain and determined. He didn't have kids and didn't understand the pressures teens faced.

Pastor James, a very average-looking man—thin, medium height, mousy brown hair and brown eyes—gestured to the three chairs in front of his desk, wordlessly inviting them to sit. Josh sat between his parents. The pastor settled into the chair behind his desk.

He spoke directly to Josh. "Your mother tells me you're having homosexual feelings. Is she correct? Are you?"

Josh stared at the desk and nodded wordlessly.

"Have you acted upon the feelings?"

Josh squeezed his eyes shut and his face turned red. He gave a quick shake of his head.

"Congratulations, Josh," Pastor James said enthusiastically. "The ability to refrain from the lifestyle is a strong indicator for successful treatment. Other indicators are the intention to follow our Lord Jesus Christ, and family support and commitment."

Josh had all of those.

Pastor James continued, "Both your parents are here today. Strong family support. Check! Are you willing to do what you need to do to help your son with this affliction?"

"Absolutely, Pastor," Dad said. "A hundred percent. We'll do whatever it takes for Josh to return to righteousness."

Jenn nodded next to him.

"Josh, are you committed to living biblically?" the pastor asked.

Josh looked up. He stared straight at the man across from him and said clearly, "More than anything I want to be right with the Lord Jesus Christ. I want my shame to be gone."

"Well, you've come to the right place. We'll start with prayer. We'll end with prayer. It always comes back to prayer, to your relationship with the Lord. We'll pray in your home, in your room, in youth group. You'll be an example, Josh, for our whole community. You have a special calling: to show sinners who are less committed and weaker a true and righteous path toward God's love. Let us pray." He bowed his head and reached out his hands. The four of them made a circle of connection. "Jesus, in Your name we pray. Lord, help Your child Josh to know he is not alone in his misery, but rather that You love him deeply. Remind him that You do not condemn him for homosexual feelings and temptations, and that You only ask him to desire a righteous path. Turn him away from homosexual lust and relations.

"Lord, release Josh from the hold of the devil. Drive the evil from his soul. Jesus Christ, deliver Josh from his present state of mind so that he can be free to live a morally dignified lifestyle. Lord Jesus, uncover the deep needs at the root of Josh's same-sex desires.

"Lord, guide Josh's parents, Jenn and Steve. They are Your willing servants, no matter how hard the road. They have failed you in some way, Lord. They are ready to do better. Forgive them as they repent of their sins. In your name we pray. Amen."

Mom gave Josh's hand a squeeze before they unclasped hands.

Pastor James said, "We can start on your recovery right now. I know this will sound harsh, but there are very clear steps that will lead to your healing. Josh, trade places with your father. Jenn, they need to work on their relationship. A proven factor in male homosexuality is desperate longing for connection with the male parent. Steve, I'm sure you did not intend for Josh to have a defensive attachment. It happens when fathers are not committed to their children. Josh needs to increase his masculinity by spending less time with you, Jennifer, and more time with Steve participating in traditionally male activities."

"My dad's around as much as any of the dads," Josh responded. "Well, more, since he doesn't commute. And he coached my soccer team."

Dad said, "Josh, don't argue." He stood up and pointed to his chair. Josh slid over.

Pastor James explained, "Josh, I imagine you *think* you have a close relationship with your father, but you wouldn't be having these feelings if you truly did." Then he went on more gently, "As I said, this is going to be hard to hear. No family wants to know that they have damaged their child, but if treatment is going to work, you have to be committed."

Shame filled Josh. Pastor James was blaming his parents for his weakness. It wasn't their fault. But Dad had told him not to argue back, so he didn't say anything.

"We are committed," Dad insisted. "It's just... well, you're right—it's hard to hear."

"Of course. This is a lot to take in," Pastor James said, kindly but firmly. "I'll tell you a few more things before our time is up. Then I'll give you a booklet and some other resources that you can take your time with at home.

"You will also need to find a cause of trauma," Pastor James went on. "Most likely sexual trauma. A babysitter, a grandparent, a teacher. Some male figure in his life sexually abused Josh."

"Nothing like that ever happened to me," Josh declared.

"Most people can't remember," Pastor James replied knowingly. "But it is a fact that homosexual feelings are caused by sexual abuse. Did he go to childcare when he was young?"

"No, of course not," Mom said. "I was home with my children, like I am now."

"Perhaps at a gym for a short time?"

"Yes, I took them to childcare at the gym," Mom replied. "He always loved it."

Pastor James nodded. "Yes, some kids crave that attention, because it is missing from their male parent."

"They were all girls at the gym." Mom sounded confused.

"The men hide in the back until parents are gone. They're very sneaky." Pastor James held up his hands to stave off more comments. "We won't be able uncover this now. It will take a lot of time with a qualified counselor."

"We have an appointment on Monday," Mom told him. "I got the name of a therapist from a doctor."

"Is he a Christian counselor? That's very, very important. I can't emphasize that enough. You do not want someone encouraging these thoughts... or behaviors." Pastor James shivered.

"I'll ask," Mom replied. "I hadn't even thought of that. This is very overwhelming."

"The third thing should help with your confusion: prayer. Nothing is as clarifying as prayer and building your relationship with Christ. He will take away these sinful thoughts and feelings, if you actually believe in Him. The pamphlet I'll be giving you will have some specific prayers. You can't say them too often. You need to shore up your faith. Prayer will be the wall of defense against Josh's unnatural lusts. And Josh," he added, holding up a finger, "pray as if your life depends on it, because it does."

Pastor James continued, "Josh, you are not alone in this struggle. Many young people have succeeded in being cured. I know you'll be one of them. I highly, highly recommend that you go to an Exodus or Resurrection Ministries program as soon as you can. You'll meet inspiring Christians who give you faith and strength like nothing else. Maybe your family can go together. Do you have any questions?"

Josh looked from Pastor James face to the desk. He shook his head. He was back on the roller coaster of horrible feelings, feeling more sick and hopeless than when he arrived. He hadn't ever been abused, he was certain of it. He was too close to his mom and not close to his dad? They caused him to have homosexual attractions? That didn't make any sense, but he wasn't supposed to argue. He wasn't praying enough? He prayed so many times a day. They weren't praying right?

Finally, Dad spoke up. "No questions. Thank you for your time."

"Of course. Let's end with prayer." They held hands while Pastor James spoke to God on their behalf.

They rose when he finished. Pastor James handed Mom a pamphlet. She opened her bag to put it away, then pulled out an envelope. Her hand shook as she handed it to Pastor James.

"Pictures, from the witness on Saturday. I made doubles because I thought you'd want them."

"Thank you, Jenn. You are so thoughtful! We'll get these up on our public ministry board as soon as possible," Pastor James replied. "God bless you."

TEN

Jenn

Jenn held in her tears in the car. *Abused*. The word was a vise grip on her heart. How could she have been so oblivious and naive? She desperately wanted to reach behind and grab Josh's hand, to apologize and ask for his forgiveness. But apparently that was part of the problem: she needed to discourage their connection. Holding herself back was his treatment.

"Jenn, I'll take you home," Steve said. "Then I can drop Josh off at school before I head to work."

Josh sat forward, poking his head between their seats. "I can't face school after that. Can I please just go home?"

"Of course," Jenn said.

Steve looked over at her. He shook his head, eyebrows raised. What was he trying to signal? That Josh should go to school after all he'd been through?

"Josh, you have to man up," Steve said flatly. "No more lying around feeling sorry for yourself. School. Practice. Home. And then youth group. You've got to get back in the game. Sorry, dude."

Jenn looked back at Josh. He looked ready to cry. He sat back hard against the backseat. "All right."

"Do you have everything you need?" Jenn asked. "Your lunch and backpack?"

Steve gave her a glare. Oh! She was doing it again. This was going to be hard. She was so used to caring for her son. Pulling back from that was going to be a huge adjustment.

The phone was ringing as she walked into the house. She rushed to the family room to see who was on the line: her parents. It was probably Mom, since her dad rarely called. She wasn't ready for a conversation yet, so Jenn let the machine pick up.

Her mom's voice came through after the beep. "Jennifer, it's Mom. I'd like to know how Joshy is doing. Please call me when you can. You're all in our prayers, of course. My morning spirit circle is praying for all of you, too. Love you. Call me back as soon as you can."

Suddenly exhausted, Jenn sank down on the sage-colored couch. Her eyes glazed, and she stared at the blank TV across from her. There was a slight reflection from the windows. She saw flecks of dust on the screen sparkling in the sunlight. If she weren't so tired, she would hop up and clean it, but she just wanted to sit. Her mind was a jumble of thoughts. She wondered how Josh was doing. He'd probably just gotten to school. Hopefully Steve had walked him in, because he didn't have a note.

She considered calling Sara or Lindsay or Mom to let them know what Pastor James had told them. It was difficult to believe Josh had been abused, but Pastor James was so certain. Her mind rifled through every adult they knew, every occasion when Josh was out of her sight. She thought about Thanksgivings at Steve's aunt and uncle's house. He used to take naps there alone in a room. Or Christmas at both grandparents' house. Or gatherings at the Bishops'. Or church. The list went on and on. He'd been out of her sight hundreds of times before he started kindergarten.

To stop the thoughts, she tried praying but couldn't get in the right state of mind and spirit. Instead, she turned on the TV, something she normally only did during the day when she was really sick. But she needed a diversion. She flipped the channels until she came to *Family Feud*. That would be distracting enough. When it finished, she considered getting up to do laundry but instead watched *The View*. In the middle of the show, the phone rang. It was her mom again. She sighed, turned off the TV, and picked up.

"Hi, Mom. How are you?"

"Fine. How is Joshy?"

"Josh is struggling. He's still struggling." She did her best to keep her voice even. "We had pastoral counseling today. It's good to feel the support of the church. I know it will help. And your prayers, too."

"I'm sorry, sweetie."

"Me, too, Mom." A tear leaked from Jenn's right eye. "It's laundry day. I have to get it finished before I get Rachel. Thanks for your prayers. We need them."

"Can't you tell me more about what he's struggling with? Specific prayers are more beneficial."

Jenn sighed, "I'm having a hard time understanding myself, Mom."

"I know I'm an old lady, but that just means I've seen a lot of life," her mother stated clearly.

Jenn smiled to herself. She hated to keep anything from her mom. She knew Josh wouldn't like it, but her mom could be trusted with this. She said, "Well, Mom, he's struggling with homosexual thoughts."

"Oh dear," her mom said slowly. After a long pause, she asked, "Are you sure?"

"We're not sure of anything," Jenn said quietly. "We're getting treatment. Pastor James is confident that Josh is a great candidate for therapy."

"Well, that's good. I imagine it's from living so close to San Francisco. You may want to move back home, you know. Have him in an environment more conducive to Christian values."

Jenn rolled her eyes. Her mother had been trying to get her to move back to Orange County since 1987, the year Jenn and her family moved to Dublin. Of course she would use this opportunity to make her case yet again. "Good try, Mom."

"You can't blame me for wanting my kids close."

"No, I can't," Jenn agreed. "And now I'm starting to see things from your side."

Tenderly her mom said, "I'm sorry things are hard... for Joshy and for you. I love you both, very much."

"Thanks, Mom. I love you, too."

"We're praying for your family."

"That means a lot to me." Jenn's voice cracked.

"All things are possible with God."

"I keep reminding myself that He is walking right next to me."

"Yes, He is. God loves you, and Josh, more than we can possibly understand. Reach out to Him whenever you need comfort. And to me, too, dear."

"Thanks, Mom." Suddenly Jenn started to sob. "Mom?"

"Yes?"

"Pastor James says someone sexually abused Josh."

"What?" her mom exclaimed.

"That's a cause of same-sex attraction."

"Oh, honey. Are you sure?" Pain and confusion came through the phone.

"I'm sure he said it. It's made me realize that Josh was away from me hundreds of times when he was little. I thought I'd done such a good job with them. Now I know I didn't."

"Jenn, you and Steve are great parents. What does Josh say?"

"Josh doesn't remember being hurt, but the pastor says that means he repressed it or was too young," Jenn explained, her voice high and tight.

"I don't know that that's true. Pastor James must be mistaken."

"I wish you were right." Jenn felt sick inside with the enormity of telling her mom about her failure.

"I am right," her mom insisted. "I am certain that you and Steve are great parents, whatever your pastor says."

It was sweet to hear that her mom had faith in her as a parent, even if Jenn didn't believe it anymore. "I'm glad you know, Mom. Don't tell anyone. Okay? Not even Dad, please."

"Oh, honey, I won't. But your father won't condemn Josh, or you. God is the only judge—and you know He is a loving God. You know that, right?"

Jenn knew her mom was trying to be a comfort, but she wasn't succeeding. She didn't understand the secular influences that could pressure Josh into thinking the homosexual lifestyle was acceptable. Suddenly, Jenn was too overwhelmed to keep talking. She nodded and muttered something noncommittal. "I gotta go, Mom. Give Daddy my love. 'Bye."

Jenn hung up, not even certain her mom had said goodbye.

After dinner, Steve took Josh and Rachel to youth group. Usually Jenn did the driving, but this gave Steve and Josh more time together. When Steve and the kids got home, Jenn waved from the family-room couch where she was watching *American Idol*. Josh ignored her and stormed upstairs, obviously upset. Steve and Rachel came into the family room.

"What happened?" Jenn asked, her brows furrowed with a question.

Steve shrugged. They both looked at Rachel for an answer.

"Pastor James asked everyone to pray for him," their daughter explained. "He said Josh has been having impure thoughts. Josh got so embarrassed that he turned totally red. What's the pastor talking about?"

"Oh dear," Jenn said. She patted the couch, indicating that Rachel should sit next to her. Steve sat in the recliner.

Jenn eyed Steve. He eyed her back. She guessed he wanted her to take the lead on this one. She was hesitant to tell Rachel without asking Josh first; she'd already broken her agreement with him by telling her mom, but she didn't want Rachel hearing this from anyone else, so she plunged ahead.

"Your brother has been having some homosexual thoughts."

"Josh is gay?" Rachel exclaimed, her eyes wide with shock.

"No," Jenn corrected, "Josh is not a homosexual. He's confused. He understands this and is working on healing. Dad and I are getting him treatment."

Steve spoke up. "We don't want this to change how you feel about him. Josh is still a good person."

"In fact," Jenn said, "his honesty and commitment make me even more proud of him. If anything, you should have more respect for your brother, not less."

Rachel looked confused but nodded.

"Do you have any questions?" Steve asked.

Rachel asked, "Does Sara know?"

"Yes," Steve replied. "Josh confided in her first."

"Do Poppy and Nana know?"

Jenn reluctantly admitted, "I told Nana today. I asked her to keep it private for now."

"You did?" Steve challenged.

Jenn sighed. "It's hard for me to keep anything from my mom, you know that. She took it well. She's supportive."

"What about Grandma?" Rachel looked at Steve.

"I haven't told her," Steve replied. "And I don't plan to. She's not tolerant about these things. I'm afraid she'd write a horrible letter to Josh. He doesn't need harsh criticism right now."

Jenn was relieved to hear that. Her mom was one thing, but Marilyn's judgmental attitude would not be helpful to any of them.

"Does this mean he isn't Christian anymore?" Rachel asked.

"No!" Jenn and Steve said at the same time.

Jenn was shocked that Rachel was calling into question Josh's faith. He was as devoted as anyone.

Steve said, "Josh is committed to living his Christian values. I'm confident his faith will be even stronger after this test. Every Christian is tested, Rachel. We're all sinners. That's why Christ died for us."

Jenn stepped in. "As Christians we don't throw away the gift of the resurrection. Josh is choosing to devote his life to Christ. He's an example for all of us."

The phone rang. Jenn looked at the caller ID and sighed. It was Lindsay.

"I'm going to get this. I haven't updated Lin in a while." She picked up the cordless phone and walked into the living room.

"Michael just got home from youth group. He told me that we need to say extra prayers for Josh. What's going on? How can I help?"

The love and concern in Lindsay's voice cut through Jenn's numbness. Her eyes welled up. "Oh, Lindsay, it's a nightmare." Jenn needed Lindsay's full support more than ever in her life. Josh wouldn't understand, but she told her friend the details of their last two days. "I didn't tell you before now because that would make it real. But Pastor James convinced me that we need to face this head on."

"You know we're going to be there for you and Josh one hundred percent. Whatever you need, you tell me."

"Thank you, so much. We need your prayers. And please, please keep the specifics confidential. Josh doesn't want it spread."

"Of course." Then Lindsay suggested, "Let's have a prayer circle in his bedroom. All those powerful prayers will bring Jesus right there to strengthen his soul."

"Josh isn't ready for something like that. So public. He's very upset after youth group tonight."

"He doesn't need to be there. We'll do it while he's at school. Like a spring cleaning—he'll come home and just feel the Godly spirit. I don't need to tell people the details. You know people will have heard that he's having impure thoughts. What sixteen-year-old boy doesn't? How about I arrange a series of prayer circles? Josh's room will be the first stop."

Jenn considered the offer. Pastor James said that they needed to be fully committed. She knew she and Steve had to be shining examples of Godly commitment to their children.

"That would be great, thanks," Jenn agreed. "I'm so scared for him, Lindsay. He's so fragile. It's too much for a boy to have to deal with."

"God never gives us more than we can handle, Jenn. You know that."

"I keep telling myself He has a plan for us and I'm not to question. But it's hard. So hard."

"You're wise not to question," Lindsay reminded Jenn. "Trust in the Lord—and the power of prayer."

Usually those words were a comfort, but tonight they rang hollow. After Jenn hung up, she went to face Josh.

ELEVEN

SUNDAY FEBRUARY 22, 2004

Josh

Of course, Mom knocked and walked in while Josh just wanted to hide. He'd been sitting on his bed, hitting his fist into his baseball mitt like when he lost a game during his childhood.

He took one look at her and declared, "I don't want to talk. To anyone. About anything."

She didn't leave. He was barely containing his fury.

"Josh, I have to tell you something. You're not going to like it. I'm sorry. This is all getting out of hand," Mom explained.

Josh stared at her hard without saying a word, hoping she could see that he needed space.

She spit out, "I broke your confidence. Sometimes a secret is more harmful than helpful. The devil lives in secrets."

Rage exploded in his chest. "Who did you tell?"

"Rachel asked us what Pastor James was talking about. I wanted her to hear it from us. And I want her to know what you're going through."

Josh glared at his mother. He punched the mitt in his hand so hard that his knuckles hurt. Everything was totally out of control. He punched the mitt again, driving out his shame with pain.

"Lindsay called because Michael told her about youth group. She wants to support us. She's my best friend. I tell her everything. I asked her not to tell anyone else anything besides what Pastor James told the youth group. She said she would keep it private."

"Anyone else?" Josh could hardly speak.

"Nana," Mom practically whispered. "I can't keep secrets from her. She loves you. She had no judgment at all. She's just worried for you. Her prayers will work better because she knows what to pray for."

Adrenaline surged through him. Feeling trapped in his own room, Josh leapt up. All those people talking about him, learning about his shameful feelings, was absolutely unbearable. He got his track shoes out of his closet and put them on in silence.

"I'm going for a run," he declared.

"Josh, don't you have anything you want to say to me?" Mom asked cautiously.

"No," he barked.

"It's late to be out alone."

He stared at her. She looked scared, but he couldn't take care of her right now. He had to calm down before he made everything even worse.

"Mom, I'm going to explode if I don't go for a run," he begged, tears pushing at his eyes. "Please move."

Reluctantly she stepped aside. He stormed down the stairs and slammed the door as hard as he could.

He hit the sidewalk hard with each stride, feeling the shock up his legs. He pushed as hard as he could until he was panting, his mind entirely focused on breathing. The adrenaline left his body and he stopped to sit on the wall at the Johnsons'. He panted and wiped his eyes until he was ready to go home.

God doesn't give you more than you can handle, he thought. He had a purpose in those people knowing, even if Josh didn't understand it.

As he walked back, he realized it was a relief that everyone in his family knew. At home he didn't have to pretend he was okay anymore.

Mom and Dad yelled goodnight as he went up the stairs—and thankfully neither of them followed him. In the middle of his pillow was an index card:

Love you, Josh.
♡ Rachel

He smiled at her sweet gesture. He put the note along with his mitt in the second drawer of his bedside table. All his anger was gone. He was left exhausted and only wanted to be asleep. His phone dinged. It was a text from Sara.

goodnite

nite sweet dreams

He didn't feel so alone anymore. He said his prayers, thanking God for his loving and supportive family. He was committed to being cured and making them all proud.

The next afternoon, Mom drove carpool. Josh said "hi" to her when he climbed into the passenger seat, but otherwise ignored her. He turned, chatting and joking with Joe, Phil, and Grant in the back. They had no idea what was wrong with him, and he was going to do what he could to keep his secret. After his friends were dropped off and he was alone with Mom, he looked at his phone. There was a text from Sara.

BTWN class. FWIW <3

He smiled. Every day she'd been sending him silly things since he'd told her. He texted LOL back.

"Josh?" Mom interrupted.

"Yes?" he replied.

"I had a prayer circle for you today," Mom said.

"What?" Josh felt his heart speed up. "With who?"

She tried to sound casual, but he could tell she was nervous. "Just a few women from church. Lindsay organized it. They're all good people. And we weren't specific about why we were having it."

Josh sighed and stared out of the window. "Thanks, I guess."

"That's the right attitude, hon. I'm proud of you."

"I'm trying, Mom. Really, I am." He was desperate to feel differently.

"I posted a lot of prayers around the house. I didn't have time to frame them, but we just need them up. We'll surround ourselves in prayer, like Pastor James suggested."

Josh nodded.

"One other thing..." Mom said carefully. "I took down your posters."

"What? Why?" Josh was confused. He swallowed the ball in his throat. "What's wrong with them?"

"We, well, you need something more masculine on your walls. You and Dad can pick something out."

"Half Dome isn't masculine?" Josh asked.

Mom told him, "We need external changes to represent the internal changes you want to make. This is an easy and small way to do that."

Josh was silent.

Mom prodded him. "Josh?"

"It's not small to me," he mumbled. "I feel the Holy Spirit in those places. Did you throw them away?"

"Of course not!" Mom rushed out. "They're safe. I bought a special protective tube for them. It doesn't have to be forever, Josh. Just while you're getting cured." She reached out to squeeze Josh's arm. "This is sad for all of us, you know."

"I know, Mom. I'm sorry to cause you more work."

It was his fault, not hers. She was doing so much to help him, and he'd wanted to bury his head in the sand. He had to be as committed as his mom.

"Josh, there's no need to feel bad. Just keep working hard like you are. You'll be cured soon, and our life can return to normal."

He nodded at her and prayed to God to heal him.

This had been the longest week of his life. On Saturday he got to do nothing, which was great. He didn't crack a book. But on Sunday he had to go to church. The thought of going to worship was nauseating, but he didn't ask to stay home. He had to show his devotion. *By faith he can be healed.*

They stopped at BART for Sara. He got out of the car and gave her a big hug before letting her slide into the middle. She'd really made an effort to cheer him up, texting him little things each day, full of hearts. She understood, or sort of understood, what he was going through.

When the five of them walked into the sanctuary, there was a ripple of energy. It was embarrassing to know people were talking about him. Pastor James made a big show of hugging Mom and then whispered to them all, "I've got some great news. Find me after the service."

Dad started to slide in first, like usual, but Mom stopped him. She made Josh go in first, followed by Dad. He'd wanted to sit by Sara, but he didn't argue. He avoided eye contact with the stranger next to him, closing his eyes and praying.

Dear God, give me strength and faith. Guide me in following You.

He put the people around him out of his mind and focused on the energy and rhythm of the praise band. He raised one arm, moving to the rhythm. His eyes closed in prayer and his lips parted. He prepared himself for worship, getting ready to invite in the Holy Spirit. He felt his heart open up.

By the time the worship leaders started speaking, he felt peaceful and filled with grace. The sermon, on accepting what God put in your path, landed in his heart. Senior Pastor Williams said it was a sign of spiritual maturity to trust God even when life didn't make sense to you. God was giving him an opportunity to deepen his faith and trust in Him.

And then his family was held up in the pastoral prayer and his fragile peace flew away. In the past, he'd been proud to be a part of this prayer. Today he had to remind himself to be grateful to be mentioned rather than embarrassed. He leaned over, elbows on knees and head in his hands, trying to take in the words. Dad put his hand on Josh's shoulder.

The second the service ended, Josh asked, "Can we leave?"

"Sure," Dad agreed.

Mom shook her head. "Pastor James wants to see us. He told me to find him in the back of the sanctuary."

"Can I stay here until everyone clears out?" Josh asked. He couldn't face talking to anyone.

Dad looked at Mom. She gave a small nod. Mom chatted with any congregants who approached them, while the rest of her family sat in place. When the sanctuary was almost empty, Mom signaled to them. They walked to the back to talk with the youth pastor.

"Great news!" he exclaimed. "I have a few resources for you, including a wonderful opportunity for Josh—there's going to be a conference in April."

"Wow," Mom said. "Where?"

"It's in Tracy, only thirty miles away, and it's during

Dublin High's spring break, just before Easter. The Lord is taking care of you. This will be amazing—for all of you. The teens are there for eight days, and parents join in on both Saturdays. Here's a flyer about it. You can sign him up right away. Praise Jesus!"

"Praise Jesus," Mom echoed. "Josh, isn't this great?"

I guess so, he thought but said, "Thanks."

"Absolutely!" the pastor replied. "I know you're going to be one of the success stories, Josh. Our Lord Jesus has a plan for you."

Josh gave a small smile and nod. He didn't want any attention, though he was grateful to know there was a good treatment.

Pastor James exclaimed, "And here's a great book to give you guidance as a parent. It's my gift to you."

Mom took the flyer and the book. *Prevent Homosexuality* was in bold black letters on the cover. Underneath, in smaller letters, it said *A Guidebook for Christian Parents.*

Josh looked around. Could anyone read it? He willed his mom to hide it in her bag or turn it around, but she left it facing out for the world to see.

"Thanks," Dad said, not seeming to share Josh's discomfort. "The Lord is showing up in our lives."

The car was strangely quiet on the drive to Mimi's for brunch. Rachel usually filled up the silence, but even she understood what a weird position he'd put their family in. He made them all freaks.

Josh watched Mom read the flyer from Pastor James. She passed it to him.

He read:

Join us for

RESURRECTION MINISTRIES FREEDOM BRIGADE

April 3 to 10, 2004
FREEDOM FROM HOMOSEXUALITY THROUGH THE
POWER OF JESUS CHRIST

*Do you struggle with Same-Sex Attraction (SSA)? Are you
between the ages of 15 and 25? You are not alone. You have
Christian allies in this battle for your soul. You can be
transformed by God's amazing grace. Learn the root causes of
your SSA and the treatment that can set you free.*

*If you seek and submit your whole life to the Lord, you will find
freedom to live in sexual and relational wholeness according to
God's design. We will discipline and inspire you for the path
ahead.*
Sudden, radical, complete change is possible.

Josh zeroed in on those words: *Sudden, radical, complete
change is possible.* They could *cure* him. He felt hope rise.

Mom said, "This is exciting, Josh! It's just what you need.
God is watching out for you."

"If I do this, will I still go to that other doctor on Monday?"

Mom replied, "Yes. If he confirms he's Christian, we want
you to meet with him. This retreat is weeks away. You need
help right now."

Sara asked, "Are you sure this is a good idea, Mom? I've
heard some of these things are really mean."

"From who?" Mom asked with heat in her voice.

"My roommate has a friend who's pretty down on Christians because her family stopped talking to her when she came
out. We've had dinner a few times. I explained to her that not
all Christians are bigoted against gays—that we hold up the
possibility of healing because of God's love, not hate."

Dad said, "You know we'd never stop talking to you guys. No matter what, right?" He looked into the rearview mirror.

The girls nodded. Josh didn't feel so sure.

"Right, Josh?" Dad pressed.

"I guess," Josh finally replied.

"No. Not 'I guess.' You understand what I'm saying? I don't want you to worry about that. We're not kicking you out of the house. We're not cutting you off. We're getting you the help you need. We're all on the same team here."

Josh bit his lip and nodded. Dad meant it to be kind, but it was a lot of pressure. What if he couldn't be cured?

But he replied, "Got it."

Mom said, "Sara, I trust Pastor James's judgment. If he says it's a good organization, then I'm confident this is right for Josh and our family. I'm sure there are some people who hide their bigotry behind their Christianity, but that's not us. Our passion comes from our desire to live biblically and to bring others to the salvation that our Lord Jesus Christ offers. I'm sure this conference will be in line with our family values."

"We all have to go?" Rachel asked. She sounded upset.

"I don't know, Rachel. We'll do whatever they say is best," Mom replied, using her self-righteous voice. "Josh's well-being is the most important thing right now."

"I didn't mean that, Mom. Of course... whatever Josh needs. It's just..." Rachel paused. She sounded like she might cry. "We aren't going to go to Monterey, are we?"

Mom's face softened. "Oh, they are the same dates, aren't they? I'm sorry, hon. We have to postpone. Maybe in the summer?"

Josh felt terrible. He sighed. "I'm sorry, Rach. I know how much you wanted to see the otters and the penguins. You guys should go."

"It's okay, Josh," Rachel soothed her brother. "Summer's soon enough."

"I'm ruining everything. For all of you," Josh said. He leaned back his head and closed his eyes.

Sara replied, "Joshy... of course not. You aren't ruining anything."

"Josh," Dad said, "don't be dramatic. It's fine. You'll meet with these people and take care of the problem. Got it?"

"Yes, sir," Josh said like he agreed, but he wasn't so certain. One second he was faith-filled, and the next he was a doubting Thomas. He wanted to believe, but his faith kept slipping away.

TWELVE

Jenn

Monday morning Jenn called the therapist after her prayers. His voicemail picked up, so she left a message: "Good morning, Kyle. This is Jenn Henderson. My son, Josh, has an appointment tonight at seven o'clock. I need to confirm that you're a Christian and will provide counseling in line with Christian values. I hope you understand our need to know the answer to that question before he meets with you. Thank you."

Kyle returned her call when she was grocery shopping. She picked up the phone in the cereal aisle.

"Hello?"

"Hello, Jenn? This is Kyle Goss."

"Thanks for getting back to me."

"Of course," Kyle replied. "To answer your question, yes, I'm Christian. I attend church on Sundays."

"So your treatment with Josh will be in line with Christian values?"

"Not all my clients are religious. However, my work is deeply grounded in Jesus's teachings."

Jenn was relieved. "That makes me feel so much better."

"Good," Kyle said. "So I'll meet you and Josh tonight?"

"You'll see Josh, but not me," she explained. "Steve will bring him. We're having them do more things together at the suggestion of our pastor."

"All right, then. I look forward to meeting Steve and Josh tonight and perhaps you on a different date."

Jenn hung up. Tears pressed against the back of her eyes. She leaned on the cart, exhausted and overwhelmed. She had just gotten off the phone with a therapist for Josh. How did she get here? She felt like a child, naive and unprepared. Up until a week ago she had known, without a doubt, that she was raising her kids right.

But that feeling was entirely gone. Good parents didn't raise a child with same-sex attraction. Jenn fretted about Josh from the moment she woke up until she went to sleep. Her head was filled with what she should or shouldn't say, and what she should or shouldn't do. She questioned her instincts constantly. She'd start to hug Josh or ask about his day and then stop herself because she was damaging him.

Jenn obsessively reviewed his childhood, thinking back on every mistake she had made. They had let him get involved in cross-country instead of football. He helped with the dishes like his sisters. The whole family went camping together rather than it being father-son bonding time. Their poor choices had hurt their son.

She was tired and insecure, but she didn't want to show or tell anyone. She'd never felt so supported, yet so alone.

"Excuse me," a woman said.

Jenn was blocking the oatmeal. She pushed forward despite her misery, grabbing some Frosted Mini-Wheats and continuing down the aisle.

. . .

That night Jenn lay in bed reading the book that Pastor James had given her. It was hard to take in the information. She realized now that she and Steve had made so many errors. The reasoning was outlined clearly. With each page her spirit sank lower and lower until she felt sick to her stomach.

"We shouldn't have given him a name that started with the same letter as mine," Jenn told Steve as he climbed into bed.

Steve looked confused. "What are you talking about?"

"It made him identify with me. It's even worse since he looks like me. And now I'm scared for Sara. She looks like you, and you share a first letter." Jenn's voice cracked. "Why didn't anyone tell us these things before they were born? All I cared about was giving them biblical names."

"Are you sure that's what the book says?" Steve sounded incredulous. "I've never heard anything like that before."

Anger flared up in Jenn. "I'm not stupid, Steve. I can read a book. It says it's best to name sons after their fathers, so they'll have strong masculine identities, especially if they favor the mother. We can't take his name back now."

Steve took a deep breath. He looked like he wanted to say something, but he suppressed it.

"What?" Jenn barked.

"I think we need to focus on the future and not the possible mistakes we made in the past. He has his name; he looks like you. What does it say we need to do now?"

"All the stuff Pastor James told us. He needs to spend more time with you and less time with me. He must only do masculine activities—I guess he doesn't set the table anymore. And we have to find the root cause, the sexual abuse that traumatized him." Jenn's eyes welled up. "I think about that over and over and over. If he can't remember it, he had to have been so young. I just can't believe it was my dad or your dad or... How could it be anyone we know that we trusted him with? It makes me think about awful things—with our Josh." Jenn started sobbing.

It was horrifying to know that Josh had been sexually abused and she hadn't stopped it.

Steve took the book from her lap and wrapped his arms around her.

"Jenn," Steve spoke quietly when she was done crying. "It's good you're doing a lot of reading and that we're doing everything we can to help Josh. But... this book may not be one hundred percent true."

Jenn pulled away from her husband and looked at him incredulously. "You don't believe Pastor James is guiding us well?"

"I didn't say that. I just know you can't believe absolutely everything you read. People have strong opinions. I find it hard to believe that Josh's name would make him a homosexual."

Every time Jenn heard that word her stomach churned. She picked up the book and waved it at Steve. "This is the Christian way. We are Christians. We must have faith, or we'll jeopardize Josh's recovery. I need to know that we're in this together, Steve."

"Jenn, you know part of being a Christian is listening for God's truth for yourself. That's why we pray. I've been praying a lot, just like you, and listening for God's guidance," Steve reassured her. "We're together in this. We both know Josh can be cured through faith. I just don't want you beating yourself up and hurting our family. Kyle told me we have to be gentle with each other and trust in God's love. I think he's right."

Jenn leaned back against the headboard with her eyes closed. The words echoed in her head: *gentle... trust*. She felt very far from either of those things. She was full of blame and fear. She wanted to take action, do something, fix this problem, not be gentle and trust that it would work out.

"What else did he say?" They hadn't had a private moment to talk about Josh's first appointment earlier that evening.

"I didn't have much time with him—maybe ten minutes in

the beginning before he asked me to leave so he and Josh could speak alone. Next time I need to take something to read. The waiting room only had old *Newsweek*, *People*, and *Better Homes* magazines. He walked Josh out to me after they were done and said that thing about being gentle and trusting God."

"Well, what did you talk about in your ten minutes?"

"He asked about who was in our family and what brought us there. He wondered whether any of our friends or family were homosexual. He asked about our church and how we're feeling as a family."

"What did Josh talk about with him?" Jenn probed.

Steve shrugged. "I didn't ask, and he didn't tell."

"You didn't ask about it?" Jenn was shocked.

"No. It's private. Josh and I don't talk about things like that," Steve said. "I'm sure your book thinks that's just fine."

Jenn smiled with a snort. "You're right. I just hate not knowing."

"Guess it's a guy thing. I don't need to know. I don't want to know."

They made the changes that the book and Pastor James suggested. No more movies as a family on Fridays, so that the kids could watch gender-appropriate films. That meant Josh and Steve watched thrillers, adventures, or science fiction and the girls watched romantic comedies. Jenn discouraged Josh from doing anything in the kitchen other than taking out the garbage. He and Steve spent time in the garage building something or other. Jenn and the girls got mani-pedis on Saturdays while Josh and Steve watched sports with Mark and Michael.

Jenn avoided interacting with her son as much as possible, though they did have family dinners together. She drove him places only if they couldn't make another arrangement. She didn't go to his games, ask him about friends or school, or watch

TV with him. She missed Josh. It was a huge loss for both of them, but they accepted the need for it.

Jenn fluctuated between hope and despair multiple times a day. She wished she could see some outward sign of healing, but Josh looked the same as always. He went to school, to practice, and then came home. He did his homework, ate dinner, did more homework, and went to bed. Jenn checked the history on the computer every morning to monitor his web surfing, always on the alert for anything that would undermine his recovery, but didn't find anything concerning. In fact, he hardly went to any websites at all.

Jenn reminded Steve to register Josh for the SAT, but day after day it didn't happen. She didn't want to risk her son's entire future to Steve's busy schedule, so one night, after dinner, she broke her self-imposed rule of separation and knocked on Josh's door.

"Come in," Josh called from inside.

He looked like a man, sitting at his small desk. And his room felt foreign, too. Steve and Josh had bought all this stuff during a single trip to Target. The new bedspread had a bold plaid on it. The walls were covered in posters of cars and sports teams. A few baseball players stared intently from the walls. It didn't seem like Josh at all. She supposed that was a good thing. Here was an outer manifestation of the inner change they were working for. But she felt like she didn't know this room, or her son.

"Can we register you for the SAT right now?" she asked. "We can do it online. The deadline is in two days. You don't want to miss it."

"Sure, Mom," Josh said as he closed a book. They walked together down to the computer. Jenn waved him to the chair in front of the keyboard. She pulled up a chair next to it.

"You do it," Jenn instructed him. "I'll sit here if you have any questions and give you my credit card number."

Josh filled in his demographic information. On the next screen, he chose the location of the test: Dublin High. Before paying, he had the option to fill out information about himself, including what type of school he wanted to attend. He checked off business and accounting as potential majors. Then he marked schools on the East Coast, some of which Jenn had never even heard of. She was shocked. After all they had been through, she expected him to list only nearby schools.

"Josh, you think you might go to college in New York City?" Jenn asked when he checked NYU, trying to keep the outrage from her voice.

"Yeah. Or Boston or Washington DC. I've lived in California my whole life. I'd like to be in a big city."

"With what's happening with you?" Jenn snapped. "We are not working this hard for your recovery to have you throw it away by going to a school far away. If you aren't completely cured, you'll be living at home while you go to college."

"But, Mom," Josh argued, "everyone is looking at schools all over the country. The counselors talk about them all the time."

"You are not everybody. Of course you'll go to college. I hope you'll be accepted to Cal like your sister. Maybe Cal State Hayward or even Saint Mary's. If all goes well at camp, maybe UC Davis. But New York? No, Josh." Jenn shook her head. "That is not happening."

"But—"

"Does your father know you are considering out-of-state schools?" Jenn asked.

"I guess so. Yeah."

Jenn was suddenly furious. Her son's life was unraveling entirely, and she seemed to be the only person who realized it.

Josh argued, "Sara applied to Williams and Vassar. They're out of state. Why isn't it an option for me, too?"

"You're not Sara. Don't you understand? Do you know that I worry about you—day and night?" Heat rose in her voice. "All

I think about is your future. Your future is not in New York City. Or Boston or DC. If you want to put Christian colleges on your list—BIOLA, Chapman—I'll think about you going to Southern California, near Nana and Poppy and Grandma and Grandpa. But New York City? Come on, Josh. I don't think you understand the gravity of your situation. I'm not having you all the way across the country. Or even halfway across the country. Do you know what kind of influences there will be?"

Josh tentatively suggested an alternative: "How about Vassar or other schools that aren't in a big city?"

"Josh! Stop arguing with me. You're going to college in California. Erase those schools. Put in my credit card information, and let's be done with this."

Josh did as she said. Then he stood up abruptly and said, "I need a run."

He left the room, and she heard the door slam hard. He hadn't even taken the time to change his clothes.

"Where's Josh going so late?" Steve came in.

"For a run. He's furious at me. For saying he has to go to college in California. I'm right, aren't I?"

Steve shrugged.

"I don't think I can do this." She started sobbing.

Steve wrapped his arms around her, and she rested against his chest. Then she felt another pair of arms around her. It was Rachel. That made Jenn cry even more. She wanted to be strong for her kids. To show them deep faith. But she was scared. What if Josh couldn't be cured? What would happen to his salvation then?

Jenn stepped back so Rachel could be in the middle. She held their girl while her husband held her.

"The Lord will see us through this. We have great faith in Him," she said to her daughter. "It's just not going to be easy."

THIRTEEN

WEDNESDAY FEBRUARY 25, 2004

Sara

Sara was studying in her room, glad to be alone for once. Maya was a great roommate, she couldn't ask for better, but Sara missed being in her bed with no one else around. Her sociology textbook was open in front of her. She needed to get through this chapter before class in the morning.

Her phone buzzed under her leg. Joshy was on the screen. Her heart skipped a beat.

She picked up immediately. "Hey."

A heavy sigh came over the line.

"You okay, Josh?"

"Mom hates me and doesn't trust me."

"What happened?"

"She says I can't even consider going to college on the East Coast. Like I'm a totally irresponsible pervert."

"You're not! You know that, right?"

She could hear him sniffle on the other end.

Finally, he said, "This camp has to work, Sara. It just has to. I don't know..."

Sara's heart fell. "Josh, promise me you won't hurt yourself again. No matter what. You have to have faith."

She waited for his reply.

"Josh, promise me," she practically shouted.

"Okay," he said, but she didn't believe him.

"Can you promise to call me or come to me before... Josh. Please say you will."

"Yeah, I can call you if I..." Eventually he finished his sentence, "Lose faith."

She replied, "I'm glad you called me now."

"Really?"

"Yes. Day or night. I was so scared when you were in the hospital. No matter what happens, Josh, my life is way better with you in it."

"Are you sure? Wouldn't you all be better off without me?"

"No, Josh, not even the tiny, tiniest bit better," Sara replied. Then she prayed out loud, "God, please help Josh so he knows deep, deep in his heart that his sister needs him. And loves him. No matter what. Guide him to keep faith in your unfolding creation and will. Amen."

"Amen," Josh replied. "Thanks, Sara. I love you, too. I feel better."

"Phew," she responded.

"What are you doing?"

"Studying for class. Tonight's reading is the sociology of sports. It's all about the rituals associated with sports and how that gives people meaning in their lives—kind of like church does for us. It's interesting, actually."

"I can't wait for college," Josh said.

"Keep your eye on that prize," she replied.

"You're right," he said. "Thanks, Sara. I'm fine now. You can get back to your studying."

"Are you sure?" she asked.

"Yeah."

"Call me—day or night. Anytime you need to, okay?"

"K."

"Love you," she closed.

"You, too." He hung up.

Sara stared at the phone in her hand. She replayed the conversation. Had she said the right words? She wanted Josh to have faith he could be cured, but she didn't want him to kill himself if he couldn't be. Just that thought brought her to tears; weeks of pent-up fear and sorrow poured out of her.

Maya walked in while she was crying. There was no hiding her distress. Her roommate walked to her bed and sat down close.

"What's the matter?"

Sara stared into Maya's hazel eyes. Did she trust her? Sara was so tired of hiding that she suddenly didn't care if Maya hated her after telling her the truth.

"I'm afraid you will hate me, so I haven't told you the whole truth about my family," Sara said.

"What, no! How could you think I would hate your family, for being anything...?" Maya sounded hurt. "I'm not... Please tell me."

"You know how my brother was in the hospital?"

Maya nodded.

"He tried to kill himself."

Maya's hands went to her mouth... in horror? Sorrow?

"Oh my God, I'm so sorry," Maya said. "It's awful, but nothing to be ashamed of, to hide from me. I promise."

"Because he has same-sex attractions," Sara continued.

Maya practically scoffed, "Also nothing to be ashamed of. You know I support gay rights one hundred percent, right?"

"And our family is Christian."

Maya's eyes went wide.

Sara said, "The kind of Christian that's against gay marriage."

"Oh fuck." Maya sat back with her hands over her heart. She seemed to be making sense of it layer by layer. "Oh... oh... oh."

Maya furrowed her brows. "Are you like *pray away the gay* kind of Christians?"

Sara closed her eyes, started to cry again, and finally nodded. Shame poured through her.

"How is Josh doing now?" Maya looked so concerned.

"Terrible," Sara said. "He wants to be cured."

"It's not a disease," Maya replied. "There is no cure for liking what you like. There's just hiding it."

Sara whispered, "That's not what our ministers say."

Maya replied, "I'm not going to argue with you about this. I just know that being gay isn't something to be ashamed of or fixed. No matter what your ministers say."

"How do you know that?" Sara asked. "What does your religion say?"

"My family is lots of different religions: liberal Christian, all kinds of Catholics, Evangelical, reform Jewish and Muslim. I was raised nothing but got exposed to all of it. My Great Aunt Teri is so Catholic that she goes to church more than once a week and she says, 'God doesn't make mistakes and it is not mine to judge, only to love.' My mom says that's what we believe."

Sara sighed. "Do you hate me now?"

Maya snorted. "Mine is not to judge, only to love."

"Really?"

"It's easy with you. For other people, not so much."

Sara smiled, just a little.

Maya asked, "Have you told Josh you love him?"

"Oh yes!" Sara explained. "That I love him, no matter what happens. That he can call me anytime night or day. My dad says it, too. It's my mom that's the big problem. She's set in her ways. And to be honest, Josh is, too. He really wants to be cured. So if I say I love him no matter what happens, he gets upset and asks if I think he can't be cured." Sara started to cry. "I'm afraid of upsetting him by saying the wrong thing. I want what he wants, I believe in him, and I will love him no matter what happens."

"Have you said that to him?"

Sara shrugged.

Maya replied, "Well, to me that sounds like the right thing to say to him."

"Please don't tell anyone on the floor," Sara asked. "I don't want to be the freaky Christian girl at Cal."

"I won't. Your secret is safe with me." Maya snorted. "Ironically, you are in your own type of closet, aren't you?"

"Yeah, coming out as Christian in Berkeley?" Sara shuddered. "I'm not that brave."

Maya smiled. "Thank you for trusting me."

"You don't hate me?"

"When I was young, I was jealous of people who had church. First communion dresses, bat mitzvahs, and youth group seemed hella dope. I didn't like that we were nothing, but I see now how we got to be everything by being nothing."

Sara was confused. "Does that mean you don't hate me?"

"I don't hate you," Maya assured her. "I promise."

Maya hugged Sara. "And I'll keep your secret until you say otherwise."

"Thanks."

Maya crossed to her bed and got out her phone to text someone. Sara turned back to her textbook, grateful and relieved that Maya knew her secret. Her mind wandered to her brother. Before she could concentrate on her reading, she had to send him a text. It took a long time, but it was worth it:

i want wut u want & luv u no matter wut.

FOURTEEN

Jenn

Jenn drove to an appointment with Kyle Goss. After a few weeks of meeting with Josh, this was her first time seeing him in person. He'd reached out, saying he wanted to know about her goals for Josh.

Kyle welcomed her warmly into his office. She had imagined him as white, but he wasn't. He had dark-brown hair, brown eyes, and light-brown skin. Maybe Middle Eastern or Hispanic. Maybe he was mixed black and white.

"It's nice to meet you, Jenn," he said as they shook hands. "Sit wherever you like." He pointed to a dark-green love seat and coordinated chair. She looked between the two pieces of furniture and finally chose the love seat. He settled into the chair across from her. She noticed a box of tissues on the small table between them.

"Whenever I'm working with a teen, I ask to have some time alone with each parent. It's best to know one another and for me to learn your goals. So, please—tell me how you are doing. What are your concerns and hopes for Josh?"

"I want him to live his life in conformity with God's will as expressed in the Bible. He cannot be homosexual, so he needs to eliminate any unhealthy attractions. He's getting pastoral counseling on occasion from the youth minister at our church. And he'll be going to a camp to treat same-sex attraction. But that's not until April—during Easter break. We want him to be cured as soon as possible, so he's seeing you."

Kyle nodded slowly and pursed his lips. "Do you have any other concerns? School pressure, grades, attitude?"

"He's a very good student. I worry that he works too hard, but he seems fine with it. I'm concerned that he doesn't understand the gravity of his situation. When he registered for the SAT, he indicated an interest in colleges on the East Coast—including New York City. He argued with me when I pointed out that it would be dangerous for him. I was stunned."

"Why is that?" Kyle sounded curious.

"You think it's appropriate for him to live in New York City? I don't let our children visit San Francisco without me. He doesn't need those kinds of influences. He would be exposed to people who might encourage him to be homosexual."

Kyle asked, "Do you mind if I play devil's advocate here?"

"Go ahead," Jenn replied, though she didn't like the sound of it.

"What if Josh is gay and he can't change that?"

She flinched at the words *Josh is gay*. She took a breath and asked as calmly as she could manage, "You can't cure him?"

Kyle replied, "I asked, what if he can't be changed?"

"The flyer promises that complete recovery is possible through God's grace. I believe in God's grace, and I know He'll offer it to Josh."

"The flyer for the conference he'll be going to?"

Jenn nodded.

"Some of those programs can be very harsh, bordering on abusive." Kyle looked concerned. "Kids can be locked in closets, given shocks, and pressured to reveal very personal information publicly."

"I'm sure this program is not like that. Pastor James loves Josh. He would never recommend something to hurt him. Do you believe Josh can be cured?"

Kyle's voice was calm. "Some treatments will make Josh more depressed. He's responding very well to therapy with me. Do you agree that he is doing much better than a few weeks ago?"

"Josh is depressed because he's afraid he's homosexual. He feels hopeful that he will be cured; that's why he is doing well right now," Jenn explained. "When he's cured of his same-sex attraction, he won't have anything to be depressed about."

"I just want to make sure you and Steve know this camp might make Josh's depression worse. For some kids the pressure is too much, too fast."

Jenn shook her head. She couldn't believe she had to explain this to Josh's therapist. He was supposed to be the expert, not her.

Jenn said, "If Josh had cancer, would you tell me not to give him chemo because it will make him feel bad? No, you would understand that the chemo was ultimately for his own good. This camp is the chemo to get the cancer of homosexuality out of my child."

Then Jenn started to cry. Not just pressure pushing at the back of her eyes. Not just a few tears rolling down her cheeks. She buried her face in her hands as moisture poured from her nose and her eyes. Kyle sat patiently, not saying a word, until she stopped.

Eventually Jenn stammered, "I... I'm so scared for him. All the time. It's a constant anxiety eating at me. I've never, ever had to deal with anything like this in my life. Suddenly I question everything. I used to believe I was a good parent. I knew we were living right. And now I've discovered we made so many mistakes. My poor judgment is putting Josh's soul in danger. It's all my fault."

"Josh is a wonderful person," Kyle reassured her. "Every parent makes mistakes. You've given him an amazing base. He has a strong relationship with God and Jesus. We talk about that a lot."

"That will help him, right?" Jenn grasped at this straw of hope.

Kyle nodded. "Enormously. It can be the difference between life and death in these situations."

Jenn started crying again. "He's not going to try to kill himself again, is he?"

"I can't know for certain, but I don't think so. He's showing strong signs of moving past the desire to hide from himself... and from you."

"I'm so tired." Jenn sighed.

"So is he," Kyle said. "Please be gentle—with yourself and with him. These things take time. Don't expect an instantaneous change in either of you. Pray for strength, guidance, and compassion."

"Do you have prayers you can give me?"

"I like the Serenity Prayer."

"From AA?"

"It's good for many situations. Asking God to give you courage, serenity, and wisdom can help all of you."

Jenn let those words wash over her. *Courage. Serenity. Wisdom.* She was lacking all three.

God, open my heart to your truth. Make me a servant for your holy will. Jenn nodded at Kyle.

"Thank you."

"This is a faith journey for you as well as for Josh. Can you grow as a person of faith to move from expectation to acceptance? Be gentle with yourself."

Jenn nodded. That word again: *gentle.*

She left Kyle's office with a little more hope. She was still confused, but she wasn't as mad at herself for being confused. At home she Googled the Serenity Prayer, cut and pasted it into a Word document, changed the font to make it nicer, and printed it out. She glued it on a card with a flowered border. She went to her room, sat at the edge of her bed, and read the prayer out loud:

> *God, grant me the serenity to accept the things I cannot change,*
> *The courage to change the things I can,*
> *And the wisdom to know the difference.*

The beautiful, and elusive, chill of the Holy Spirit filled her soul. God was telling her to accept this prayer. She placed the card by her bed. Maybe courage, serenity, and wisdom would help her to feel less anxious all the time.

A few weeks later, Jenn had a pastoral care meeting with Pastor James. Jenn was grateful that he'd made time for her throughout this ordeal to offer support and guidance. After they prayed, he asked if Josh was ready for camp, which started on Saturday.

"Do you have any questions?" he asked Jenn.

"No, I think we're all set. Steve and I are looking forward to being there with him. I'm nervous, but I keep saying the Serenity Prayer. It helps a lot."

"Excuse me? The Serenity Prayer!" Pastor James scowled.

"The one from AA. Josh's therapist suggested it to me. He thinks we need to be gentler, give Josh time, and not be so anxious."

"Josh doesn't have time," Pastor James replied passionately. "He hasn't yet acted on his same-sex attraction, but if we aren't careful, he will. That would be his doom. We need to cure him before he does."

"Oh," Jenn replied. Confusion rushed back in. She'd been

so comforted by Kyle's words and the prayer, but maybe it was just a distraction.

"Jennifer, it's very easy to be misguided by good intentions. I think we should look up this therapist."

"Why?"

"I question whether his practice is in line with biblical teachings."

"I asked him if he was Christian, like you suggested."

"Did you ask this therapist if his work is biblically based?"

Jenn shook her head. Her throat closed up in fear that she had made yet another mistake.

"I'm sorry. I should have been more specific. Many so-called Christians aren't. I mean, they think they are, but they're not born again. I'm afraid this person may be sending Josh signals that he should accept being homosexual. It's very common, you know. We're working against a huge anti-Christian swell."

The minister turned to his computer and asked her the name of the therapist. Jenn watched him type and read and then type some more. He pursed his lips and then exclaimed, "Ah... thought so! Jenn, he sings in the choir at the UCC church. That confirms my suspicions. He can't be trusted with Josh's salvation."

Jenn was shocked. "Are you certain? He's been helpful to me and Steve. And Josh looks forward to his time with Kyle."

"Jenn, you want Josh one hundred percent cured, right?"

"Yes."

"Then he needs to be surrounded by people who have faith in the treatment. If his therapist doesn't believe in the cure, Josh won't believe in it. This is a time that calls for the deepest faith. There is no room for any doubt."

Those words penetrated to the core of Jenn's body. Complete faith. No doubt. She didn't have the luxury of time or doubt.

"You're right. Josh should stop seeing Kyle."

. . .

Steve looked incredulous when Jenn told him about the conversation with Pastor James. "We insisted that Josh see a therapist. He looks forward to talking with Kyle, and you want us to make him stop?"

"I think Pastor James is right," Jenn replied. "All the adults in Josh's life need to be on the same page. Kyle might be encouraging Josh to accept his same-sex attraction."

"I've gone along with everything you asked. We redecorated his room. I don't call Sara anymore. I drive Josh whenever I can. He and I watch sports and 'masculine' movies. But this?" Steve shook his head. "I'm not sure it's a good idea."

Heat moved through Jenn's body. She was so mad that she didn't care if she hurt Steve's feelings. She practically yelled, "What I asked? This is not about what *I* want. This is about what *our* son needs. It's not my fault. It's our fault. You're the one who's been a poor role model. You always favored Sara, and he could tell. We all could tell."

Steve looked outraged. He raised his voice, too. "That's ridiculous! I don't love Sara more than I love Josh or Rachel. You're not making any sense."

She shot back, "Are you going to be supportive of his recovery or not?"

"Of course I am," he countered. "You're too hard on him."

"I'm not angry with Josh. I'm angry with myself. And you." All the heat went out of her voice. She softened. "I'm sorry. But it's true."

"Jenn, this is just one part of Josh." Steve's voice got quiet. "You have to see all of him. He's a good kid. We can be proud of him for working so hard."

"He needs to be focused on his recovery, not distracted by college in New York or a therapist who doesn't believe in his transformation. This is the most important thing in his life, in our lives. Don't you see?"

"He needs to know we're on his side. He's done everything

we asked him to do. Give him a break. I'll agree to stop taking him to see Kyle, but you have to be kinder to him."

Jenn sighed. "I'm terrified for him."

"Me, too. But we have to show him that we have faith if we want him to have faith. We need to surrender *our* lives to God if we expect him to."

Those words were a blow to Jenn's stomach. Steve was right. She *was* trying to control everything, not giving control to God and Jesus.

"Will you say a prayer over me?" she asked. "For surrender."

Jenn knelt in front of Steve. Her husband prayed, "Lord, we ask You to guide Your servant Jenn to live in accordance with Your will. Help her to let go of the sin of control. Let her surrender to Your will in all things. Guide her in being the best mother she can be to Sara, Josh, and Rachel. Help our family to avoid immoral practices and help us to refrain from judging those who engage in them. In Jesus's name we pray. Amen."

"Amen," Jenn echoed. Surrender to His will. *I will surrender to His will.*

FIFTEEN
SATURDAY, APRIL 3, 2004

Josh

Josh woke to the smell of Nana's pancakes. Mom only made them on special occasions: birthdays, Christmas, Easter. He rolled over in bed. Apparently going to be cured made the cut. Nervous and touched, his heart rode his ribs like a roller coaster. He'd been praying to be healed for so long that he wasn't as hopeful as Mom, but he kept his doubts to himself. Maybe his parents' faith would carry him.

They didn't talk about the camp while they ate, but all five of them were at the table. That didn't happen on Saturday mornings—another sign of how important this day was for their family. They were all counting on Josh to get better.

After breakfast Sara followed him upstairs when he went to get his bag. She closed the door to his room behind her.

"Are you okay?" she asked.

He shrugged.

"I'm a little scared for you, but excited, too. If it works, you'll be happier, right?" She stared at him. "You want it to work, for you, yeah? Not just for Mom and Dad?"

He nodded. "More than anything."

"Well, then I want it for you, too."

Josh teared up.

"Joshy, you know that no matter what, I love you?"

He nodded.

"I have met some good people who are gay and proud of it."

Josh looked at her, and nodded, hoping she would go on.

She said, "Listen for God in your own heart, more than anyone else. Okay?"

"You don't think I can be cured?" he asked.

"I didn't say that," Sara said. "I'm just saying, God's will might be more complicated than Mom and Dad think it is."

"Ready?" Mom called from the bottom of the stairs.

"Coming," Josh yelled down.

Sara gave him a big hug. She felt solid and warm, and he let himself relax into it for a moment. When they separated she pretended to spray him.

"Just in case," she said. "To keep the monsters away."

Josh laughed. Maybe the spray would work on his insides.

Rachel, Mom, and Dad were in the entryway when he came downstairs. The family formed a circle around him. Mom and Dad prayed for his full recovery through the love of Christ, and Sara and Rachel asked that Josh know the love of Christ. He prayed for both.

Alone in the back seat, Josh stared out the window as they traveled east on the 580. His right leg kept shaking—and his left joined in every once in a while. He didn't try to stop them. Soon he'd be surrounded by strangers and have to hide his nerves.

The cinder-block church looked like a Home Depot or Costco. The parking lot was already filled with cars and SUVs. He didn't realize that so many people would be here. Guess he wasn't alone in this struggle.

"You ready, Josh?" Dad asked after he pulled into a spot.

"I am!" Josh pumped his fist like he was getting amped for a game—putting it on, hoping it would turn his nerves into excitement.

A woman with long brown hair greeted them with a wide smile as they walked into the building.

"Welcome! I'm Donna, one of the local hosts. We're so glad you're here, ready to receive the transformative blessing of our Lord. This is going to be an amazing, Jesus-filled week of healing and release. Find your name tags right here. The symbol on the corner tells you which spirit circle you're in." She looked at Josh. "They will be your family this week, but also for the rest of your life."

"Thank you. We're glad to be here," Dad said.

Mom searched the name tags. All three had the same symbol on the upper right of the badge: an Easter lily. Donna looked at the tags in Mom's hand.

"Oh, goody! My husband is one of the leaders of Josh's spirit circle. His name is John."

Mom gave her a questioning look.

"Our daughter struggled with SSA," Donna explained. "With the guidance and support of Exodus Ministries, she's cured. She's getting married in June. I can't tell you what an incredible journey it's been. At first, I was devastated, but now I know it was part of God's plan to call us more deeply to His work. Before Kathy's troubles I was a Sunday-morning Christian. Now I'm a twenty-four/seven Christian. What a blessing it's been. Oh, listen to me going on. You'll find out for yourselves."

Donna's enthusiasm was intense. Mom probably liked hearing that this whole experience was a plan to bring their family closer to God.

Pointing, Donna said, "Josh, you can put your things in Faith Hall and then go into the sanctuary for the opening program. Welcome to your home for the week. Welcome to your 'people' for always."

The sanctuary was enormous—at least three times bigger than their church. The front was already filled. The size of the space and the crowd was intimidating. They slid into a pew and looked around. He thought everyone would be sad and serious, but it felt more like a celebration. A band was playing, and people walked up and down the aisles hugging, shaking hands, and chatting. A huge banner filled the back of the chancel. The first line said, RESURRECTION MINISTRIES: FREEDOM BRIGADE. Underneath that it said, CHANGE IS POSSIBLE. Flowers and balloons covered the chancel, adding to the party feel.

The kids looked normal. A few boys and girls had short, spiky hair, but most of them looked like regular teens. Their moods were like his, not hyped up like the leaders on stage.

Nearly everyone stood, moving to the beat of the loud praise band. Josh closed his eyes and blocked out everything other than the music. The lyrics filled his soul. He opened his heart to the Holy Spirit like Sara had suggested. *Heal me, Lord.*

He felt his shoulder drop and his heart rate slow. He took a deep breath and let himself float in prayer.

"Welcome, everyone!" A voice interrupted his meditations.

A man with gelled blond hair was at the mic. He waved at people in the crowd, pointed at others, and mouthed *welcome* over and over again. The music faded away. The congregation sat.

"Welcome, everyone!" he repeated.

"Thanks, Doug!" a few people yelled back.

"We are so excited to have you with us for this Jesus-filled week of healing and release with Resurrection Ministries. Are you ready?"

A few people in the crowd spoke back: "Yes."

"I can't hear you." Then he said even louder, "Are you ready?"

"Yes," the crowd shouted. Mom joined in.

"I still can't hear you! Are you ready?!"

"Yes!" the crowd answered. Josh heard Dad joining in with Mom.

"That's more like it!" Doug said from the chancel. "Let's start with a song, my favorite."

The band began to play, and the words flashed on the screen. Mom, Dad, and Josh stood up and joined in with the crowd. Josh sang out, too. It felt so good to be part of something, to be with people who knew what he was going through.

When the song ended, Doug began his speech, "I'm just going to come right out and say it. We're all here today because our lives are affected by the sin of same-sex attraction. You or someone you love is struggling with homosexuality. Look around this room. Go ahead. Right now, look around. Look at these wonderful people and know... you're not alone. Everyone here knows what you're going through. Raise your hand if you're here for the first time."

Most of the crowd raised their hands, but a lot of them didn't—probably a quarter of the room. Mom looked shocked.

"I want to praise you for being here, for making a commitment to living a biblically based life. You know that Jesus is the only answer, and here is where you'll find Him. All homosexual relationships are sinful. That's just a fact. It's also a fact that everyone can go from having homosexual attractions to having heterosexual attractions. Change is possible."

Someone yelled out, "Change is possible."

Change is possible, Josh repeated to himself.

Doug smiled. "It sure is, amen. I'm living proof of that. I have been set free from the sin of homosexuality. It wasn't easy giving up that lifestyle. I wrestled with the devil for my soul... and I won!" The crowd cheered. He went on, "I count my blessings each day that I live my life in conformity with God's will as expressed in the Bible. I know what you're going through. And I know your suffering can end. Jesus died on the cross for our sins. He died for you so that you may be saved. Are you going to throw that gift away?"

Josh mouthed the word "no".

"No," came a few voices.

"Are you going to throw the resurrection away?"

"No!" shouted even more voices.

"No. You are not. We're here to guide you on that path. We will equip your children to walk in freedom from same-sex desires. But our emphasis is not to simply change one's attraction. No! We are called to discipline all of us, parents and children, into a deeper walk with Christ and allow Him to do transformational work in the world through us. Your children are especially blessed to be on this sacred path during Holy Week. This week we will live the crucifixion and the resurrection." Then he shouted at the top of his lungs, "We are Resurrection Ministries!"

The band started up with a loud guitar. The congregation rose up, cheering. Energy filled the room. Everyone sang; people swayed and clapped; many were crying and singing. They were surrounded by people dealing with the same issues, some who had come through to the other side. These people were living examples of God's grace and mercy.

Josh turned up his face and hands to the Lord. He closed his eyes and swayed to the music. A chill moved down his spine. The Holy Spirit was pouring into him—filling him with faith and hope.

After the opening, they were sent to their spirit circle—ten kids and their parents. The leaders were like Doug, all excited to be there. They started by having them say their names and a bit about their journey. The other kids were quiet, just saying their name, grade, and school. Only one of them, Ashley, had much to say. She'd been to two of these camps before and told them to expect a roller coaster of feelings.

Some parents shared lots of details about what their family had been going through and others just said where they came from and who was in their family. It was obvious a couple of them were skeptical and one of the moms cried when she said her husband wouldn't come because he didn't believe in this treatment. Her son, Dominic, looked like he wanted to disappear.

Their family was last to go. Josh said his name, grade, and school. He was the only kid from Dublin High. Mom teared up when she said that she loved Josh so much and wanted his soul to be at peace with God. She looked so ashamed that Josh could barely look at her. Dad brought up Sara and Rachel and that they were all one hundred percent committed to Josh.

Some of the families had been dealing with this for a long time while others were new to this "situation." The leaders said there would be lots of prayer *and* lots of instances of good Christian fun during the week. It wouldn't be all work. In fact, building Christian community among the teens was central to the treatment.

Josh studied each kid as they went around the circle. Five girls and five boys. Mira had spiked hair and wore a flannel, but she was the only one who looked alternative in any way. Not that it was a problem that she looked like that. It was just none of them "looked gay," except maybe her.

Pamphlets were handed out describing the therapeutic process. The leaders kept saying over and over again that all of these young people could change with deep commitment and hard work, but then they'd switch and say it might take a while. They seemed to be talking more to the parents than the kids, telling them not to be attached to immediate and complete transformation. God was in charge here, not them. Surrendering their child to God's will was their spiritual task.

God's will. Like Sara had said. *Listen directly to God.*

Josh had been here for only a few hours, and he already understood what Ashley meant about the roller coaster.

In the afternoon, the three of them had private time with Andrew, Josh's counselor for the week. He asked about their family and was particularly interested in what kinds of activities they liked to do together. He was delighted that they attended church regularly and that Dad had been one of Josh's soccer coaches.

"Now for the difficult conversation." Andrew switched to a somber and empathetic tone. "Abuse. We know there was a root trauma. Have you uncovered it?"

He leaned in, hanging on every word. He probably thought he was being a good listener, but he seemed like a used car salesman from a bad movie.

There was silence, and then Mom shook her head. "I've been thinking and thinking. So has Josh, right?"

Josh gave a small, noncommittal nod.

"A teacher, a grandparent, a scout master—it could be anyone," Andrew said. "Josh, you have no recollection?"

Josh shook his head and said quietly, "I don't think there was anything."

"Denial is the enemy of healing. It must have happened when you were very young, under four years old, or it was extremely traumatic. It's one of those two things. We'll do good work together to help you uncover it."

Josh slouched in his chair, wanting to disappear. He had absolutely no memory of being abused and hated that Mom blamed herself for being neglectful.

"Are there any practicing homosexuals in your lives? Friends, family, coworkers?"

"Absolutely not," Mom said as Dad nodded.

"Who?" Mom asked.

"At work. We have a lot of employees." Dad shrugged.

Then he continued, "Safeway is an openly tolerant workplace—a lot of homosexuals work there. And I have a cousin who I'm pretty sure is gay."

Mom exclaimed, "What?!"

"Justin," Dad said quietly.

"But he's married," Mom replied.

"Was married," Dad corrected her. "Remember, they got divorced two years ago? I'm pretty sure this is why."

"Those poor children. Why didn't you tell me?" Mom asked.

"I'm sorry, Jenn. No one said anything to me outright. I'm not absolutely certain, but my mom alluded to never hosting Thanksgiving again, since he's not welcome in her home. She didn't say why, and I didn't ask."

"Well, there's your root cause." Andrew sounded excited, like he'd closed a sale on a car. "Did Josh spend time with this Justin when he was young?"

"Justin is the nicest guy ever," Dad protested. "He wouldn't hurt Josh."

"He wouldn't see it as hurting. They think differently—people who choose to live the homosexual lifestyle."

"Josh, don't listen to him," Dad countered. "You don't need to be afraid of Justin."

Mom slapped at Dad's arm. He looked at her, and she gave him the look—the big-eyed look that said *be quiet*. Dad raised his hands in surrender.

Josh was confused. He hardly knew Dad's cousin. Once a year they had Thanksgiving together, but there were lots of grown-ups there. He was never alone with Justin. But Andrew wasn't looking to him for confirmation.

"I know this is hard to hear," the counselor said. "I was resistant to my root cause for a long time."

Mom asked, "You struggled with SSA?"

"Yes, of course. That's why I'm so committed to this ministry." Andrew beamed at them.

"And you're cured?" Mom asked. "Are you married?"

"I'm still on my journey. God hasn't put a wife in my path, but I know He will when the time is right. Just like He will for Josh, praise Jesus. Well, our time is up. We've already made a lot of progress," Andrew went on. "I know this will be a fruitful week for Josh. He's going to deepen his relationship to Jesus, strengthen his masculinity, heal from his root trauma, and weed out his same-sex attraction. I'm excited and hopeful for our time together."

After dinner with his spirit group, but without his parents, Doug welcomed them back to the sanctuary. Josh sat with the other teens. Toward the end the parents were invited to do a laying-on of hands on the children. The kids bunched up in the front of the sanctuary. Travis from his group was on his right and a kid from a different group was on his left. He didn't know where to look so he stared at the back of the neck of the kid in front of him. His brown hair was starting to curl around his ear.

"Awkward," Travis whispered.

Josh looked at him and smiled. "Yeah."

They got pushed close together.

"Sorry if I need a mint!" Travis quipped.

"You're good," Josh replied.

"Thanks." Travis looked relieved and sad, reminding Josh they were going through the same thing. Maybe they'd be friends in this struggle.

Parents gathered around them in concentric circles with their hands resting on the back of the person in front of them. The whole group linked together by touch. Josh couldn't see his parents, but he felt them in there. Love and faith were being poured into him.

Doug prayed out loud from the inner circle: "Lord, thank You in the name of Jesus. God, thank You for the power of the Holy Spirit. We ask that Your presence fills us with wisdom and revelation so that we may follow You, love You, and serve You entirely. Bind up all distractions and show us Your will.

"Lord, we ask for Your blessing on these children. They are ready to live a surrendered life. Jesus Christ, our Lord and Savior, we know You have not given them more temptation than they can bear. They are ready to reject homosexual desires and turn their mind to whole-some thoughts.

"Lord God, these babies have been wounded by their pasts. We know they can only be healed through Your mercy. I call on You and Lord Jesus to save these children. We know You want to protect them from homosexual behavior. They are ready to work with you, Lord, so that they may be agents—no, warriors—for Your will on Earth. In Jesus's name we pray, Amen."

Everyone in the room echoed, "Amen."

After the service Josh had to say goodbye to Mom and Dad. He waited with his spirit circle. He wanted to look faithful and hopeful, but he was actually just scared. The girls were on one side and the boys on the other, clumped into pairs and trios.

Dominic and Luke were chatting. He'd forgotten the name of the other kid standing with them.

He asked Travis, "What's his name? The guy from Modesto?"

"Andres," Travis replied.

"Thanks." Josh tried to think of something else to say or ask but was coming up with nothing. Awkward. Every other group had something to say to each other.

Travis leaned in and whispered, "Have you heard of or seen *The Eternal Sunshine of the Spotless Mind?*"

Josh shook his head.

"It came out a few weeks ago. You can erase anything you don't want to remember," Travis said. "I wish they had a machine like that, but for us. We stick our heads into a tube and presto chango."

"Like the Star-Belly Sneetches' machine," Josh said.

"Yeah," Travis said. "Or a wave of the wand in Harry Potter."

Shocked, Josh asked, "You've read Harry Potter?"

"All of them so far. It's the best!" Travis replied, his eyes practically glowing. "You didn't get into it?" He looked incredulous.

Josh bit his lip. Should he be honest? If not now, when would he ever be? Travis shared the same terrible situation as him, that's why he was here.

"Not allowed," Josh said. He wiggled his head and shrugged. "Magic. Incompatible with God's laws."

"Me, too," Travis said. "My parents have no idea I've read them—I did it at school."

Josh said, "One secret was enough for me. Too much, actually. Guess I'm obedient."

"Were you allowed to watch *The Wizard of Oz*?" Travis asked.

"Yeah. It's a family favorite," Josh replied.

"Us, too. After I realized it had witches and they approved, I didn't feel so bad about sneaking Harry Potter," Travis said. "Magic from their childhood was okay, but not new magic? What hypocrites, right?"

Josh felt his mind twist into a jumbled up Rubik's cube. Before he could give it more thought Andrew got their attention by shouting to the whole group, "Here come your parents."

Josh looked over at his mom and dad, heading their way. His heart twisted. Maybe they were hypocrites, but he wanted their approval so much that it hurt.

Andrew directed, "Give your father your cell phones in surrender and trust, and then say goodbye."

Adrenaline poured into Josh. He wouldn't be able to text

Sara or Dad. He and Travis exchanged looks. They'd be in this together.

Josh swallowed hard as he reached into his pocket. His hand shook as he surrendered his phone. Dad noticed and nodded at him.

Mom gave him a huge hug. It felt nice. He leaned against her for much longer than allowed. He missed his mom under these new rules they had to follow.

When they pulled apart, she said, "I am so proud of you, honey. I want you to walk this week surrounded by the Holy Spirit. You are a special person, Josh, especially touched by God. There's a reason for this struggle that will be revealed to us in time. I love you."

"Bye, Mom. I love you, too," Josh said. "But not too much!"

Mom laughed. It was nice to see her smile. He was going to put everything he had into this week.

"I love you," Dad said. Then he hugged Josh, and whispered into his ear, "No matter what they say, I have always loved you. From the moment you were born."

Josh welled up. When they parted, he saw that Dad had tears in his eye, too.

"I know, Dad. I always have," Josh replied.

Dad pushed something into his hand. It was a stack of quarters.

"In case you need us."

Relieved at the lifeline, Josh smiled. "Thanks, Dad."

They hugged again.

"Come on, Josh," Andrew interrupted. "We'll take good care of him. I promise."

Josh tore himself away and joined this group of strangers, filled equally with hope and doubt.

SIXTEEN

SATURDAY APRIL 3, 2004

Jenn

Jenn watched Josh walk away with his "family" for the week. Even taller than Andrew, his dark brown hair poked above the others. She ached with love for him. Steve wrapped an arm around her, and she leaned into his support. They watched until Josh disappeared into a room and the door closed tight. She pulled away from Steve and looked around. They were surrounded by parents watching their sons and daughters walk away from them. All of these people were entrusting their precious children's souls into the care of Resurrection Ministries.

"God, watch over Josh. And heal his unnatural yearnings, in Jesus's name. Amen."

As they drove home, Jenn chastised Steve, "I can't believe you didn't tell me about Justin."

"The poor guy is being shunned by half his family. I don't see how it helps to have more people speculating about him."

Jenn was hurt. "Do you think I would be rude to Justin? Shun him?"

"No," Steve said. "It's just none of our business. His life is his life."

"It's our business where our children are concerned," Jenn challenged.

"They see him once a year for three hours over dinner. It's not going to hurt them. I don't care what that guy said. Justin's a good person. Jenn, he was an usher at our wedding. Do you actually think he would have hurt Josh?"

Jenn took a breath and exhaled. "No. I guess not."

"You know I work with people who are practicing homosexuals. It's not like it's contagious."

"I never said it was," Jenn said. "You're treating me as if I'm in the wrong here. Who's a homosexual at work?"

"Bethany," Steve said with a shrug.

"Your secretary?" Jenn's head dropped forward and her mouth opened in surprise. "But she's beautiful."

"Remember how I told you that you didn't need to be jealous of her?"

Jenn nodded.

"Now you know why." Steve winked.

Jenn's eyes got big; she shook her head. "She's really a homosexual?"

Steve nodded. "The world is changing. It's complicated, Jenn. I'm not going to compromise my Christian values, but sometimes being Christian means being respectful of people who don't share my beliefs. You choose the people you're around every day, but I don't have that luxury. I work with all kinds of people, and I'm responsible for creating a good working environment for each of them."

Jenn patted Steve's arm. "I love that you're a great boss. But we have to be in this *all* the way for Josh. We have to believe—be a team."

"We are a team. And like all teams, we each have a position.

You play the mom part, and I'll be the dad part. You have to trust me, okay?"

Jenn nodded. *Surrender*, she told herself. *I'm surrendering.* Steve squeezed her hand.

"I wonder about taking Rachel to Monterey this week—like we planned before all this. What do you think?" Jenn asked.

"Great idea," Steve replied. "She'd love it."

"We need more mother-daughter time. You'll be at work. Josh is in great hands. Why not?" Jenn was excited. Things were looking up and she was finally getting back to her confident self.

Most motels were already fully booked, but after eight calls Jenn reserved three nights somewhere suitable within walking distance of the aquarium. She surprised Rachel on Sunday as they were driving home from dinner at the Bishops'. Rachel squealed in delight. They packed that night and left by ten in the morning. Two-day passes to the aquarium would give them plenty of time with the penguins, the otters, and the jellyfish. Whenever Jenn worried about Josh, she reminded told herself to let go—Josh was in God's hands. This was Rachel's time, so she focused on her youngest child, which meant they went to every scheduled penguin feeding while they were there.

During one of the feedings, Jenn slipped away from Rachel, saying she had to use the bathroom, but she actually went to the gift shop to buy stuff for Easter. She chose small stuffed animals for each kid: a penguin for Rachel, an otter for Josh, and a jellyfish for Sara. They'd roll their eyes, but Jenn knew they loved that she still hid baskets for them.

In the jellyfish exhibit the Holy Spirit poured into her body, sending a chill through her spine. She felt utterly connected to all of God's creations. At once she felt both small and big, like she was a tiny atom in God's heart. She was entirely at peace for the first time in two months.

When it was time to head home, Jenn felt restored in the

Lord and prepared to return to her life. She and Josh would both be transformed this week, more certain of their faith and their relationship with their Savior.

On the way home, Jenn's cell rang, and Rachel picked up because she was driving.

Jenn heard Rachel say, "Hey, Josh, it's Rachel. Mom's driving, so she can't talk now. Want me to give her a message? How's your camp?"

Rachel listened for a bit.

"Oh," she said into the phone. "That's too bad. I'll ask her." To Jenn, Rachel said, "Josh wants to come home. Can we go get him?"

"How is he calling me? He doesn't have a cell phone." Jenn was incredulous. Josh was supposed to be on his way to a cure, not quitting his treatment.

"Mom wants to know how you're calling her." Rachel listened to Josh's reply. "He's at a pay phone. There's one in the church. Can we get him?"

"No!" Jenn declared. "Tell him no. He needs to stick this out."

"You heard, huh? Sorry, Joshy. We'll see you on Saturday. I miss you. The house is too quiet when you're gone."

"I love you, Josh," Jenn yelled, hoping he had heard her.

"He says he loves you, too," Rachel said to Jenn. Then into the phone she said, "Bye, Josh. Cheer up. It's almost over... two more days until you come home."

After Rachel hung up, Jenn asked, "How did he sound?"

"Not good," Rachel said matter-of-factly.

"What did he say?"

"He said, 'Ask Mom if I can come home,'" Rachel said in a low voice, mimicking Josh.

"What else?"

"Nothing." Jenn felt, more than saw, Rachel shrug.

Suddenly Jenn plummeted back into a pit of anxiety. The

calm mood brought on by two blissful days surrounded by sea life instantly evaporated. She started to question again: was he homesick? Resisting treatment? Had she made a rash decision to tell him to stick it out? Should she talk to him?

After she parked in their garage, she hit redial. The phone rang and rang and rang. She counted to twelve, but nobody answered the pay phone. In the family room she dug through the papers on her desk to find the emergency contact number at Resurrection Ministries and dialed.

A woman answered the phone.

"Hello. May I please speak to Josh Henderson? He's attending camp this week."

"May I ask who's calling?"

"This is his mother, Jennifer."

"Hello, Jennifer, this is Donna! Remember me from the first day? My husband is John, one of Josh's spirit circle leaders."

"Yes, Donna. Of course I remember you." Jenn was relieved to hear a familiar voice. "How are you? How's camp?"

"Blessed and wonderful, praise God!"

"Josh called while I was driving—may I speak to him?"

"Oh dear," Donna said in an ominous voice. "Talking with parents is counter to the program. I'm sorry to hear he called you. You know I'll have to report him."

"Excuse me?" Jenn asked.

"For his own good. Andrew, John, and Elaine will need to know so they can adjust treatment as needed. Josh knew that calling outside was forbidden without express permission from Andrew."

Jenn's stomach sank. She got a metallic taste in her mouth. She sighed. Tentatively she asked, "Do you know how Josh is doing?"

"Well... because my John is with him, I *have* heard a few stories. I don't want to alarm you," Donna said slowly, "but apparently Josh is having difficulty with complete surrender.

It's common, so don't be too concerned. Andrew knows how to handle this type of oppositional behavior. He's a very experienced leader."

Despair for Josh coated her lungs. Jenn bit her lip. "I'm so sorry. He's never been oppositional before."

"For some reason SSA can open the door to all kinds of unwanted behaviors and attitudes. That's why you were wise to just nip this in the bud. We'll have him shaped up by the time you get him on Saturday... or at least further on his way to recovery. I'll hold you, and him, in my prayers tonight. Good-bye," she said cheerfully.

"Thanks," Jenn squeaked out. She was teary once again. This roller coaster of emotions was exhausting.

She dialed Steve at work. He reassured her that she'd made the right decision: Josh needed to see this thing through. That gave her the strength to stay home rather than run out to Tracy to see him.

But it didn't stop her from worrying about her son.

SEVENTEEN

THURSDAY APRIL 8, 2004

Josh

"Josh?" Andrew sounded annoyed.

Josh looked up from his plate. He'd been lost in non-thought again.

"Will you lead us in prayer?" His tone made it clear he was repeating the request.

Josh nodded and reached out his hand to the boys on either side of him: Travis and Dominic. It felt nice to be connected to the others that were sharing his tragic struggle, but he suspected they were hiding behind lies like he was.

"Dear Lord. Please open our hearts to the mystery and power of Your love. Help us to live in harmony with Your will for us. We thank You for this food which sustains our bodies and for our families that sustain our spirits. In Jesus's name we pray. Amen."

Andrew led the conversation as always. He brought up March Madness like it was still a thing, but it had ended on Sunday. Josh had missed the final game to be here. The boys looked at each other, but no one corrected Andrew. It was dangerous to cross him in any way—even for facts.

Josh's outrage had boiled over in the last session. Andrew yelled at him, trying to get him to accept things that were not true. Some of the other kids made up stories about neglect or abuse, just to get him to move on. But Josh refused to admit to a lie. He'd never, ever been alone in a room with Dad's cousin Justin.

When Andrew finally gave up on him, Josh asked to go to the bathroom. He used the time away to call Mom on the pay phone with the change that Dad had given him. Rachel picked up and passed on the message that he had to stay. Ever since he'd hung up, he'd been afraid that someone had seen him at the phone, and he would be disciplined.

Donna walked up to the table while they were eating their baked chicken. She gave him the side eye and then whispered into Andrew's ear. He nodded slowly.

Fear tasted like metal in his mouth. They knew what he'd done.

After dinner, back in their therapy room, the group sat in silence. So much for the fun that Doug had promised their parents. Everyone was too scared to be themselves. They were like frightened rabbits waiting for their turn to be tormented by the wolf.

God, give me strength.

"Josh, come with me. The rest of you stay in your chairs in silent prayer. You're being watched so I will know if you are following my directions. Do you understand?"

The others nodded.

Andrew led him to a room with two chairs. Doug sat in one.

"Sit," Doug commanded.

Josh swallowed hard and did as he was told. Andrew left him.

Doug spoke, "I've been getting reports about you, so I know what you've been doing while you're here."

Josh nodded.

"You've been defiant and questioning. Your intelligence and leadership have led you to believe you know better than God."

Josh bit back his response, but his head shook slightly.

"Are you challenging me right now?" Doug asked.

"Sir, with all due respect, I *do not* believe that I know better than God."

Doug stared at him. "But you believe you know better than Andrew?"

Josh nodded.

Doug sat back. He thought for a moment. "Go on. Tell me where Andrew is mistaken."

"He jumped onto the idea of my dad's cousin being my abuser. I barely know the guy. Andrew asked my parents one question, 'Is anyone homosexual in your family?' My dad said *maybe his cousin*, but he isn't certain. And now Andrew believes if I 'accept the fact that Justin abused me' God will cure me by faith."

Josh exhaled. He was trying not to tear up. He continued, "My parents taught us that lying puts you outside of integrity. Dad drilled into me: integrity and faith. How can I be cured by faith with a lie?"

"You don't want to feel this way anymore, do you?" Doug said.

"No, sir, I don't. Truly, I want to be cured." Josh pushed back tears. "But lying to God is impossible. We can't lie to Him, can we? He knows my heart."

Doug looked stricken, his face as white as a zombie.

"God knows I hate that I feel the way I do, but He knows that I feel it," Josh explained. He stared at Doug, hoping he had an answer.

Doug stood up abruptly. "I think it is best if you be given time to talk to God directly. Follow me." Doug showed Josh to a small room with a mat on the floor and nothing else. Josh walked in and Doug shut the door. Josh jumped when the deadbolt turned. He stared at the door; the slit of the keyhole was empty. He'd been locked in.

They won't kill me, Josh assured himself. *God is here, too.*

He sat on the mat. Alone for the first time in five days, he took a big breath and felt his shoulders drop. He let tears seep from his eyes. He'd desperately wanted camp to work, to be cured of his attractions.

He thought about his conversations with Kyle. There hadn't been many, but the therapist suggested Josh listen for God directly, not someone else's words about God. Kyle was confident God did not care who Josh loved.

But Kyle didn't understand that Josh would lose his whole family if he...

He couldn't let himself imagine that option. He pushed aside any thought of living the homosexual lifestyle.

Could he lie and tell them he didn't feel the way he did every time he took Travis's hand? Like he told Doug, there was no lying to God, but other people didn't know what was in his heart. Lying was an option, but that was not showing integrity. Lying to his mom and dad could not be his solution.

Could he be honest that he hadn't changed on the inside, but wouldn't act on his feelings? He would never get married or have a family. He could be the fun uncle. Would Sara let him be around her kids? Would Rachel? Mom? He didn't have to be alone with them.

Josh started to cry. Not little tears, but big sobs, like when he fell as a kid.

"God, help me. Please," he whispered in a prayer.

How could he avoid temptation? He could live alone or with his parents... or maybe one of his sisters. He wouldn't act on his desires. He was good at that. Catholic priests gave up sex for a lifetime for God. He'd be like a priest, living his faith by being celibate.

His heart lifted a little.

Foreswearing same-sex behavior wasn't lying. He considered. Could he promise celibacy? To his parents? Andrew? Himself? And God? It would be hard, but it was way better than losing his church and his family.

He could abstain from acting on his impulses, he knew he could. He'd already done it. For the first time in months and months he felt at peace. Maybe even years.

God had answered his prayers. *Thank you, God.*

He could tell Andrew and Doug that he'd found a solution that was pleasing to God and would satisfy his parents.

Exhausted, Josh lay on the mat and fell into a deep sleep. When he woke, breakfast was on a tray by the door.

EIGHTEEN

SATURDAY, APRIL 10, 2004

Jenn

On Saturday, Jenn and Steve got up early to make the drive back to Tracy. Jenn told Steve she was too excited to eat, but actually she was too scared to have an appetite. She was afraid Josh was mad at her, she was afraid he wasn't cured, and she was afraid to hear what they were going to tell her about Josh. She had no faith that this camp worked.

Donna was again greeting people at the door as they arrived.

"Welcome back," she said to them. All traces of enthusiasm and excitement were gone. Jenn felt like she had done something wrong.

"Hello," Steve said.

"How's Josh?" Jenn asked, worry shading her voice.

"You'll be reunited with him soon enough," Donna explained in a formal voice. Her eyebrows arched up. "You'll get a full report from his counselor after worship. Just go right into the sanctuary."

Jenn felt thoroughly dismissed. The energy in the sanctuary

was a stark contrast to her mood. The band was playing raucous music, and there was a lot of excitement in the room. None of the kids were there, but seats were roped off in the front, presumably for them. Jenn walked as close as she could to the teen area. At nine sharp, Doug stepped out onto the stage.

"Blessings, parents and family!" he yelled into the microphone.

"Blessings, Doug," the well-trained crowd yelled back. Jenn didn't join in.

"Parents, family members, you should be so proud of your children! They did the work of the Lord this week. The Holy Spirit has been in the house! Please stand up and give them a big round of applause as they come in."

The congregation stood and cheered. Jenn and Steve rose with them. At the front of the sanctuary, the doors on both sides swung open. The kids filed in one at a time, following their spirit circle leaders into the saved rows. They were singing. Jenn could barely make out the song, but as more kids filed in, she recognized the comforting and powerful words: *Our God is a Loving God. Through Him we are saved.* Her pulse raced in anticipation. She turned her head, searching for Josh. She recognized a few of the leaders, but not all of them. Then, on the right, Andrew was coming through the door. She grabbed Steve's hand and pointed. Kids filed in behind him. Josh would be coming through soon. Jenn focused on each face. Josh was the last person from his group. He wasn't smiling or singing like the others. She waved, but he only looked ahead.

"I know you want to see your kids, but we have a special ceremony first," Doug said over the singing. "Your reunions will be well worth the wait."

The kids stood in the reserved rows. Jenn saw the top of Josh's crown above the crowd. *He needs a haircut*, she thought automatically. She stared at the back of his head, willing him to look for her, but unlike most of the other kids, he didn't turn around and wave to his family. The words to the song flashed on the screen. Everyone joined in the singing. When it was over, they all sat. Josh slouched, so Jenn could no longer see his head. The pit in her stomach got bigger.

"This week has been filled with the work of the Lord! The spirit is in the house!" Doug yelled.

The congregation cheered.

Then people came forward and started giving testimonials. Middle-aged people, young adults, and teens spoke about the transformative love of Jesus Christ and the power of complete surrender to God's will. Person after person reminded the crowd that change was possible. They told stories about their own journeys away from the temptations of the homosexual lifestyle and to the transformative love of Jesus.

After the testimonials, Doug invited the teens and spirit circle leaders to come to the left side of the chancel. In neat rows they stood facing their families. Josh was so far to the back that Jenn could not see him very well, but she tracked where he was standing.

Doug spoke to the parents. "Families, you have entrusted your children's souls to us. We have honored that trust with hard work and dedication to bring your children in line with biblical living.

"Parents, do you promise to keep faithful to God and our Lord Jesus Christ regardless of the secular and ecumenical pressures that may tempt you away from an unholy life for yourself and your children? If you agree, please say, 'We will.'"

Jenn took Steve's hand and together they said, "We will," along with the crowd.

"Spiritual warriors," Doug said to the spirit circle leaders, "you are doing God's most holy work. We thank you for what you have given to these young souls. What you have done here this week will ripple out into the world, bringing our Earth a little closer to God's kingdom.

"Let us pray. Lord, thank You in the name of Jesus. Watch over these beautiful children. Lead them away from same-sex attraction and guide them toward healthy, biblically based living. Transform them with the power of Your Love..."

Doug's prayer went on and on. Jenn turned her attention to where Josh stood. She searched for any indication of how he was doing. She wanted to know that he was happy, or just okay, but he was too far away for her to see his facial expressions.

She returned to listening to Doug's ongoing speech: "...commit to a full and complete transformation through our Lord Jesus Christ? Do you promise to avoid temptations both physical and spiritual?"

One of the teens walked to the center of the stage. She spoke into the mic in a shaky voice. "I renounce homosexuality and commit to my faith in God and our Lord Jesus Christ."

"Amen!" cried Doug as the young woman crossed to the right side of the stage.

Another teen stepped to the middle. His voice was strong as he said, "I renounce homosexuality and commit to my faith in God and our Lord Jesus Christ."

"Amen!" Doug shouted, and this time he was joined by other voices from the crowd.

That teen was followed by another, and another, and another speaking into the mic and then being affirmed by the congregation with a loud, "Amen." Some cried when they spoke. Others cheered. Some were serious, but most spoke quickly and got it over with. Clearly many of them did not like public speaking. Josh was comfortable with a microphone, so that wouldn't be a problem for him. The group of teens on the right grew as the group on the left dwindled. Soon there were just a few teens surrounded by the spirit circle leaders, including Josh. Jenn saw Andrew whisper something to him.

Josh walked slowly to the microphone. He stood there, looking out at the crowd, his face sad. Jenn's hands got clammy.

She was nervous for him. He was waiting too long. Josh just needed to speak—it would only get harder if he kept standing there.

He stooped over. Very slowly and with little emotion in his voice, Josh said, "I renounce homosexuality and commit to my faith in God and our Lord Jesus Christ."

Jenn's stomach dropped; something wasn't right.

After worship the families were reunited one by one in meetings with the spirit circle leaders. Steve and Jenn were directed to a waiting room. Other parents were there, too. Jenn was way too distressed to make conversation with these strangers, so she pulled out her phone and opened solitaire to look like she was playing rather than listening intently to the conversation around her. She didn't want to talk, she only wanted to hear.

The parents introduced themselves to one another and shared their stories.

"This is our third camp," came a low male voice. "We did one through Exodus and the other was also through Resurrection."

"Your child isn't cured?" a mom asked, sounding confused and disappointed.

The dad replied, "I used to pray for a full recovery. Now I pray for celibacy. She's committed. We know she is, but she refuses to date any boys. She says she doesn't want to be a liar."

Another parent said, "This is our second camp. Our son needed a strong tune-up. We hope this will get him back on track. The forces for accepting himself as homosexual were getting too strong. We took him out of the public high school and have been homeschooling him."

The first mom asked, "Is that going to be a problem for college? How old is he?"

"He's a senior. He'll be going to Chapman next year—close to home and surrounded by people who share our Christian values."

"You came from Southern California for this?" Steve asked, his leg shaking up and down. He was as nervous and jumpy as she felt.

"This was an easy drive. One of the camps was in Texas."

Steve whispered to Jenn. "Guess we were lucky this was so close."

Jenn nodded. She was shaken. When she signed Josh up, she believed this would be a one-time treatment. Complete transformation was promised. This was supposed to be the end of their journey, but from the sounds of the other parents, that was unlikely.

Jenn's phone vibrated. She looked at the screen. It was Sara.

When will u b home?

Jenn texted back.

In a bit. Let u know when we leave.

The couples were called in one by one. The parents wished the others well and offered to pray for them as they left the group still waiting. Eventually Jenn and Steve were alone, nervous and lost in their own ruminations.

"Do you think this is a bad sign?" she asked Steve. Her eyes welled.

Steve sighed. "Someone had to be last."

The door opened, startling Jenn.

"Here we go," Steve sighed.

Andrew beckoned them into the room. Josh was standing in the middle of the large space. Next to him was a black

Naugahyde couch and a folding metal chair. Jenn started to rush to Josh, opening her arms to give him a hug.

"Stop!" Andrew said. "A verbal greeting is called for."

Jenn felt like she had been slapped. Her face flushed. It had been a long time since she was embarrassed enough to turn red.

"Hi, Josh. I missed you," she said.

Josh nodded. Then he put his hand out to Steve.

"Yes, a handshake is a good masculine greeting for your father. Nice work, Josh," Andrew said. "Have a seat."

They settled into the couch, with Steve sitting between Josh and Jenn. They were sandwiched in so close together that Jenn couldn't see Steve's or Josh's face.

"I'm here to give you a report on Josh's progress this week. As you know, it's not been easy for him. He is extremely resistant to treatment, though he may have had a breakthrough yesterday. Wouldn't you agree, Josh?"

Jenn's mood lifted a little when she heard the word *breakthrough*. Maybe Josh was transformed.

"Yes, sir." Josh stared at the ground.

Steve asked, "What do you mean by resistant?"

"We spend time on the parts of the treatment each day: parental relationships, root trauma, same-sex attraction, and prayer. His strength is in prayer. He's able to pray for himself and others and accept prayers on his behalf. However, he insists that his relationship with each of you is fine. I trust you will not encourage that thinking. And he's in denial about a root trauma, even though we uncovered it when you dropped him off. We encouraged him to speak about the abuse from your cousin Justin, but he claims it goes against his integrity to lie. As I said, he is in denial."

Jenn's feelings about the counselor's report were a swirl. It was sweet to hear that Josh said his relationship with each of them was good and she was glad that he didn't want to lie. She also found it hard to believe that Justin had abused Josh.

But mostly she wanted her son to be cured. For that he needed to surrender to treatment. That was why he was here, to surrender his life to God.

Andrew kept going. "As for the same-sex attraction, Josh has decided that he knows better than we do and isn't willing to submit to a faithful path. He claims he can *abstain* but that he cannot *lie* about what he is feeling. Pledging abstinence is a wonderful start, let me be clear about that. But if he doesn't believe God can remove his unhealthy impulses, then He can't. By faith all things are possible, but doubt ties God's hands."

Jenn blinked. "Josh isn't cured?"

"It's usually a long process. I'm sorry if you misunderstood. Not many of our kids are entirely changed in one week. There are more camps, and we have a list of wonderful counselors who can work with him on an ongoing basis." Andrew handed them a piece of paper.

"*Change is possible*," Jenn declared. "That's what you said. Change is possible."

"Of course it's possible. That's true. Just not in the case of Josh right now. But I haven't given up hope on him. Not in the slightest. As I said, his prayer life is beautiful. That's not true for many of the other teens. The journey back to a right relationship with God isn't short, but it's rich and meaningful. I wish you all the best."

He stood up, clearly finished with them, and opened the door they hadn't come in through. They stood up, too. Andrew shook each of their hands and escorted them to the entryway where only Josh's belongings were left. Slowly he picked up his backpack, pillow and suitcase and Steve took the luggage from Josh's hand. Jenn wanted to hug her son, but she resisted the impulse. Her eyes burned. The entryway was empty and cold. All the signs and balloons were gone. They were the last family to leave.

In the car, she faced forward so Josh could not see how

upset she was. Resistant to treatment, oppositional, homosexual: those were not the words she wanted to hear about her son. *Cured.* That was the word she was longing to hear today. *Cured.*

Jenn had nothing to say to her son. Apparently, neither did Steve. They drove along in silence all the way home. She looked over at her husband. Steve's jaw was clenched, and his hands twisted on the steering wheel. He was as upset as Jenn. It felt much like the ride from the hospital.

Two months had passed, and Jenn feared they were no closer to a cure.

NINETEEN

SATURDAY, APRIL 10, 2024

Sara

Sara and Rachel were watching a re-run of *Full House* when they heard the front door open and shut. Sara looked at Rachel, who shrugged. They rushed to the entryway to find the rest of their family.

"Surprise," they shouted in unison and raced to hug Josh.

They'd hung a big, homemade sign that said, WELCOME HOME, JOSHY. WE MISSED YOU!!!!!!

"You said you would text when you were on your way!" Rachel chastised Mom. "We were gonna be waiting! Josh, we made you a mocha cake—come see."

"Thanks, guys," Josh said without enthusiasm. "I'm not hungry. Maybe after dinner. I'm going to rest."

Sara looked at Dad, her eyebrows pulled into a question. Dad shook his head. He watched Josh walk away, then explained quietly, "It's been a long day. Camp wasn't so good for Josh. We're all disappointed."

"Baking a cake was a very sweet thing to do for your brother," Mom assured them. "Thank you." She hugged them tight.

"I'm going to talk to him," Dad said, and went upstairs.

Rachel said, "I'm going back to the show. You coming?"

Sara shook her head.

"Was it bad?" Sara asked her mother when they were alone. She felt as sick as her mother looked.

Mom nodded. "Could you please go for a walk with him after he's done talking to Dad—before dinner?" she suggested. "It might help. I'm scared for him, Sara."

"What happened?"

Mom sighed. "I don't know all the details. They didn't say that much, and Josh didn't tell us anything on the way home, but basically, he didn't surrender and..." Mom's voice cracked. "Well, he's not cured."

Sara rubbed Mom's arm and said, "I know this is hard for you, but Josh is an awesome person and he's going to be fine. I'm certain of it."

"Thanks, Sara." Mom hugged her. "That means a lot."

Sara didn't tell her mom that maybe she was the one making life worse for him. She had to be as careful around Mom as she was around Josh.

Sara waited for Dad to come down and then went to Josh's room. Hopefully he'd feel the love, rather than feeling ambushed. Josh leapt at the chance to walk.

"Tell me about it." Sara started the conversation when they were on the sidewalk.

He shook his head. "The spirit of everything felt right, but the words..." He stopped and sighed. "They're encouraging us to lie, I can tell. I think they may be liars, too."

"I did a search in the psych library," Sara replied, "and there's no evidence that conversion therapy works. I'm sorry, Josh. I know you were hopeful."

"I've decided to be abstinent," he replied. "That way I can live biblically and be honest. Who needs to know? No one. I'll be that crazy bachelor who lives with his parents when he's forty." A tear slid down his cheek.

Sara put her hand out to stop him. "Oh, Josh."

"It's the only way." He looked at her. Desperation in his eyes, he asked, "You'll let me see your children, won't you? I promise I would never, ever harm them."

"Oh, Josh..." Sara started to cry. "I have never, ever thought for a second that you would. How can you think that? Of course, no matter what you... you will always be in my life. I've met awesome gay kids at Cal. They're in couples... and they're just, just—Josh, they're just like us. I'm not afraid of them anymore." She rushed on. "I've never been afraid *of* you. Only afraid *for* you."

"Really?"

"I swear."

She hugged him tight, wanting to squeeze out his doubt with her love.

When he broke away and stepped back there were tears on his cheeks. "What about Mom?"

"It's only been two months," Sara said. "I don't know if she can change, but I like to think she can—with more time. She's scared for you, too, but for her it comes out as mean, sometimes."

He laughed. "That's what Dad said, too. It seems like she hates me."

"She doesn't, not at all," Sara said. "She wants to control everything in our life like when we were kids. It makes her feel safe. I'm not sure she knows how to be a mom to grown-ups. Not that we are really grown up, but you know what I mean."

Josh stared off. Sara waited.

He finally spoke. "Dad's secretary is a lesbian. She has a life partner, and they have a child together, like Ms. Hodder."

"Really?" Sara was shocked. "Wow. He told you that?"

"Yeah. He had tears in his eyes when he told me. Like he

wanted me to know that... it's possible." Josh stopped. "I can't imagine..."

"Having a life partner?" Sara asked.

Josh nodded.

Sara shrugged. She stared at him.

After some time, she said, "I can see it, Josh. Now that I've gotten used to the idea. Truly I can. You don't have to decide anything forever right now, but our world is changing."

"Our church isn't," he said. "Or Mom." He stared off again and then asked, "Can you tell her what you told me about the research?"

She nodded even though he wasn't looking at her. "Give her time. I have faith in her, and God's ability to open her heart."

"You really believe God doesn't hate the sin?" Josh asked.

"To be honest, I started thinking that a while ago, Josh, before you..." She couldn't bring herself to say *hurt yourself.* "I thought there wasn't any reason to bring it up, but now I'm so sorry I didn't. If you had... if you had actually died..." Her voice broke. She cleared it and went on, "I would have hated myself forever."

She shook her head at the thought. "Jesus asked us to love. Since you told me, God keeps sending me: *Faith, hope and love, but the greatest of these is love.* I don't see how you loving someone hurts God."

Josh bit a trembling lip and tears streamed down his face, but in a sort of happy way. He nodded and then hugged her tight. She wrapped her arms around her tall little brother. He felt strong and solid. Perhaps she had said the right thing.

At the dinner table Dad said, "You'll be glad to know your brother got an 'A' in prayer at camp. I think he should show off his skills by leading our prayer."

"Hear, hear," said Rachel.

Mom winked at Dad, then bowed her head.

Josh spoke clearly and emphatically. "Merciful God, we thank You for this glorious bounty. May the spirit of Your love and Your son fill our souls, that we may be guided to do Your will for us on this day and in all the days to come. Amen."

Josh's words felt strong and true. He loved God.

When she looked up, Mom asked, "Are you too old for Easter baskets?"

"I want my basket," Rachel said, "until I'm eighteen! And I don't want to hunt for it alone." The others laughed.

Mom knew the answer to that question because she had asked it last year, too. Sara was certain she already had three baskets ready for the morning. It was silly, but it did make Sara feel loved. Mom's heart was in the right place—it was her faith that was misplaced, but maybe it could be turned right again. Maybe they could come through this stronger as a family.

Sara looked at Josh and squeezed his hand, grateful that he knew she was on his side. He smiled at her and gave a little nod.

TWENTY

SUNDAY, APRIL 11, 2004

Jenn

Easter was usually one of Jenn's favorite days of the year. She loved watching her kids hunt for the baskets she put together, going to church to hear about the physical resurrection that brought her salvation, and then dinner with their closest friends. But this year it was hard.

Most of the church service washed past her, but the sermon grabbed her attention. Pastor James said, "Jesus was killed on the cross, died, and rose again for *you*. You do not have to do anything for the gift of His sacrifice besides believe. It was a gift freely given by God for you, because you are sinful. And by your faith you shall be saved. Isn't God glorious? Didn't He make a beautiful design? And He did it for you. For each of you, because He loves you completely."

God's love filled Jenn in that moment. She felt Him holding her, telling her that she was saved. Then she thought about Josh, throwing away the gift of the resurrection. It was unfathomable that their family would be in heaven without Josh—it wouldn't be heaven if Josh wasn't there. The grace she felt from God's love dropped away again.

After the service Pastor James gave the whole family a warm greeting and big hugs.

He looked intently at Josh and solemnly asked, "How are you?"

Josh tilted his head noncommittally.

Pastor pushed him. "Wasn't camp inspiring? Did you feel the Holy Spirit?"

Steve replied, "Josh was praised for the depth of his prayer life. I'm very proud."

"Praise Jesus!" Pastor James replied. "May the blessing of the resurrection fill your lives today. I'm sure you feel it more strongly than ever. A tested faith is a stronger faith." And then he moved on to greet the next family.

Steve had put a great spin on it with Pastor James, but Jenn knew she'd tell him the rest of the story soon. She spent the afternoon obsessing over their next steps while she made short-cake for Easter dinner at the Bishops'. Her mind kept returning to the conversation with Andrew and the pledge she had made to commit to Josh's soul. She looked over the list of camps and counselors that they had handed out yesterday. She decided that a month-long camp over the summer, along with weekly counseling with Pastor James, was the best strategy to keep the momentum going.

That evening at the Bishops', Jenn and Lindsay were alone in the kitchen putting the finishing touches to the meal. Everyone else was in the family room playing *Celebrity*. From their behavior, no one could tell her family was in crisis.

"So? How did it go for Josh? He looks great," Lindsay said.

"Oh, Lindsay." Jenn choked up.

Lindsay put her arm around Jenn and gave her a squeeze. "Take your time. What's happened?"

"He's not cured. Not at all. They said it might take a long time. I thought it was going to be over by now, but he needs more treatment."

"I'm so sorry, Jenn. I know you were so hopeful." Lindsay made a sad face. "You must be so disappointed."

Jenn nodded.

"But you have to keep faith in the Lord," her friend reminded her firmly, sounding like a schoolmarm.

"I have faith. Sometimes that feels like all I have," Jenn said.

"No! Don't say that—you have us. We're with you every step of the way," Lindsay said. "You know that, don't you? Every night you're in our prayers."

"That means so much to us. Some of the parents at camp said the whole experience brought their family closer to God. I'm fighting for that for our family." Then Jenn sighed and said, "But others said it's torn their family apart. To tell you the truth, I'm exhausted. I just want a rest."

"You're the mom," Lindsay replied. "You don't get that luxury, do you?"

Jenn shook her head. She didn't get to wallow in self-pity. She had to push on through and show faith.

The meal was delicious: salmon with lemon dill sauce, fresh asparagus, homemade rolls, and strawberry shortcake with whipped cream, but Jenn hardly tasted the food. She went through the motions but didn't feel the spirit. They were there to celebrate Easter, but her soul wasn't light with the good news of their Savior's resurrection. It was heavy with the knowledge that Josh needed more treatment and the sinking suspicion that he didn't want it.

· · ·

After dinner, as Jenn drove her to BART Sara asked, "You okay, Mom?"

"Well, as you know, Josh didn't make the progress we hoped for," Jenn said. "It's hard for me. I worry about him constantly."

"He thinks you don't love him anymore," Sara told her, "and that he's a total disappointment to you."

"Oh, Sara. That's simply not true. Not at all. I love him very much," Jenn explained to her daughter. "I just need to show it less. That's part of the remedy."

"Don't you think that's messed up?" Sara asked, charged with emotion.

Jenn asked. "What do you mean?"

"What kind of treatment tells a mom to ignore her sons and a dad to ignore his daughters?" Sara asked with heat in her voice.

Shocked at Sara's attitude, Jenn replied, "Daddy's not ignoring you."

"Practically." Sara's voice cracked. "He won't talk to me on the phone. He tells me to ask you if I want advice. We hardly ever spend time as a family anymore. I didn't do anything. Why am I being punished?"

"You aren't being punished," Jenn said. "We just don't want to make the same mistake with you that we made with Josh." Carefully, she added, "We don't want you to start having same-sex attraction."

Sara laughed. "I assure you, Mom, you don't have to be worried about that."

"Really?"

"Yes, I'm as straight as they get, I promise. I'm like a zero on the Kinsey scale."

"The what?" Mom had no idea what she was talking about.

"You know, the human sexuality scale that goes from zero to six. Zero is all the way straight and six is all the way gay," Sara explained.

Straight? Gay? Jenn hated that Sara was using those words so casually. "No. I don't know. Where did you learn about such a thing?!"

"Intro to Psych," Sara explained. "It's been around for a long time, like since the fifties. I'm surprised you haven't heard of it."

"We never learned about it at BIOLA, that's for sure," Jenn said. Then she was hit by an awful thought. "Have you ever...? With a boy?"

"No." Sara laughed. "I'm not even dating anyone. I just know who's attractive to me, and it's not girls."

Relief flooded Jenn's body. She didn't even realize she'd been so anxious for Sara. Until recently, she'd thought her kids told her everything, but now she knew better. Sara and Rachel might have secrets, too.

"What about Rachel?" she dared to ask.

"She can't stop talking about the cute boys in her classes, so I think you're safe there," Sara said. Then she spoke cautiously. "Is it so bad that Josh is gay?"

Those words were still like a slap to Jenn. "Excuse me?!"

"I've met a lot of great kids who are gay. Some are even Christian."

"Being homosexual is incompatible with scripture," Jenn insisted. "You know that!"

"I know God loves Josh," Sara said.

Jenn had the sudden, awful realization that Sara was losing faith in Josh's transformation. A vise clamped up her throat. Jenn looked at her daughter. She was a child in an adult body. Her faith had never been tested. Sara didn't have the spiritual strength to fight for Josh's soul.

She doubled her resolve to be a moral example for their kids. She'd have enough faith for Sara and Josh—like the footprints in the sand. She'd carry her children across the desert of doubt. She was strong enough to do that for them.

Sara broke the intense silence. "Are you allowed to tell Josh that you love him? Or give him anything?"

"Yes," Jenn squeaked out with a nod. "I'll talk to him, I promise."

TWENTY-ONE
SUNDAY, APRIL 11, 2004

Josh

The whole day was a disaster—so much for the glory of the resurrection. Church was embarrassing. Dinner at the Bishops' was totally awkward. Mom put on an act, but it was obvious she was very upset with him. After all that, he had to cram in homework. Spending the week at that camp meant he had to do all of it today.

Mom knocked and walked into his room—without waiting for his consent. A flash of frustration shot through him, but he smashed it down. He wasn't even going to give her a fight.

She looked at the textbooks spread out in front of him on his bed and said, "Shouldn't you be working at your desk?"

He looked up at her, bit back his retort, and sighed. "If you want." He started to stand.

"No, Josh. Sorry. You can do your schoolwork however you like," Mom said from the doorway. "You're a good student. You don't need me telling you how to study."

Josh sank back onto his comforter. He put his math textbook on his lap and grabbed a notebook, ignoring her. Mom kept standing there, not talking but not leaving. He ignored her, pretending to read. He knew he was being passive aggressive, but he just wanted her to go.

Finally, she asked, "Josh, will you tell me what happened at camp?"

He slowly looked up at her. "Do you really want to know what they did to me, your shameful son?"

"I do want to know. Of course I want to know. I'm not ashamed of you," Mom chastised him while defending herself. Quietly she said, "I'm afraid for you."

Josh closed his eyes and blinked them a few times. He mumbled without looking at her, "They kept asking me about all the ways Dad disappointed me or ignored me or made me feel like I wasn't a man. I couldn't think of any. Other kids lied. They made up stories just so they could earn food and free time."

"What do you mean, earn food?"

"I never went hungry," Josh explained, still mumbling. "But kids who *made more progress* got good food. At first, I lost dessert, then fruit. Eventually all I got to eat was PB and J." His eyes welled up. He shrugged.

"Oh, Josh. I'm sorry. I had no idea."

"They screamed at me, Mom," Josh said, energy building in his voice. Looking her straight in the eyes, he said, "They yelled in my face, telling me I had to love Jesus or I would go to hell. It didn't matter to them that I do love Jesus. They kept doing it, especially when I didn't make up some story about Dad's cousin Justin."

He looked back down at his bed. "That was the day I called you. Then I was put in isolation—for two nights. They wanted me to have time to 'talk to God.' It was better than being yelled at. I still like talking to God."

Mom stood there, not responding. Eventually she said, "I'm glad you like talking to God. It will save your life. I'm sorry camp was hard." Her voice was flat, like a robot's. "It's for your own long-term good, though it may not seem like that right now. I know it seems like I don't love you, but that's not true. It's the farthest thing from the truth. I love you as much as any mother has ever loved a son."

Mom teared up. Her voice was full of emotion as she said, "Do you understand? It's like chemo for cancer. It hurts all of you, but it's only meant to destroy the disease."

Cancer. He understood her thinking, but no longer believed in her treatment. There was no chemo, no cure.

Was he God's mistake? Sara didn't think so. Ms. Hodder didn't seem like she was sinning.

He'd always had faith in his parents for wisdom and guidance, but they couldn't lead him in this. Mom preached humility and surrender, but she was so attached to being right that she wasn't practicing either.

He closed his eyes and opened himself in prayer. The Holy Spirit poured into him, ripping the scales off his heart. He looked at his mother, seeing her anew. Mom was a hypocrite who cared more about her reputation on this Earth than God. Her certainty in this situation was simplistic and insulting rather than comforting.

His mind and heart raced but he only said, "Okay."

Mom stared at him, waiting for him to surrender to her will, but he couldn't give her more.

He asked, "Can I get back to my work? I have a lot to do before school tomorrow."

"Yeah." Mom nodded. "Goodnight. Thanks for talking with me."

He looked up at her. She appeared sad. He searched for something true and kind he could say. "I miss you, Mom."

"Me, too, Josh." She looked at him with longing.

When she left, he clenched his fist and shook it at the closed door like an old man in a movie. She was so frustrating; what she wanted was impossible: for him to be open and honest *and* not feel the way he felt. She couldn't admit that she was disappointed in him. His heart clenched. Being a disappointment to his parents was what was most unbearable.

He wiped a tear from his eye. He was so tired of feeling this shame. Would it ever go away?

God, what do you want me to learn from this burden? He prayed. Then he added: *God, please open my mom's heart to Your wisdom and love, too. Amen.*

Handing her over to God helped. He didn't need to pray for his dad. Somehow, he knew Dad was asking God the right questions himself.

Josh's heart pounded the moment he walked into English. For four days he'd been trying, talking himself into staying after class to talk to Ms. Hodder. Today he was going to do it. She was the only gay person he knew, and she was so *out* and proud about it. A large picture of her family sat on her desk, and she sprinkled her lessons with stories about her wife and two kids. He was going to speak with her, but wanted to sound casual, not desperate. His mind kept drifting from *The Great Gatsby* as he rehearsed what to say.

He looked at the small poster he'd stared at all year:

This classroom is a safe space

His heart pounded as he considered what to say:
"*What day is the GSA meeting?*"
"*I think I want to go to GSA, is that okay?*"
"*Does GSA meet here?*"
It didn't seem possible, but when the bell rang his heart

pounded even harder. He slowly packed up while everyone poured out of the room.

"Coming?" Michael asked.

"I have to talk to Ms. Hodder. I'll find you after." Josh swallowed hard. He hadn't told his friend. He wasn't ready. Who was he kidding? He'd never be ready; he probably didn't even have the courage to actually go to a GSA meeting. Just thinking about asking the question gave him a heart attack.

He was alone in the classroom. Well, Ms. Hodder was at her desk. He looked up at her. His hands went clammy, and his head started spinning. He was too chicken to do this; he had to get out of there, but his legs wouldn't move. His chest was so tight he couldn't breathe. He heard panting.

Ms. Hodder crossed to his desk.

In a very calm voice she said, "Look for five things in the room and tell me about them."

He stared at her.

"Look around the room." Her blonde eyebrows rose as she insisted. "Tell me five things you see."

"The... the fla..." His chest was so tight it was hard to talk so he pointed at the U.S. flag.

"That's one, what's two?"

"A chair," he said.

"That's two, what's three?"

He looked around. "The white board."

She nodded.

His lungs loosened, making space for more air. "The trash can and the door."

"You did it." She smiled at him. "Do you feel a little better?"

He inhaled and nodded. "What just happened... to me?" he asked.

"It looked like a panic attack. You have something you are scared to tell me, right?"

He teared up.

She took a deep breath and put her hand on his arm. "Take your time. You are safe in here. And what you say in here, stays in here."

He hung his head. Tears streamed from his eyes. So much for not crying. He looked up.

"I'm gay, but I don't want to be. I won't ever fit in anywhere."

"Sweetie, I have had many people tell me they are gay, and so far, not one of them wanted to be at first. You are brave to tell someone. Thank you for trusting me."

Josh swept a tear from his cheek and wiped it along his desk. He smeared it in a long line and then watched it evaporate.

"I'll never fit in anywhere... I'm Christian. I'm not like those other happy rainbow kids."

"That can make it harder." She sounded so sympathetic. "Do you think God makes mistakes?"

"No."

"Me, either."

He looked up. "Are you Christian?"

Ms. Hodder shook her head. "I go to a Unitarian Church—not so Jesus centered."

Josh sighed.

"But I have Christian friends who go to Welcoming UCC churches. I know you can be out and proud—and belong to a church."

"Really?" he asked.

"I'm not suggesting you do anything too fast, Josh. Give yourself time. However, I'm confident that you will find a place where you fit in."

He nodded.

"Have you told anyone in your family?"

He nodded. "All of them know. It's not... it's not good."

"Give them time, too."

"I went to a camp over Easter break."

Ms. Hodder went pale. "A conversion camp, through church?"

He nodded.

Her face went hard. Firmly she stated, "Josh, do not believe anything they told you. I like to have respect for all religions. But those camps are cruel... and utter nonsense. Those methods and ideology have been de-bunked by every credible source." Anger in her voice, she continued, "They prey on your faith and insecurity, do you understand? Do not believe them!"

His eyes went wide. And then he teared up, again.

"Thank you," he replied. "It *was* awful."

"Because you told me church is important to you, I'm going to give you information about a Welcoming UCC congregation. You can look them up on the web, too. I want you to know that it is absolutely possible to be Christian and to be proudly out, but I am *not* encouraging you to leave your church or become anything you don't want to be. These are very, very personal decisions you need to make for yourself."

He nodded.

His voice got quiet. "I want to be brave enough to go to a GSA meeting, but I'm scared."

"They're on Thursdays at lunch, in this room. You're welcome anytime. And," she continued, "it can change your life in very dramatic ways. I know who your friends are."

He swallowed. "It's not like... we don't... my friends aren't the ally types."

"Josh, you get to come out to whoever you want, however you want, whenever you want. Don't let anyone pressure you."

He nodded.

"And some people will surprise you with their support," she said.

He gave a little nod. "My Dad and sisters have been..."

Urghh, he thought, as he teared up yet again. He cleared his throat. "They *have* been great."

"That's wonderful."

"Am I ever going to stop crying when I talk about this?" he asked.

"Eventually, yes," she replied, "but don't be ashamed of your tears. They're telling you that you are doing something important. Listen to your body. In my opinion, our bodies are very honest."

He'd been fighting with his body for a very long time, doing his best to ignore it, but maybe that was like lying to God. Pretending he didn't feel something didn't make it true.

She continued, "Your tears may be telling you to slow down, or to speed up. No one can tell you from the outside. Only you can know—from the inside." Very gently she said, "Not knowing is hard, but often that is the right place to be. You are brave to be right where you are."

A chill traveled down his spine. *Brave?*

"Thanks." Josh didn't feel brave, but it was nice to know that someone thought he was.

TWENTY-TWO
FRIDAY APRIL 16, 2004

Jenn

The next morning, when Jenn went out to the front yard to get the newspaper, her gaze was caught by some color at the end of the driveway. She walked closer: in bright-pink chalk the word *faggot* was written on the concrete.

A hot wave passed through her body, leaving her nauseous and her lungs clamped tight. *Josh can't see this.* She ran into the house to catch Steve before her son came out of his room. She found her husband getting dressed in his closet.

"What's wrong?" he asked as soon as he saw her.

In a jerky voice, she managed to say, "Out front... You have to fix this. Please clean it up before he leaves for school."

"What are you talking about?"

"Someone wrote something horrible... about Josh... on our driveway. I can't even say the word. Please. Wash it away." She started crying. "How can anyone be so mean? I don't understand. Our Josh is a good person. He's good and kind and beautiful..." Steve started to give her a hug, but she cut him off. "Now, please. I don't want Josh to see. He's so fragile."

Jenn was shaky as she served breakfast to the kids. They were still eating when Steve walked back in, damp from the hose spray.

"What're you doing, Dad?" Josh asked, looking puzzled.

Jenn shot Steve a look, but he was prepared. "A dog made a mess in the driveway," he said. "I was cleaning it up. But now I need to change. Jenn, can you take the kids to school, so they won't be late?"

"Sure."

When Josh and Rachel finished breakfast, they piled into the Land Cruiser for the three-and-a-half-mile drive to Dublin High. Jenn pulled into the drop-off lane to let them out.

"I love you, Josh," Jenn cried after him as he slammed the passenger door.

"What about me?" Rachel asked.

"You, too." Jenn smiled at her daughter. "It's not a competition."

"It sure feels like it... these days." Rachel scowled before slamming the back door.

Jenn shook her head and sighed. There was no way to win. She watched Josh yell out a greeting to his teammates Scott, Joe, Grant, and Phil. They let him into their circle and did that handshake thing she didn't understand, with a fist bump at the end.

Someone must have cracked a joke because they all laughed. Josh looked like nothing was wrong in his heart. Was he pretending, or was he actually happy?

He looked like he fit in with those boys. Did they know? Had one of them written on their driveway even though they'd been friends for years? She studied the scene, looking for any sign of hostility toward Josh but didn't detect any.

She considered parking and going to the office to report the graffiti to the principal but decided drawing more attention to Josh would not help their situation. She drove home, her hands gripping the wheel tightly to prevent them from shaking. Sitting in her prayer chair to calm down was the last thing she wanted to do. Maybe she should take up running.

That evening, Jenn went to find a sweater in her bedroom and was startled to see Steve sitting on the flowered comforter, the phone on the bed next to him. His skin was blanched, and his eyes were red rimmed. Cortisol put Jenn's body on high alert.

"That was my mom," Steve said. He leaned over and started sobbing—not quietly but actual sobs. *James must be dead.* She sank down onto the bed next to Steve and wrapped her arms around him, while he leaned his head into her. She stroked his hair, her eyes burning.

Jenn asked gently, "Your dad... He's passed?"

Steve shook his head. He pulled back and looked at Jenn. "She... doesn't want to see Josh again," he stammered out. He cleared his throat. "My mom."

"What?" Jenn was confused.

"She heard that he's gay... from someone at church who knows Lindsay's mom."

A knot tied in Jenn's stomach.

Steve said, "She... I knew she would disapprove, but I didn't think she'd cut him off. She called to tell me that the rest of us are welcome. But not... not Josh." His eyes bored into Jenn. "I'm never, ever doing that to him. No matter what happens. It's not an option."

"No, of course not."

Jenn leaned against her husband, at a loss for words, her stomach churning. This wasn't going away; it was getting worse. She'd been so naive, never once considering Josh would be ostracized by his loved ones.

"She'll change her mind when he's cured," Jenn said, sounding more confident than she felt.

Steve shook his head slowly. "I'm afraid I'll never forgive her, even if she changes her mind. How can she do this to our son? To me? To all of us?"

"I don't know."

"I told her that I won't go anywhere Josh isn't welcome... but she didn't care." Steve looked incredulous. "She said that was my choice, but she isn't going to compromise her Christian values."

"Oh, Steve, I'm so sorry." Jenn wept, too. "Did you talk to your dad?"

"Mom said she spoke for both of them." Steve punched the bed. "I just want to hit something," he said through clenched teeth. "You know what I thought about after she hung up?"

Jenn shook her head.

"Justin. And Aunt Michelle. I didn't do or say anything when my mom banished him from her home. Do you know what that makes me?"

Jenn shook her head.

"A coward."

"No, Steve."

"Yes," he insisted, "I'm a coward. I didn't stand up to my mom; I didn't call Justin. I just let it be. Not out of any principle —but because it was easy. I didn't say anything to you because I didn't want to talk or think about him. That doesn't make me righteous. It makes me lazy, and disloyal."

"You're a good cousin to Justin."

"Not when he needed me. Not when it was hard." Steve blew out his breath. "I don't know if he'll forgive me, but I'm going to apologize."

Jenn couldn't think of anything to say that would be helpful to her husband. She studied his face as he stared at the wall in silence; it was clear that he was thinking by the way his eyes darted around.

"I'm not going to tell Josh about my mom," Steve said. "He

doesn't need this right now. It's not like he sees her often. He might not notice. Agreed?"

Jenn nodded. "Absolutely."

Steve looked desperate. "Jenn, promise me. No matter what happens to Josh, or any of our kids, we won't cut them off."

"Of course not."

"Even if Josh stays homosexual?" Steve pushed.

Jenn took a breath to calm herself. "I can't imagine a scenario where I would give up on Josh's salvation. But that doesn't mean I would cut him off." She added carefully, "But if he were a heroin addict, would you want me to come around to supporting that?"

"If one of our kids was a heroin addict, they would be welcome in my home—would they be welcome in yours?"

Jenn heard the challenge in Steve's voice. *His* home and *her* home, as though they would be two different houses. Jenn's pulse picked up. Her head was light, and she felt dizzy.

Deliberately, she chose her words. "I want him cured. All the way cured. I will never give up on his salvation. If he were a drug addict, I would never stop fighting for his recovery. If he had cancer, I would fight for his physical life."

"But would he be welcome in your house?" Steve demanded.

"Yes, Josh will always be welcome in my, in *our*, home," Jenn agreed. "But I won't stop praying for his recovery. Will you? Are you just giving up because it's a hard fight? I am never, ever giving up on Josh... or Sara... or Rachel."

Steve nodded. He looked satisfied with her reply.

"Do you know something?" Jenn asked, terrified of the answer, but needing to find out. "Has Josh told you he's given up on his transformation?"

"Josh hasn't said anything directly, but it seems that his spirit is not in the fight anymore," Steve replied, searching Jenn's face.

A wave of emotion passed through her body. She had just stopped crying, and now tears were streaming down her face again.

"I can't pretend that doesn't tear at my heart." She appealed to her husband. "How can it not break yours? Our Josh living the homosexual lifestyle? I want him to have a normal life: respect, church, children. I can't just give up on him. Have you? Can you imagine heaven without him? All of us with God, but without Josh?"

"Jenn, I haven't given up on him," Steve replied. "It's just..."

"What?" Jenn's heart hammered hard.

Steve sighed and stared into Jenn's eyes. He was thinking about his words.

"What, Steve? Just say it, please."

"I haven't given up on his salvation, but we can't push so hard that we shove him away from us altogether. I've seen that in some families. So have you."

"I don't want him to think we've given up on him," she pleaded.

"Me either, Jenn."

She took a slow breath. Steve had said the words she wanted to hear, but she wasn't so certain that they meant what she wanted them to mean.

On Thursday morning Jenn walked with Lindsay in the neighborhood. Their conversations had become increasingly awkward giving Jenn the feeling Lindsay had say something but held back. Jenn was the same. She avoided talking about Josh with Lindsay. Not so long ago she would have told Lindsay all about Marilyn's behavior, but today she wasn't interested in hearing her friend's thoughts about her mother-in-law.

After walking, Jenn gathered Josh's laundry. She checked the pockets of his clothes before she dropped them in the wash.

Mostly they were empty, but in the back of a pair of jeans she found a folded piece of paper. She opened it up and read:

Welcoming and Affirming Church

Wherever you are on your personal journey, we will love you and embrace you just as God does. We seek to live out Jesus's love on earth.

Jenn's breath caught, and her stomach dropped. How was Josh learning about another church? *Kyle Goss!* He was encouraging Josh to embrace the homosexual lifestyle. No wonder Josh was giving up hope. She was furious—with Kyle, with Steve, and with herself. Pastor James had warned them about secular dangers, but she hadn't taken his concern seriously enough, and now Josh was paying the price. She dropped the jeans into the washer but didn't start the load.

Jenn grabbed her keys and raced to Kyle's office.

She resisted the desire to pound on his office door but restrained herself and sat in the waiting room. It was ten-thirty, and though she was furious with Kyle, that was no reason to interrupt someone's appointment. She sat on a couch, thumbing through the old magazines, looking at the posters on the wall, and rereading the note from the so-called church.

At ten to eleven, the door swung open. Kyle looked surprised to see her. He said a warm goodbye to the woman leaving his office and motioned Jenn to come in with a tilt of his head.

"Hello, Jenn," Kyle said. "How's Josh?"

"Have you been seeing him against my wishes?"

Kyle shook his head. "No. Steve told me you were going to focus on his other treatment."

Jenn held up the paper in her hand and waved it in front of

Kyle's face. "How could you give this to him?" she yelled. "You know it goes against everything we value."

"I see you're upset about something," he said, very calmly. "Would you like to have a seat?"

Rejecting the offer to sit, she challenged him. "I'm furious that I trusted my son to you, and you betrayed us."

Kyle sat down. "I don't know anything about that piece of paper."

"You didn't give this to Josh? Encouraging him to find another church?" She put the paper on his desk. Slowly Kyle read the flyer.

Jenn sat down. When he finished, he looked up and said, "This isn't from me. It's the church I attend, but I didn't give this to Josh. It would be unethical for me to encourage Josh to attend any religious community besides the one you have chosen for him, most especially my own."

Jenn glared at Kyle. "You lied to me. You told me you're a Christian. You knew exactly what I meant when I asked that question."

"I answered honestly. My work is deeply grounded in Jesus's teachings," he replied calmly.

Jenn said challengingly, "You don't live a biblically based life."

"On the contrary. I turn to the Bible on a daily basis. It's rich, complicated, and contradictory scripture. I wrestle with it every day to try to understand what enduring truth is in there and what is human bias."

Jenn shot back, "It's all enduring truth."

"Slavery, polygamy, stoning?" Kyle questioned. "Those are enduring truths?"

"You know what I mean!" Jenn retorted.

"With respect, I don't know what you mean." Then his tone of voice changed along with the subject. "I understand this is hard. I have had to wrestle with these questions for myself.

That's part of a life of mature faith. I'm sorry, but I have another client arriving very soon. I need to be ready to meet with him. I'd be happy to schedule time with you, if you like. And with Josh, if you decide you want that. Josh is a lovely human being. He has a deep well of faith, and he loves you very much."

Jenn stood up. She stammered, "B... But what about..." She waved the flyer.

"I don't know." Kyle shook his head. "You'll need to ask your son."

Jenn felt deflated as she left. She'd been so full of righteous indignation as she drove over, and now she was just confused. Slowly she walked to her car. Sitting in the Land Cruiser, she prayed to God, asking Him to take away her confusion and guide her on a righteous path. *Surrender*, she reminded herself. *Surrender to God's will.*

She was waiting to speak with Josh when he got home. He walked into the family room and blanched when he saw the flyer in her hand.

"Mom, let me explain—" he started.

"Where did you get this?" she asked calmly.

"At school. From a teacher."

Jenn was stunned. "A teacher is handing out religious flyers to kids? Dublin High is a public school. Separation of church and state. I'm going to get him fired."

"No, Mom!" Josh pleaded. "She wanted to help me."

"Help you? What kind of help involves luring a child away from his religion? It's wrong, Josh. She needs to know that."

Josh dropped onto the couch. He buried his head in his arms, obviously very upset. Jenn was being too hard on him again. She sat next to him and put her arm around him. He leaned into her. Even though she knew she was going against his treatment, it was sweet to have him close.

She said gently, "Josh, you didn't do anything wrong. She knows better. Don't beat yourself up about this."

"I shouldn't have gone to her with my doubts."

"I wish you had come to me or Dad."

Josh popped his head up and stared at Jenn. "Really, Mom? Come to you? With my doubts? Like you want to hear about it."

"I do, Josh," Jenn said. But if she were being honest with herself and him, she didn't want her son to have any doubts.

"Complete and immediate transformation. That's what you want, Mom. I've tried—for years. You have no idea." Josh shook his head, looking pained. "I've thought about this and prayed about this so much. I'm left with either God not loving me at all or loving me just as He made me."

Jenn didn't like either of those choices. The best option was that Josh surrender his life to God. He had to refocus.

"Why did you talk to that particular teacher?" she asked.

"She's the GSA adviser, so she understands what I'm going through."

"The what?" Jenn quizzed him.

"The Gay-Straight Alliance," Josh mumbled.

"What?" Jenn yelled. "You've been going to that group? After all Dad and I have been through to help you? Are you so willing to throw your salvation away?"

"No. I don't want to throw my salvation away. Or my relationship with my Savior. That's why Ms. Hodder gave me that flyer. She says I don't have to pick between being honest about who I am and loving God. She told me there are some churches that think being gay is part of God's plan."

Jenn was speechless. She wanted to scream at Josh and shake him. They were working so hard for his complete transformation through faith, but she was losing him. She had pledged to protect him from secular influences at Resurrection Ministries, but clearly, she was failing.

"She's enticing you to come to her church?" Jenn was incredulous.

"It's not her church."

Jenn stared at him.

Josh said, "Really, it's not her church. She's a Unitarian."

"That's supposed to make me feel better?" Jenn retorted. "You're getting spiritual advice from a Unitarian. It is absolutely unethical for her to encourage you to leave your own church."

"Promise you won't get her fired," Josh begged. "I'd hate myself even more if that happened."

"Josh, no... there's no reason to hate yourself."

"Come on, Mom!" Josh stood up. His face was red and contorted. "You're crazy! Do you even listen to yourself? You can't have it both ways. Either I'm an abomination or I'm not!"

He stormed away, and she heard a door slam upstairs.

Jenn was shaking. Josh had never, ever screamed at her like that before. Her first impulse was to call the principal of Dublin High to report that teacher, but she no longer trusted her own instincts. She considered Lindsay despite their tensions, but rejected the idea. Her platitudes about the simplicity of surrender wouldn't be helpful. She had no idea what Jenn and Josh were going through. Steve would tell her to leave it alone, so she called her mom for sympathy and advice.

Jenn told her Mom the story and asked, "Do you think I should call the principal?"

"Well, dear, I think it would cause Josh to trust you less. Do you want that?"

"No, of course not. I just want him healed. He's given up on his own transformation. It's devastating. His salvation is at stake!"

Her mom said, "To be honest, I'm not so certain about that."

"What?"

"It just seems like this issue became so important to our pastors out of the blue. I blame that Anita Bryant."

"What are you talking about?" Jenn asked her mother.

"She got all worked up about it, and then everyone followed. No one used to care about such things."

Jenn was confused to be hearing her mother talk like this. "Are you sure?"

Her mom insisted, "I absolutely never heard a word about homosexuality in church until you were a teenager."

"Because everyone agreed it was wrong."

"I don't know that that's true," her mom said. "Remember Uncle Bob?"

"Grandma's brother? Of course."

She hadn't thought about him since Valentine's, but her great uncle was a wonderful man. He always treated her with such respect, as if her opinion mattered.

When he gave her that real SLR for her sixteenth birthday it was like he'd looked into her soul.

He handed it to her and said, *For you to show the world what you see, because you are the only one who observes creation through your eyes. Each of us is a unique gift from God, and when we reveal our true selves we honor Him.*

She'd been too self-conscious to tell anyone about her calling to take pictures, but he'd seen it. And then she started going to witnesses and the camera allowed her to stare unabashedly at people, study all the beautiful faces filled with the Holy Spirit. She was free to trap the fleeting nature of rapture onto film and print it out for the world to see. It brought her closer to God.

"Remember his friend Joe?" Mom asked. "The one he lived with? We included him in all the family gatherings; we just didn't talk about it."

"Yes..." Jenn said, her mind reeling as she took in her mother's implication. "But they sang in the church choir?"

"Everyone knew they were special to each other."

"Uncle Bob told you he was homosexual?!" Jenn nearly screeched.

"No. We just didn't make a show of it." Mom was calm. "They never hurt anyone. Uncle Bob sure loved Jesus."

She thought back to Uncle Bob and Joe. Suddenly she saw them in a whole new light.

"That's why Joe came to family events even after Uncle Bob died?"

"We weren't going to just abandon him. We were the only family he had. Even if we never said so. What is it they call that? You know, President Clinton's words?"

"Don't ask. Don't tell."

"Yes, that's it. I guess we were ahead of our time," Mom laughed. "We didn't ask, they didn't tell, and we all got along just fine."

"Are you saying you don't care if Josh has a..." Jenn paused for the right words. "A special friend when he grows up?" Jenn's stomach churned at thought.

"Well, dear, of course I want him to change. He's my precious grandson. I want him to have a good life. But I've been doing a lot of thinking and praying ever since you told me, and if Josh decides to lead a homosexual lifestyle, I don't think God will be bothered. And if our Lord isn't bothered, why should I be?" her mom said.

Jenn's throat got tight. "Does Daddy feel the same way?"

"Oh, goodness, dear. Your father and I don't talk about things like that. But I'm sure he'd go along, like he usually does."

"You don't think Josh will go to Hell?" Jenn asked.

"I'm not a theologian, dear, but God has forgiven much worse." She continued, "I love Uncle Bob, and I *know* I'm going to be with him in heaven. You cannot possibly believe that I'm more loving or forgiving than God."

More loving than God? Jenn was confused by her mother's question. No human was more loving than God. And He had rules they were supposed to follow. Was her mother suggesting they get to pick and choose?

"Mom, I'm glad that you have room in your heart for Josh."

"And my home, dear," Mom replied. "You, too, you know. I pray for you every day. For guidance and wisdom."

Jenn teared up. "Thanks, Mom."

TWENTY-THREE
FRIDAY, APRIL 23, 2004

Jenn

The next morning Jenn got a text from Lindsay.

> Starbucks @ 10:00?

Her stomach clenched when she saw the request. Their walk yesterday had been awkward. The whole time Jenn sensed that Lindsay was on the edge of saying something unpleasant.

Lindsay was pulling away. Was she going to pull a Marilyn and cut them off? That would have seemed unbelievable a few months ago, but Jenn was learning again and again that she didn't know what was inside other people's hearts and minds.

Jenn replied in the affirmative but didn't bother with any further pleasantries.

Through the widow, Jenn spotted Lindsay staring off into the distance. Her face confirmed Jenn's fear. She got herself a tall decaf, added cream and sugar, and then sat with her friend, perhaps former friend. This was a nightmare.

Getting right to the point, Lindsay said, "Jenn, you know we love you all, as much as we love our families."

Jenn stared without saying a word, not wanting to make this easy for Lindsay, forcing her to actually say the words.

"Please don't hate me... it's just that... well, Mark and I have decided we can't keep exposing our kids to Josh right now. Michael looks up to him; he wants to be like Josh. You have to understand. When Josh was open to treatment, he was a fine influence. But now..." Lindsay shook her head.

Jenn's heart pounded hard. She took in a breath, trying to steady it.

"Say something," Lindsay begged.

Jenn started to speak. She stopped. She took another breath. "What makes you believe that Josh has given up on treatment?"

"He told Michael. Well, he said he would never do another camp again. And he says he's quit youth group."

Jenn felt nauseated. She stared at the table, blinking back tears, keeping her exterior under control. It wasn't a surprise, but hearing this from Lindsay was a blow, physically and emotionally.

Lindsay took Jenn's hand. "I'm sorry, honey. My heart is breaking... for all of you. You're so important to us. But we just can't risk our kids' salvation. You understand, don't you?" Lindsay asked as she wiped her eyes.

Jenn bit her lip. She did understand. Before all this, if the tables were turned, she might very well have drawn the same line. She'd always been certain something like this would never happen to her because she'd done everything right. Done everything God had asked of her.

She never realized that God might ask her to choose between being kind and being steadfast.

She gave a slight nod.

"We're still praying for you," Lindsay said, her eyes red. "I hope it's just for a little while... until he gets back on track."

Jenn just stared wordlessly at Lindsay. Her head buzzed. There was nothing to say.

Very gently, as if she were soothing a child, Lindsay said, "You may not want to hear any advice from me... but if he were my son, I'd move him to Valley Christian, now. We're moving Michael and Abigail there in the fall. The secular influence is just too overpowering at DHS."

Lindsay squeezed her hand, stood up, and gave Jenn a tender kiss on her cheek. Then she walked out of Jenn's life. As far as Jenn was concerned, eighteen years of friendship had just ended.

Jenn put her head in her hands and cried silently, even though she was embarrassing herself in public. She prayed in her head.

Lord, guide me to do Your will. Please God, help me to understand. I'm doing my best to carry out Your will on Earth. I know I'm being tested, but why? Why would You put these feelings in Josh and not take them away, when all he wants to do is follow Your path...?

Cold shame stopped Jenn. She shouldn't be asking God why she was being tested. They'd lost Steve's parents, and now the Bishops. Her faith was wavering. More than ever, she needed to feel God's love, but instead she felt abandoned and alone. She turned her head to the wall so no one could see her. After her tears ran out, she drove home.

Lindsay was right: Valley Christian would get Josh back on track. God had spoken through Lindsay. Jenn hummed with certainty through the evening, but waited to approach Steve with the idea until they were alone in their bedroom at the end of the day.

"I think Josh should transfer to Valley as soon as we can get him enrolled," Jenn asserted.

"For the last quarter of his junior year?" Steve looked doubtful. "What about his AP classes?"

"They have AP classes at Valley. Those will be the easiest ones to transfer into, because it's a set curriculum."

Steve shook his head. "I don't know that Josh needs such a big change. He's very fragile. That might tip him over to a bad place."

"He is suffering, *right now*. Can't you see that? He told me he feels like a loser! He's going to keep hating himself until he roots out the same-sex attraction. We have to do everything we can to help him."

"I don't know that Valley will help him, Jenn."

Jenn's neck tensed, and she eyed her husband. "You don't condone him going to the GSA thing, do you? Did you know about it?"

"I've been doing some reading," Steve explained tentatively, "on the PFLAG website."

"The what?" Jenn questioned.

"Parents and Friends of Lesbians and Gays. Bethany thought it might be helpful to me... to us. I'm not sure anymore that complete change is possible. Most psychologists say you can modify behavior, but not attraction."

Jenn's pulse raced. Steve was giving up, too. "They aren't spiritual leaders, are they? We are talking about a spiritual transformation, not a psychological change. Andrew said there was no reason to give up on Josh. Doug said there would be secular pressures. *With God all things are possible.* You know that! He needs to have faith, or there's no hope for transformation at all."

"I need to think about this, Jenn... and talk to Josh," Steve said. It felt as if he were placating her, but he wasn't saying no. "Why now?"

Jenn let out a big sigh. "Lindsay had a 'talk' with me at Starbucks today. The Bishops don't want their kids to be around Josh until he's cured."

"Shit!" Steve exclaimed, his eyes big. Emphasizing each word, he asked, "Are you serious? When were you going to tell me this?"

"I didn't want to say anything in front of the kids," Jenn defended herself.

Steve closed his eyes and took a moment before he spoke. "You were right to wait till we were alone. I guess you learn who your real friends are at a time like this."

"She said it wasn't forever. Just until Josh is committed to a cure. Can you blame them?" Jenn asked. "We might make the same choice, if the tables were turned."

Steve stared at her, fury burning in his eyes. "No, Jenn, I would never make that choice. And I'm sorry to hear that you would."

Jenn's stomach dropped. She felt sick, and her eyes welled up. She'd never felt this separate from Steve before, never seen him so angry. She struggled for the right thing to say, to assure them both that they shared the same values, but her mind was blank. Anything she thought to say might make him angrier and grow the rift between them.

Steve stood. He started to leave but turned at the doorway. "I think we need time as a family. Can we please do something fun tomorrow—the five of us together?"

"Of course," she agreed quietly, grateful he wanted to do something to bring the family closer. "What do you want to do?"

"How about hiking Mount Diablo? Then dinner and a movie out? Nice family time where Josh isn't the focus or the problem."

She nodded slowly. Steve was right. It had been too long since they had family time. "That's a great idea. I'll talk to Sara and Rachel. You ask Josh. How about we plan to leave around two?"

Steve nodded and left. Jenn said a prayer in her head.

Dear God, help me find the words I need to hold up Your will for my family. In Jesus's name I pray. Amen.

April weather could be all over the place in the East Bay, but it was a perfect day for a hike. Jenn put on a happy face, but she was acutely aware of the tension between her and Steve. She'd packed a backpack full of snacks and water bottles.

They let Rachel pick a movie for all of them, ignoring the rules about feminine and masculine films. Excited to see one of her favorite childhood books come to life, she picked *Ella Enchanted*. They'd eat at Applebee's and then go to the seven-twenty show.

During the hike on Mount Diablo to Rock City, everything felt normal, just like their family. Steve and the kids climbed over the amazing formations while Jenn watched from a distance from a flat, red stone.

She took out her camera, hoping God would give her a clear focus. Her family was a small cluster in the middle of large, beautiful red walls. They were the center of her world but only a small part of this landscape. She zoomed in on them. Rachel must be telling a story because the other three were looking at her. Suddenly they all laughed, and she pressed the shutter, capturing the moment.

She looked at the picture she'd just taken on the small screen. They were so happy together. She zoomed in on Josh; his head was tipped back, and he looked up to the heavens with such joy on his face. She hadn't seen that in him for so long that she had forgotten it was possible.

She wished she was like Steve and trusted, even for a moment, but she was consumed by the need to stop their life from becoming entirely unraveled. She didn't know if her concern was too extreme or Steve's was too minimal. Yes, she was on edge all the time, but that seemed like an appropriate reaction to the kind of crisis they were dealing with.

Steve walked over to Jenn and sat close. Eventually he broke the tense silence. "Josh is a great person. They all are. You can be proud."

She replied, "I don't feel proud these days."

"I have faith he'll be fine, whatever comes."

She looked at her husband. "But maybe not fine in the way that matters most to me."

So gently, like he was soothing a broken-hearted child, Steve replied, "You might need to redefine what matters most."

Jenn's heart skipped a beat. "What if I can't, Steve? I'm afraid I can't, and I'm going to lose him altogether." *And you, too,* Jenn thought, but she didn't want to make this conversation more complicated.

Steve replied, "I have faith that you can."

"What?" Jenn asked.

"Every day I pray for you, Jenn," Steve said tenderly. "For you to open your heart and accept Josh."

Fury exploded in Jenn's chest. She hissed at Steve, "You pray for *me* to accept *him* being homosexual rather than for Josh to be cured! How is it that we're not on the same page about this? We're a team. You and me. One team. United in the one true faith. When did you get traded?"

Jenn could not bear to look at Steve. She was so mad she wanted to scream at him, but instead she stormed away, not caring what her kids noticed or thought. She rushed back down the trail toward their car.

As she walked, Jenn replayed the conversation in her mind, becoming less certain of what she'd heard. Did Steve actually say he wanted Josh to be homosexual? That was unlikely. But he did say that Jenn was the problem in their family. Well, maybe not exactly. The more Jenn thought about it, the less she was hurt and the more she was embarrassed. By the time she got to the SUV she felt sheepish. Jenn didn't have a key to the car, so she sat down on the hot wooden railing in the shade. She watched a dragonfly land gently on a rock.

She pulled out her camera and zoomed in on it. It had a bright blue head and stripe on its body. She clicked and clicked, taking image after image as it lifted into the air and flew away. She watched it become a small speck in the sky and then disappear altogether.

When her family came down the path half an hour later, Jenn was still taking close-up pictures of the beauty around her, looking perfectly calm.

"Sorry to rush off, I had to go to the bathroom," she lied to her kids. "Are you ready for dinner and *Ella*?" She only wanted to go home and crawl under her covers, but she pushed aside her desires. They were going to have cheerful family time.

"Bring your camera, Mom," Rachel directed. "I want to see the pictures you took."

Jenn grabbed the bag before slamming the car door.

Rachel looped her arm through Jenn's, chatting about her plans with her friends to go to the mall tomorrow after church.

As soon as they sat in the booth, Rachel pulled out the camera. The three kids hovered over the screen. She'd yet to fill up her photo card, so every photo she'd taken with the camera since Valentine's Day was there. They started from the beginning, leaning in close, laughing and pointing every few photos.

"Look at your face!" Rachel squealed and Josh shoved her.

She turned the camera around to show her parents. A less than flattering close up of Josh filled the screen. Had he been sneezing? Yawning? Running? Josh grabbed the camera and found an equally embarrassing picture of Rachel to display.

They continued, reviewing the past two months—reminding

Jenn there were good times right alongside the pain. Josh's games. Her trip with Rachel to Monterey. Family picnics. Her children right there, across the table from her, teasing each other. She'd been so afraid she missed the joy and love even as it was happening.

"Josh, you look like a model in this one!" Rachel declared.

She turned the camera around so Jenn and Steve could see it. Josh was standing by a large boulder staring off into the distance. He did look like a model in a magazine.

As she took that shot she wondered what he was thinking about. It was hard to read his emotion as he gazed at the awesome view. Was he worried, content, optimistic, hurt? Would he ever come to her again with his greatest hopes and fears?

"Mom, you really are a great photographer," Sara said.

"Thanks," she smiled. "You do look like a model, Josh."

Her handsome, sweet son shrugged. Love welled up. She looked around the table. He meant the world to her, all of them did. She took Steve's hand and rested her head on his shoulder. He'd been right. It was good just to be together as a family—laughing, planning, and reminiscing.

"No way, Mom. No way!" Josh replied when Jenn casually suggested that he transfer to Valley Christian.

"We're just thinking about it," Steve reassured Josh. "We wanted to know your preference."

"I don't want to be some new freak at Valley Christian, that's what I think," Josh said.

"There will be fewer distractions there, Josh," Jenn said. "You can focus on your recovery."

"We aren't forcing you. Just think about it," Steve said.

"I don't need to think about it." Josh was adamant. "Valley Christian is not for me. What about track? You want me to just stop my life?" He stood up. "I can't take this anymore," he said, and stomped out of the family room.

"You didn't even encourage him to do it, Steve," Jenn scolded.

"I agreed to ask his opinion," Steve countered. "I didn't agree that it was a good idea to move him to Valley. We asked. He answered. As far as I'm concerned, he's staying at Dublin High." He left her alone.

"God, my Lord and Savior, guide my words and my actions," Jenn prayed aloud. "Lord, please, I beg of You, keep my family together. I have never wanted anything but to love my family, love You and Your only son. I surrender my life to you. Amen."

TWENTY-FOUR
SUNDAY, APRIL 25, 2004

Sara

Sara reached for her froyo and felt the buzz of a call at the same time. She handed her cup of cookie dough topped with peanuts to Maya and dug the phone out of her pocket. Best Bro was on the screen. He was calling without texting first. Her heart sped up and she hit accept, but it was too late.

She hit call back, but it went directly to his voicemail. She trailed behind her friends walking back to the dorm.

"You okay?" Maya turned around to ask.

"It's Josh," Sara said. Maya knew why Sara was scared.

She hit redial, and her phone rang at the same time. She meant to hit pick up but sent it to voicemail by accident. She stopped walking and stared at her phone.

Call me, Josh. I'm waiting for you, she sent out with her mind. *Wait, wait, wait,* she told herself.

Best Bro popped up on the screen, and she hit accept.

Josh rushed out, "I can't take it. I can't take her. I cannot be in the house with her!"

"What did she do?" Sara asked.

"She wants me to go to Valley Christian," he replied.

She pulled in her lip and bit it. That tracked. Of course VC would be Mom's next move. They'd had a lot of fun yesterday, but it was obvious Mom was barely holding it together.

"What does Dad say?"

"I can do what I want," he replied. "Stay at Dublin. She was *furious* at Dad for not backing her up. She's crazy. Will she ever get it that she can't control my life?"

Sara heard cars in the background. "Where are you?"

"I left, I can't go back. I'm going to sleep at Dublin High."

"Josh... what are you talking about?!"

"I'll find somewhere safe to sleep, maybe under the bleachers, and then use the showers in the morning. I don't know how I'll eat, but I'll figure that out in the morning."

Without thinking Sara said, "Come here! It's not that far. You can sleep on my floor. You can have my bed. Please, Josh— don't sleep outside."

"Really?"

"Of course!"

"Do you have to ask Maya?"

"She'll be fine with it. Do you have enough on your BART card?"

"Lemme check," he replied, and she heard muffled sounds.

When he came back on, he sounded more like a scared boy. "I do."

She exhaled hard. She gave him step by step instructions and told him she'd meet him outside the Downtown Berkeley station when he got there. Her voice caught when they said goodbye. It would be silly to stay on the phone the whole time, but she was scared to let that connection go.

She caught Maya up who readily agreed that he could stay with them and offered to get a futon and sleeping bag from their friend Marta.

Sara called the home phone to tell her parents that Josh was okay. Mom picked up.

All her frustration and disappointment bubbled over. "Mom! What are you doing to Josh?"

Mom replied, "Sara, don't be dramatic. We're only thinking of switching schools."

Did Mom even know he'd left?

"He's furious, Mom. Don't keep pushing him so hard."

Mom replied, "Pastor James said this is when the transformation happens, when he's tested to his very limit. He has to choose."

She felt her phone vibrate. She pulled it from her ear and looked at the screen. Josh had sent a text:

> Don't tell M/D!

"Sara, are you there?"

"I'm back. Sorry," Sara spoke into the phone. "Mom, you're asking too much of Josh. Give him a break. How many times do Dad and I have to tell you that?"

"I don't understand why you *and* your father are ganging up against me!" Mom yelled. "Am I the only one who cares about Josh?" And then she hung up.

Sara stared at her phone. Her mother had *hung up* on her. She really was losing it.

Sara wiped away her tears and walked to the BART station. After that stunt, Sara was done taking care of Mom. Sara wasn't going to encourage Josh to tell her where he was staying. Let her panic when she realized Josh was gone. She might get a small taste of what Josh had been going through.

When Josh and Sara got to her room it was set for him including a big sign with rainbow flags that said *Welcome, Josh!*

Sara saw him tear up. "Thanks, Maya."

"Of course. My roomy's favorite brother can stay here as long as he needs to. I'll even sneak you food from the cafeteria."

Sara tutored him on bathroom etiquette, then they went to bed. Josh would have an early morning if he wanted to get back to DHS for when the first bell rang.

Sara's phone vibrated. It was a text from Mom:

> Sorry

She considered showing Josh, but he didn't know about their fight. He didn't need to hear that their mom was unhinged.

It's out of love, Sara reminded herself, but she was still wrong. She prayed: *God, please open my mother's heart to Your ever-present love. Help her to heal her misunderstanding and know that You do not make mistakes. In the name of Your son, Jesus Christ, I pray. Amen.*

She looked at Josh and added, *And God, pour a little extra love and faith and strength into Josh. He needs to feel You more than ever. Amen.*

In the morning Sara handed Josh two breakfast bars, a bag of nuts, and an apple from the cafeteria. "Is this enough?"

"Yeah, thanks," he replied. "Someone will share lunch with me."

Sara hesitated, but then asked, "You have... lunch friends?"

"Yeah," he said. "The kids from GSA are very nice. I eat with them now. I could eat with my track friends, too. They are either clueless or don't care." He shrugged.

"I can't believe Michael... well, it's so messed up, Josh."

Josh shrugged. "He told me it wasn't his choice, but he can't stand up to his parents."

"His loss," she replied. "I hope you know that."

"I gotta go or I'll be late."

"You gonna text Mom or Dad?"

"No. And don't you either—please. Mom will come out here and then where will I go?"

"I won't, not unless you tell me to. Your secret is safe with me."

They hugged goodbye, something they never would have done before. But Sara needed it as much as Josh did.

TWENTY-FIVE

MONDAY, APRIL 26, 2004

Jenn

Josh didn't come down for breakfast at the usual time.

Jenn called up, "Josh, food's ready."

She waited for a minute. When he didn't emerge from his room she walked upstairs. He ignored her knock. Daring to provoke him further she turned the knob but didn't push it open. No response. She pushed on the door to find an empty room. He must be furious to have left without eating. She had hoped to apologize over breakfast. Instead, she spent five minutes writing him a text:

> Sorry. We'll work this out.

She slipped her phone into her pocket, anticipating a text back. Five minutes later there was nothing. Jenn checked the setting: sounds on, ringer turned up. She put it in her pocket again so she could respond immediately. She casually explained away his absence to Rachel and Steve, speculating that he'd needed to go to school early.

More than once she checked her phone to see if he'd texted, but he hadn't. He shouldn't text during class anyway, but when he didn't reply during lunchtime, she swung between being annoyed with him for ignoring her and terrified he had hurt himself again. This couldn't be good for her heart.

By the late afternoon he wasn't home. Jenn called Carmen, his carpool driver, who reported that Josh had said he had to stay late. Jenn lied and said it was her mistake.

As soon as she hung up, Jenn dialed Steve.

"Josh hasn't come home."

"Maybe carpool is running behind?"

"Josh told Carmen he's staying late. What's he up to? I'm scared."

Steve sighed. "It's still daylight. If he's not home by the time I get there, I'll worry. But for now, I think he just needs some space from you."

"Me! Why am I the problem?"

Furious, Jenn hung up on Steve. As soon as she did it, she added shame to her rage. She was completely out of control. She texted him an apology. All this texting was going to cost them a small fortune.

Josh wasn't home by dinner, and Jenn was frantic with worry.

"Do you think he ran away?" Rachel asked.

"Why would he do that?" Jenn challenged.

"It's not like he's feeling the love here," Rachel replied.

Anger surged through her. When did her children become so utterly disrespectful?

"You're not helping, Rachel. Daddy and I are taking care of the situation. I'll let you know when we know more."

Steve looked at his phone. Flipping it open, he read a text. He sighed and then passed the phone to Jenn. It was from Sara.

Josh is here. He's safe. Don't come.

Jenn blinked at the screen. Intense, contradictory emotion flooded in. She was relieved Josh was safe, but furious that he went to Berkeley without permission. Rachel was right. He couldn't stand to be home.

"Let's go get him," she said to Steve.

Steve shook his head. "Let's trust Sara. He went to her for a reason."

Jenn ignored him and went to get her keys.

Steve followed and slowly took the keys from her hand. "Stop. Call her first. She said not to come."

Jenn glared at him but dialed Sara's dorm room. The phone rang and rang. She tried Sara's cell. Her daughter did not pick up. How could Sara leave her hanging like this? They got her a cell phone so they could be in touch. She paced around the house, fury building in her. She just wanted to get Josh home where he belonged, but Sara and Steve were thwarting her plan. Any sense of peace she felt knowing where Josh was had vanished.

"I'm going for a walk. You two eat without me." Rachel looked scared, but Jenn needed to cool off before she could be any comfort to her youngest daughter. She grabbed the leash and called for the dog.

While she was walking with Wynnie, Sara texted.

I'll call when I can.

Jenn resisted the urge to smash her phone into the street. She strode fast to release the tension in her body. Block after block she moved, pounding her frustration into the pavement. By the time she finished her loop, she wasn't burning with anger any longer. She was ready to go back home. Rachel and Steve greeted her as she walked into the dining room.

"I'm sorry, Mom," Rachel said. "I was being snotty."

"I'm sorry, too, hon," Jenn replied. "I'm not as patient and loving as I'd like to be. I'm working on it. I promise."

Rachel got up and wrapped her arms around Jenn. Jenn embraced her back. She rocked her daughter. Steve came and wrapped his arms around both of them. Jenn rested her head against his chest. At a moment like this, she had faith they could still make it through this as a strong family.

"Eat," Steve said after a while. "It'll be good for your body, and your soul."

Jenn sighed and a small smile tugged up her lips. She'd made Josh fettuccine Alfredo as a peace offering. She could eat it in honor of him instead of with him. Rachel and Steve stayed with her at the table while she ate.

The home phone rang just as Jenn was finishing her food. Steve answered and brought the handset to Jenn.

"Here's your mom," Steve said into the receiver. "I'll get on the extension upstairs."

"Thanks for calling, Sara. How's Josh?" Jenn asked.

"He's upset and feeling desperate. I think it's good he came here, don't you?"

"I suppose. I'm glad he's safe. How's his spirit?"

"Not good, Mom. That's what I just told you," Sara said.

"I'm here," Steve broke in.

"Can we come get him?" Jenn asked.

"He doesn't want to go home. I'm afraid he'll just run away again if you drag him back. Or maybe not get in the car. There are tons of street kids living on Telegraph Ave. I don't want to see Josh living like that, do you?"

"No, of course not," Jenn said. "I want him home."

"It's best for him to stay here for a while," Sara replied.

"What's he going to do, drop out of school? What about the SAT? That's crazy!" Jenn said.

"It's a long commute, but he can get to Dublin. BART's an

easy walk from here. Dad can pick him up at that end. Today he walked all the way to Dublin High from the BART station and still got there on time."

Steve said, "Absolutely."

Fury flashed through her chest. "Dad. Just Dad?" She made a fist and hit it against the wooden farm table.

"For now," Steve said gently, "maybe that would be best."

A hot wave ran through Jenn's body. "How long are we going to let him do this?"

Steve said, "Don't get ahead of yourself. Let's take it one day at a time, Jenn. He's safe right now. Thank God for that. And," his voice broke, "thank you, Sara."

"Of course, he's my brother." Sara's voice cracked. "I love him."

"We all do," Jenn said. "Sara, tell him that, okay?" she begged her daughter. "Please. Tell him that I love him."

"I will, Mom. I promise."

Rachel was staring at her when she got off the phone, a question in her eyes.

"Josh is going to stay with Sara for a few days. Just until he cools off."

"Can I send him a text?" Rachel asked.

"Sure." Jenn started to slide her phone to Rachel, then she stopped. "Use Dad's." It was devastating but true: Josh would likely ignore a text from her phone. He may have blocked her. She felt sick.

"Can I use your phone?" Rachel asked Steve as he came into the room. He handed his phone to his youngest child. She walked out of the kitchen with it.

Steve said to Jenn, "I'm going to take Josh to see Kyle on Wednesday."

She wanted to scream and yell and cry. Everything was heading in the wrong direction.

"He needs all the support he can get," Steve explained. "It was a mistake to cut him off from Kyle. I want him to have that."

Jenn felt thoroughly defeated. She nodded without saying a word.

"Are you okay?" Steve asked. He was being kind, but it felt patronizing.

In a sharp, angry whisper, so Rachel couldn't hear her, Jenn hissed, "How can you ask me that? Of course I'm not all right. I'm devastated. Josh has given up..." She took a shaky breath, trying not to cry. "My son, *our* son, has lost faith. And I have no idea what to do. No, I'm not all right, and *you* shouldn't be all right either!"

Steve offered a hug, but Jenn didn't want comfort. She deflected her husband and said, "I'm taking Wynnie for a walk."

"Again?" Steve asked.

"It's better than exploding," she snapped.

"Do you want company?" Steve asked.

"No," she replied harshly.

Jenn sobbed as she walked with Wynnie. She was grateful none of the neighbors could see her too clearly in the dark as she stormed through the neighborhood. She replayed the week in her head, imagining how it could have gone differently. It was a small comfort that things could be worse—they could be back at the hospital. By the time she got home she was only left with sorrow.

She sent Josh a text, taking the time for each word:

I love you. Please come home.

By the time Steve came to bed, she felt foolish and ashamed. She sat up to talk to him.

"Sorry, Steve," she said. "God, how many times can I say that? I can't seem to do anything right these days."

"This is hard on all of us," Steve said kindly. "None of us knows the exact right way to be."

Jenn started sobbing. "I miss my certainty. I miss us being a team. I miss my son."

"Me, too," he said. But he didn't give her a hug or sit close. He left to brush his teeth.

She stared at her phone, begging for a text back from Josh. But it didn't come.

The next morning Jenn woke up at six and immediately checked her phone from bed. Nothing from Josh. She didn't get up. Instead, she rolled over and went back to sleep. At seven thirty Steve brought her some coffee and toast.

"Are you sick?" he asked, sitting on the edge of the mattress.

"I don't know," she said. "I guess so."

Steve patted her shoulder. "You rest. Rachel and I have the morning covered. Josh just texted. He's almost at the Dublin station."

"Okay." Jenn felt like she should say more, but she didn't have the energy.

"I'll see you for dinner."

"Hmm," Jenn replied before Steve walked out the door. She doubted he even heard her. Jenn reached for the cell phone by her bed. Nothing from Josh. She rolled over and went back to sleep.

By ten o'clock she forced herself to sit up. Every movement was hard, but sleeping the day away wasn't the answer. After drinking her cold coffee and eating her hard toast, she went to her prayer chair. She needed that big hug from God more than anything. She started her prayer: *Lord, thank You in the name of Jesus. God, thank You for the power of the Holy Spirit. I ask that Your presence fill me with wisdom and revelation so that I may follow You, love You, and serve You entirely. Bind up all distractions and show me Your will for me.*

"God." Jenn's voice cracked as she spoke aloud. "I need You more today than ever. I know I keep saying that, but it's still true. Help me know what to do to rebuild my family."

She waited for the comfort of God to fill her up. She wanted the calm clarity she relied upon from a prayerful stance, but her mind raced in circles. She pictured finding Josh after school and him falling into her arms in gratitude and sorrow. She would hold him and say the right prayer to transform him. She envisioned her strong faith healing him.

Then her thoughts raced to the opposite. She imagined a look of disgust on his face if he saw her. In her mind he snarled at her, "You don't understand, and you never will. Kyle understands. God made me like this. He's not going to change me, whatever you want. He's not."

Helpless, Jenn turned to spoken prayer. *"God, please transform Josh. Open him to Your wisdom and guidance. Help him to know the divine path You have for him. Amen."*

Jenn left early to pick up Rachel from school so she could get a parking space as close as possible to the campus. Perhaps she would get a glimpse of Josh. She searched the crowd of kids after the bell rang, but there was no sign of him. This was her only chance to see him because Steve was taking him directly to the BART station after practice.

After Rachel climbed into the front seat, Jenn asked, "How's your brother?"

"My day was fine. Thanks for asking."

"Rachel, don't be smart."

Rachel sighed. "He's fine, Mom. He seemed the same as always, just tired from getting up early to take BART."

"How did he sleep? Did he get breakfast?"

"I don't know." Rachel shrugged. "Dad didn't ask him about any of that. They talked about track and chemistry."

Jenn sighed. *Track and chemistry.* She shook her head. Jenn asked, "Did you pray together before you went to school?"

Rachel gave Jenn an incredulous look. "No."

"Would you please, from now on, say a quick prayer for your brother before school? Right in his presence. It can be in your heart; it doesn't have to be out loud. But try to touch him for part of it. Okay?"

"Sure, Mom. If you want," Rachel said, but Jenn suspected she was placating her.

All of her children were slipping away.

But Steve would agree to pray for Josh. And she would pour prayers into the lunch she would send for him. She was not giving up on her son.

TWENTY-SIX

WEDNESDAY, APRIL 28, 2004

Josh

No one but Michael cared that Josh was now a GSA kid. He'd expected to walk around school like he was wearing a scarlet F, but unlike in TV shows, no one seemed to notice. He'd thought his track friends would shun him after he crossed the rainbow line, but so far no one had talked or acted different. They didn't bring it up, nor did he, and they didn't know he was staying in Berkeley. Only Ms. Hodder knew about Sara's dorm.

Josh deliberately kept his eyes on his own locker as he suited up for track. Self-conscious, he changed as fast as possible. After practice Dad was taking him to see Kyle. Did Mom know? She wouldn't like it. Dad must be very scared to go against her. Josh was ruining their whole family.

He slammed his locker door so hard it bounced open. That felt good. He wanted to do it again but stopped himself to avoid eyes on him. He swung the door around and then hit it hard to slam it shut with a satisfying sound.

"You okay?" Lewis came from around the corner.

"Yeah," Josh said. "Sorry. It's been a rough week."

"No prob," Lewis said.

They walked to the field side by side. The silence was awkward, but Josh couldn't think of anything to chat about. He knew Lewis from the team, but they'd never hung out.

"Not to make it weird, but..." Lewis looked uncomfortable. "My oldest brother is gay. He came out in college. I just... it's cool. You do you."

Josh was totally surprised. That was not what he was expecting.

"Thanks, Lewis. I mean it," Josh said.

Lewis shrugged. "I just thought... I know it's hard. Ignore the haters."

"I'm trying."

"Easy for me to say, eh?"

Coach blew his whistle. "Take a lap to warm up!"

Josh felt light as he took off around the track. Maybe this wasn't going to go bad at school at all. At the moment he was in a nice run on the emotional roller coaster. He let himself relish the moment, knowing he might hit a scary turn at any moment. But for now, he would enjoy this part of the ride.

It felt nice, safe, to be in Kyle's office again. Josh had only been here a few times, but their conversations had given him the strength to be honest with Sara. She'd been amazing. She didn't know what it was like to feel this way, but she seemed certain that God loved him even if he wasn't cured. Josh wasn't so sure, but he believed she was being honest.

"How are you, Josh?" Kyle asked after they were settled in their seats.

Josh cleared his throat. "Horrible. Good. I don't know."

"Tell me what's happened since we last saw each other." Kyle leaned in to listen.

"I went to that camp. I tried, I did, but it didn't work. I told my Mom I can't lie to God," he said. "She wants me to be an example. I did everything they said, and it didn't happen. I still want God to take away my lust, my sinful nature..."

Josh stopped. It was humiliating to say it out loud.

"Josh, if your lust was for a woman, would you think it a sin?"

Josh considered. "No..." then he whispered, "but it isn't for a woman."

"Josh, do you still pray?"

Josh nodded.

"I suggest you pray on this question: is it actually a sin to have same-sex attraction? I didn't choose who I am attracted to, nor did you. My faith tells me that if you harm other people or force yourself on them without consent, that is a sin."

"That's what your church teaches?" Josh asked.

Kyle pulled in his lips and eyebrows. He looked uncertain, but he continued, "When you're young, your parents are your spiritual guides. As you mature, you're responsible for your own spiritual path. My current church is not the one I was raised in. After college I found one that better fit my path, one that allowed me to use the Bible as a living text for today."

Josh shook his head. *Living text for today.* That wasn't his church. *God is all loving, but you must obey His laws to be righteous.*

Kyle continued, "I didn't grow up with anyone out and proud. I had to adjust my thinking as I met wonderful people who didn't live life by the religious laws I was raised with. At some point I understood that God is still speaking; Holy Books contain a mixture of enduring spiritual truths and the biases of the time in which they were written. I believe that God truly doesn't care if we eat shellfish or pork—only that we eat healthy food. Or that we rest on a specific day, Friday, Saturday, or Sunday—just that we take time to rest. And I cannot believe He *ever* wanted us to stone people to death."

Kyle explained, "People who are afraid of change tell you God only loves people who think and act just like them, but it's quite obvious that God loves diversity. Look at creation. He didn't make any two things exactly the same. Billions of people —and no two are identical. Even identical twins are not exactly the same."

Kyle stopped talking. Josh took in his words. It was like what Ms. Hodder had said. He didn't have to choose between God's love and his... attractions. Josh shook his head. It didn't seem right, but he wanted it to be true.

"What church do you go to?" Josh asked.

"I can't suggest any specific church—that would be unethical," Kyle said.

Josh snorted and replied, "Not in my church."

"Touché," Kyle laughed and then replied, "The internet is a blessing in this situation. Search for welcome and affirming churches. They often have a rainbow on their websites or a statement of inclusion."

"If I see you there, do I have to ignore you?"

"We can greet each other warmly, but no long conversations," Kyle answered.

God loves diversity.

Change is possible.

Surrender.

Those thoughts... floated through his head? Bubbled up from his gut? Stirred his heart? Spoken by God? Josh didn't know where they came from, but somehow, they gave him comfort. Maybe surrendering to God was accepting that he had been made this way *by* God. It would destroy his mom. Could he keep it hidden from her?

"What are you thinking?" Kyle asked gently.

"It will destroy my mom." He teared up. "I'm destroying my mom's faith."

"Blind faith doesn't hold up under the pains of life. Do you know the Parable of the Sower?"

Josh nodded.

"If your mom's faith withers and dies, it was shallow to begin with," Kyle said. "I know that sounds harsh. But it's not your responsibility to protect her from the path God has put before her."

A shiver ran down Josh's spine. *This is God's path for me?*

"But I love my mom."

"Loving your mom doesn't mean you have to be the same as her or protect her from who you are," Kyle said.

Josh nodded.

"I don't suggest this will be easy for her to get used to, and maybe she can't, but from what you have told me, and what I have seen of her, I expect that she will be able to set down her prejudice."

"My mom isn't prejudiced," Josh defended.

Kyle nodded slowly. "This is a big change for all of you. Each of you will manage it in your own way. Your job is to take care of you first, not your mother. Can we agree on that?"

Josh was confused. Family was everything to him. How could he leave his mother behind?

"I don't know. I can't lose her. Or make my dad pick. I can't go back there—she won't stop."

He started crying, hard this time. Ugly crying, as the girls say. Kyle watched him and passed him a tissue when he was done.

Josh asked, "Will it ever get better?"

"It will, I promise." Kyle sounded certain. "And you are doing amazingly well under very difficult circumstances. All of you—you and your mother—are *very* hard on yourselves. Can you surrender some of your control and trust a bit more?"

Josh replied, "*Surrender. And trust.* That's what they said at that camp. Over and over and over and over."

"You know the Serenity Prayer is one of my favorites," Kyle said. "Sometimes it takes a while to know what to accept and what to change. Life is a marathon, not a sprint."

Josh nodded.

"Josh, your relationship with your mother would have grown and changed even if you were attracted to women. Growing pains hurt, but they don't mean you're doing anything wrong."

Josh nodded even though his mind still swirled with confusion.

Kyle continued, "I want to leave you with one last thought. You deepening your faith and living your honest life out loud will embolden others to do the same. You will be the example of a faith-filled, honest life that your mother and father taught you to be."

Example of a faith-filled life.

That was what he wanted—more than anything else.

By being gay?!

Was accepting he was gay, being proud of it, his path? The Holy Spirit spilled down his spine and radiated out through his arms and legs to the very tips of his fingers and toes. Josh had no words, so he simply nodded.

TWENTY-SEVEN
FRIDAY, APRIL 30, 2004

Jenn

On Friday, Jenn offered to drive the kids, but Steve rejected her idea. He was kind, but clear—it was too soon for Josh. She responded with grace, but inside she was hurt. She felt so alone. In the past she would have talked this through with Lindsay, but she didn't have anyone. No one understood what she was going through.

She called Sara to plan. "Are you coming for the weekend, for the SAT and church on Sunday?"

"Dad and Josh made a plan for the SAT. I'll check with Josh about church again, but I think the answer is still no."

Jenn felt sick about being left out. "You already asked him?" Jenn asked.

"Yeah. He wants to go to church," Sara said, care in her tone, "...just not our church."

"Did you tell him that was okay?" Jenn reacted. "Are you encouraging him to give up on his transformation? Sara, he looks up to you. You can save your brother's soul with the right words. Do you understand the gravity of his situation?"

"Yes, Mom. I do, more than you know. I just don't think the same as you anymore—at least when it comes to gay rights."

Jenn wanted to scream at her daughter, but instead asked, "When did you have this change of heart?"

"I've been praying, thinking, and talking about this since Josh came out to us."

"You sound like it's a fact that he is homosexual," Jenn countered, "but there are treatments!"

"Mom, they aren't real," Sara said, as if she were talking to a child. "I know you want them to be. We all wanted them to be, including Josh. But they're a lie. Those Resurrection people make a lot of money from fear and hatred."

"Hating a sin is not wrong. This is about faith."

"I'm not going to argue with you," Sara said calmly. "I feel the way I feel. Josh is who he is."

"What about his salvation?"

"*Our God is a loving God*, that's what you taught me. How could God not love Josh?"

Jenn felt ill. Her own words were being used against her. "Well, I'm disappointed in your decision."

"I'm sorry, Mom. I know this is hard for you to hear," Sara said, her voice shaky. "I have faith you'll agree with me in time, or at least understand."

"I will never give up on Josh's salvation, Sara."

"Me neither, Mom. I'm not giving up on Josh, at all. Bye."

First Josh. Now Sara. Suddenly she needed to know where Steve stood, too. She walked around the block to calm herself and then she called her husband.

Jenn asked, "Do you know that Josh doesn't want to attend church anymore?"

Steve let out a big breath. "He has a different church in mind."

"You knew this and didn't tell me!" Jenn yelled into the phone. "Unbelievable!"

"He wants to start attending First Congregational."

"No! Absolutely not."

Steve replied, "I'm glad that he wants church in his life at all. He still loves God and Jesus. He just doesn't want the judgment."

"Like you get to pick and choose what God wants for you?" Jenn rebutted. "How naive and self-centered can he be? You support this?"

"I want him to have church, Jenn."

Jenn squeezed her hand in anger and hissed into the phone, "I don't know you. I don't know you at all anymore. Who are you? You certainly are not the man I married. We were united in this. Raising our children in *the* true faith. Instilling a sense of obligation to God and Jesus. What happened to you?"

Jenn hung up before Steve replied. She knew the answer: she was alone, entirely alone, in her desire to save Josh. Somehow Steve and Sara and Josh had all given up faith in Josh's transformation. She wanted to run away, too.

Steve was patient and kind over the weekend. He took care of getting Josh to where he needed to be on Saturday. Jenn didn't argue anymore, though inside she was angry and grief-stricken, and her family knew it.

Jenn could hardly bear to be in the sanctuary Sunday morning. People noticed it was just the three of them. They kindly asked about Josh and Sara. She didn't want to tell anyone that Josh was staying in Berkeley, so with a shame-filled heart she lied. She told them Josh was sick and Sara was studying. This was what her life had come to: lying in church. Instead of church being a comfort and a sanctuary, it was a glaring reminder of all that was wrong in her life.

She took in a long, steady breath. These words started to run through her mind:

God, grant me the serenity to accept the things I cannot change,
The courage to change the things I can,
And the wisdom to know the difference.

She didn't know what she could and couldn't change. She didn't feel serene, courageous, or wise, but if she asked often enough, she might eventually.

She'd been returning to it again and again since Josh left. It ran through her mind as she went through her days and was especially helpful in the middle of the night when she woke up in a panic. Every time anxiety started to rise in her at the thought of losing Josh, she said it. It was a small comfort that kept her from having a mental breakdown. She knew Pastor James didn't approve of this prayer, but its simple directions were just what she needed to keep her sane.

Midway through the second week of his absence, Jenn felt like she would die if Josh didn't return. Each day he was away he walked farther and farther away from her. In desperation, she turned to the only person who might be able to persuade Josh to come home: Kyle Goss. Though she'd been thoroughly disrespectful the last time she saw him, he was kind on the phone and agreed to have an appointment when she called. He greeted her warmly, and they settled in chairs in his office. He started by asking how she was doing.

Jenn hoped to be calm and reasonable. Instead, she spewed out, "I've lost my son—in this life—and I'm afraid for the next. I can hardly breathe, I'm so overwhelmed with it. I don't know what to do. I've done everything I can to help him. But he doesn't want my help anymore. He doesn't want *me*. He won't talk to me or text me or see me. I'm desperate. I need your help. Please? Convince him to come home."

"I understand it's very hard for you that he's staying with Sara. And... you can be grateful that he has a safe place to be."

"Gratitude is not high on my list right now," Jenn snapped. After she heard the words she had spoken, she said, "That sounded awful. I'm sorry."

"From what I can tell, he's going to school, too. That's absolutely remarkable for a teen who's left home," Kyle explained.

"It sounds like you think I should be proud of my son. Proud of him for running away?"

"He's making safe choices for himself."

"I want him back. I want him home. I want him in my life. What do I do?" Jenn begged.

"I can't tell you what to do. I can tell you that Josh is a lovely young man and yes, you can be very proud of him."

Jenn said, "I feel like I have to choose between my son and my Lord. I can't do it."

Kyle sat there quietly. After a few moments he said, "I know someone who was in a similar situation. She's also an evangelical Christian. When her child came out to her, she was devastated. It took years, but eventually she made peace with it."

"How?" Jenn was doubtful. "The two things are irreconcilable."

Kyle tipped his head. "It's her story to tell. Ask her. I know she'd be willing to speak with you."

"Why?" Jenn wondered.

"It's her ministry. She believes God put her on Earth for that very purpose."

Jenn stared at him, uncertainty struggling in her.

Kyle said gently, "She knows what you're going through, Jenn—more than anyone else I know."

A Holy Spirit tingle passed through her. Someone who understood her? It felt like a gift from God. Jenn nodded. "All right. I'll call her."

· · ·

Jenn's hands shook when she pulled up to Rinda's house. The woman lived in Pleasanton, just across the freeway, in a 1990s development similar to theirs. Jenn didn't know what to expect from this conversation, and that made her very nervous. She was afraid of being judged and getting into a fight with this woman who knew nothing about her or her faith, but she was desperate. And Kyle sounded convinced she would be understanding, so Jenn decided to go through with it. Steve suggested it couldn't hurt, and it might help.

The woman who opened the door didn't look like Jenn had pictured in her mind. Rinda was tall with long blonde hair and blue eyes. She wore makeup and jewelry even though it was a Friday morning. She was a little older than Jenn, but not by much, maybe in her early fifties. She exuded simple elegance. Jenn felt dowdy in her jeans.

Rinda smiled warmly and said to Jenn, "I'm a hugger. Can I give you a hug?"

Jenn laughed despite her nervousness. "Sure."

It was surprisingly nice to be embraced by this stranger.

"Come on in," Rinda said as she led Jenn through the beautifully decorated house. "I'm very glad you reached out to me. I know how hard this is for you."

Jenn teared up.

"I've been there. He's your child. There is nothing you wouldn't do for him. And your heart is breaking."

Jenn nodded even though Rinda's back was to her. She didn't trust herself to speak. Kyle was right: this woman did understand.

"Sit." Rinda pointed to the couch in the family room. Jenn admired the mission-style couch, noting that it worked in this contemporary house. Two glasses of water sat on coasters on the coffee table and a box of tissues waited between them.

Rinda asked, "Can we start with a prayer?"

Jenn was surprised, and happy, at the request. She nodded. Rinda took her hands and spoke out loud, "Lord, thank You in the name of Jesus. God, thank You for the power of the Holy Spirit. We ask that Your presence fill us with wisdom and revelation so that we may follow You, love You, and serve You entirely. Bind up all distractions and show us Your will."

Chills ran up Jenn's spine. These comforting, familiar words meant everything to her. This woman knew her heart and spoke her language.

Rinda went on, "Lord, guide us in being agents of Your love for Your child Joshua Henderson. May our words and our deeds glorify You on this Earth and be worthy of the sacrifice of Your Son. May the Holy Spirit fill us with the power to do Your will. Amen."

"Amen," Jenn echoed. "Wow. I was not expecting that. Thank you."

"For me, prayer comes in the beginning, in the middle, and at the end."

"Kyle told me you're Christian. He also said you've accepted your son's homosexuality. I guess I was expecting something different."

"I'm happy to tell you my story, but first, tell me about your Josh."

Jenn thought for a moment, then said, "He's taller than me now. I'm still not used to it. I have to look up to that little boy I used to carry around. He looks like a man, but sometimes he's a boy inside. He's in between. I guess that's normal at this age. He loves his teams: cross country, basketball, and track. He's a great student. He has the crazy notion of going to school in New York City." Rinda was listening intently. Jenn smiled and went on, "He loves God. He's the most devout of my three kids. I'm sorry. I'm rambling on."

"I asked because I want to know about him. He sounds like a lovely human being."

"He is."

"And he's gay?" Rinda asked gently.

That word was a slap to her soul every time she heard it. "Well, not exactly. He says he has same-sex attractions, but he's never acted on them. So no, not really."

"But that's why you came to talk to me. Right? To hear how I reached understanding that homosexuality is not incompatible with living biblically."

Jenn bit her lip and nodded. Her mouth was dry, and it was hard to swallow. It felt like sacrilege to listen to this woman.

"You don't need to agree with anything I say. Hear me out, and then decide for yourself. You can ask me questions. You can argue with me. It's all okay."

Jenn felt scared again.

"As you can tell, I love God, and our savior Jesus Christ. As a teen I knew without a doubt that God put me on Earth to spread the good news of salvation through Christ."

"Me, too," Jenn said.

"Ten years ago, I was to learn David was gay. He was eighteen—just starting college. My whole world fell apart."

Jenn nodded. She understood.

Rinda went on, "After a few years of immense struggle, I immersed myself in prayer and Bible study. I won't go into every thought I had, but I'll share with you the insight that allowed me to accept that God loves David. It was very profound—like being born again." Rinda asked, "The Ten Commandments are the most important rules in the Old Testament, right?"

Jenn nodded.

"Don't you think keeping them would be the most important teaching at church?"

Jenn nodded again, feeling wary.

"I realized I was breaking one of them over and over again, but no one spoke of it in church."

Jenn made a skeptical face. It seemed unlikely she was sitting next to an adulterer or a murderer.

"I break the Sabbath," Maya continued. "And I cause others to break the Sabbath."

Jenn considered for a moment.

"Us, too!" she blurted. "It never occurred to me we were breaking one of the Ten Commandments." They ate out almost every Sunday. People worked on the Sabbath so she could eat brunch after church.

"Crazy, huh? One of the big ten, but we don't follow it. We watch sports, eat out, go shopping. All on Sundays. Many Christians work on the Sabbath for various reasons, but I have never heard a sermon, not one, about the abomination of football after church."

Jenn's mind reeled, but before she formed a response Rinda went on, "I also realized that more than anything else, Jesus asks us to love one another. He tells us to throw away many rules that are in the Old Testament because they don't serve to create love in the world. Why did I feel compelled to follow one rule of Leviticus about a man lying with another man but not many of the others, like eating shellfish or wearing mixed fabrics? It seems laughable that someone would go to hell for eating shellfish. I asked myself, *Why are we elevating one law so far above the others?* Does holding strong to this one law create more love or less? When it came to my judgment of my own son, it was less."

Jenn had heard secularists make that argument about shellfish and other laws in Leviticus before. She'd dismissed it because her religious leaders knew better.

"That law is more important," Jenn said, "because our ministers say it is. How could you reject your minister's wisdom?"

"I didn't discard it lightly," Rinda replied, "I prayed on it. I asked God. I'm not saying you'll come to the same answer. But after a lot of prayer—hours and hours—it finally came down to this: I could love the child God gave me right now, or I could love an ancient law written years ago. As much as I wanted to believe that the Bible is the literal truth, I can't. I love the Bible —I read it every day—but I came to understand it can't be all be true, or we Christians would advocate for slavery and polygamy, and many other things we don't support. I don't believe our God intends for us to have those institutions. Once I realized we were choosing which parts to follow and which parts to leave behind, I listened to God more than to the minister of my church."

Rinda continued, "It was scary at first. I felt like I was unfaithful to God. It's ironic that listening the most carefully to God felt like I was betraying Him. But that's how it felt at first."

Jenn nodded. She felt disloyal simply listening to this woman. This argument was similar to what her mom had said about Anita Bryant making this an issue. Could it be that her church was wrong?

Rinda went on, "In my prayers, God told me to love David. To just love him as a holy gift. Once I came to that, everything else melted away. I knew that God loved my son, and I didn't have to pray for him to change. I never felt closer to God in my life." Rinda's eyes glistened.

"Really?" Jenn felt hope. "You felt the Holy Spirit? Telling you it's okay?"

Rinda nodded. "Absolutely. It was the most beautiful moment of my life. I came to utter peace with David. It was then that I truly surrendered my life to God."

Jenn gasped. Goosebumps rose on her arms. Rinda gave a knowing nod and a smile.

"For years I told David he needed to surrender to God's will. And all along it was me who needed to surrender. I found what God was calling *me* to do. I knew without a doubt that I had to tell others. God put me on this Earth to spread the Good Word... of His love."

Jenn let those words echo in her heart and mind. They challenged much of what she believed, but mirrored some, too. And they offered her a promise of reconciliation with her son *and* her faith. "Now you and David are close?"

"He isn't with us on Earth anymore," Rinda said softly. "David's with the Lord in Heaven."

"Oh, I'm sorry." Jenn's eyes welled up. "I had no idea; Kyle didn't tell me. He got sick? Cancer?"

"He died of suicide," Rinda replied.

Jenn's chest clenched. She went icy cold, and a wave of dread passed through her. "Oh, dear God. I'm so..." She could hardly breathe. That could have been Josh.

"I entered this journey after his death," Rinda explained. "I was furious with God. I can't even describe it. For a while I felt like I'd lost David *and* our Lord. Why didn't He listen to our pleas and change David? David wanted it as much as I did. For hours on end, we prayed together for his transformation, but it never came. David was distraught, beyond reach."

Rinda told her, "After David was gone, I realized God made David—just as he was. My son was a gift from God. My imperfect, beautiful son was a present I was rejecting. David didn't need to be transformed."

Transformed. The word cut through Jenn. She'd been praying for Josh's complete transformation for months.

"What if you're wrong?" Jenn sounded pathetic. "Am I supposed to give up on Josh's salvation because of what *you* felt?"

Rinda looked at Jenn with compassion. "God has His own path for you. I can't tell you what to do. What I know for certain is that God loves Josh even though he's gay. And he loves David even though he was gay and he died by suicide. They are saved through their devotion to Christ. That's all that's asked of us. That's my faith."

Jenn was stunned. She also believed in salvation through devotion to Christ. Josh was as devoted to Christ as anyone, and more than most. Could it be that simple? Confusion swirled in her mind and heart. Rinda sat beside her.

Jenn finally said, "Thank you... for speaking with me. You've given me a lot to think about. And I'm sorry... very sorry, about David." She welled up again.

"I'm grateful to you for listening to me. I honor David and feel close to him each time I tell our story," Rinda said. "You are welcome to reach out again if you have any questions or if you want to talk. I know it's lonely."

Jenn nodded and bit her lip. She did have another question. "Have you...? What church do you go to?"

Rinda scrunched her face and shook her head. "That hasn't been easy. I still feel evangelical, but my congregation has a hard time with my new message. My husband and I joined First Congregational, but every few months I attend my former church in Livermore. I stay in the back and feel the power of the Holy Spirit in the room. I feel God and Jesus best there. I miss it, that energy. I miss it a lot."

They prayed and said a warm goodbye. As she drove away Jenn thought about their conversation. God had put Rinda in her path for a reason. Was she a challenge to Jenn's faith or a guide to a deeper faith? Her mind spun in circles.

At home she went right to her prayer chair. She opened herself up to God, the Holy Spirit, and her Savior. She surrendered fully and then she listened.

Love your son, was all that came to her. She desperately wanted, *Love your son just as he is*, or *Love your son enough to fight for his soul*, or *Love your son but not his sin*. But she didn't get the end of the sentence. All she got was the direction to love her son.

Her stomach rumbled, letting her know it was lunch time, but she didn't move. She sat in her prayer chair, waiting to hear more, but no more words came. She wanted certainty, but she'd have to act without it. She would have to decide how to finish the sentence for herself.

TWENTY-EIGHT

FRIDAY, MAY 7, 2004

Josh

Josh left his last class of the day. His stomach dropped when he saw Mom standing in the hallway. They made eye contact before he could glance away, so there was no pretending he didn't see her. A swirl of teens passed between them, most walking by without noticing his drama.

To avoid making a scene he walked close to her. Mom said gently, "Josh, I'd like to speak with you in private. Please, come to the car?"

He shook his head slowly and spoke quietly, "I don't know, Mom. Maybe we should wait for Dad. Or meet with Kyle? Kyle wants me to invite you to a session."

"Please, just hear what I have to say," she pleaded, looking desperate. "I'm not going to fight or try to convince you of anything. I have one thing I want to tell you. We can meet with Kyle later if you want."

Josh thought. He didn't want to be trapped, but if they didn't drive anywhere and he made sure he could get away it might be okay. He looked at her and nodded. Relief filled her face. They joined the rush of teens heading for their afternoons.

In the Land Cruiser, Josh kept his hand on the door latch. Mom sat in the driver's seat; she took a deep breath and then spoke. "I want you to come home."

Josh blurted out, "No, I'm n—"

Mom held up a hand. "Please, hear me out, and then I'll listen to you. I want you to come home. That's the most important thing. You can stay at Dublin High; you can go to whatever church you want; you can have whatever you want on your walls."

"Really?" Josh asked.

"Absolutely," she replied, and she looked like she meant it.

Josh asked, "You're okay with me being gay?"

A flash crossed her face. His heart skipped a beat. She wasn't okay with it. Why was he even listening to her?

She took a breath before she spoke. "I... It's not that simple, Josh." At least she was being honest. She continued, "But the bottom line is, I love you. And I want you at home."

"I don't know, Mom. It was tense there between us. Way tense."

"You have a track meet at DHS on Saturday morning, right?" she asked even though she already knew the answer to that question.

"Yes," he confirmed.

"It starts early so it will be easier to go from home. Come for the weekend—with Sara. You can go back to Berkeley on Sunday if it's... too tense."

If you are too intense, Josh thought. He didn't reply. Mom sat back in her seat and bit her lip like a desperate teenager in a movie. He waited, seeing if she could let him be for ten seconds. He counted one, two, three, four, up to twelve. She waited, keeping her mouth shut. It would be a hassle to take BART before the test in the morning.

"I'll think about it," Josh finally said.

Mom nodded. "Okay."

"I gotta go to practice."

"Okay. I love you, Josh. That was never in question."

"I love you, too, Mom." He teared up. "I never meant to cause you such trouble. I'm sorry. I didn't ask for this, you know."

"Oh, baby." Mom opened her arms. Josh hesitated, then leaned across the emergency break into an awkward hug. "I know you didn't."

Josh wiped his face before he left the car. Hope and sorrow played tug of war in his heart. He pulled out his phone and called Dad who picked up on the second ring.

"Hey Josh, what's up?" His words were casual, but his tone was alarmed.

"Mom just asked me to come home this weekend."

"You picked up?" Dad asked.

"She didn't call; she ambushed me at the end of last period. You didn't know?"

"No... that was her decision. I'm sorry."

Josh swallowed. Dad never apologized for Mom.

Dad continued, "You know she means well. It's all out of love, but she gets controlling when she is scared."

Josh nodded though his dad couldn't see him. "She said she won't push Valley Christian and I can go to any church I want. Do you think she can...?"

"I think she wants to be someone who can," Dad replied.

Josh laughed. What did that even mean?

"If I decide to come home can you drive me to Berkeley to get my stuff?" Josh asked.

"Absolutely," Dad said. "And no pressure from me. You stay wherever it's right for you. I want you safe, Josh, and I'm proud of how you are handling yourself."

Josh teared up. "Really, Dad?"

"I'm sorry if I haven't said it enough," Dad replied.

"Thanks..." Josh considered saying I love you. It was true, but they didn't say it out loud to each other. Not like with Mom.

"I love you, Josh," Dad said.

Josh's voice squeaked when he replied, "I love you, Dad."

He called Sara for her advice after they hung up, but she didn't pick up. He texted her CM ASAP. He ran to the locker room to get suited up. Sara didn't call back before it was time to be on the field. Sara would be afraid if he didn't pick up. He debated taking his phone, but Coach was adamant about no phones at practice.

He texted her again:

NVM. At practice. I'm OK.

He left his phone in his locker and joined his team.

After practice he looked at his screen. Nothing from Sara, but there was a text from Travis. He smiled. They'd been texting since camp. Travis wasn't converted either, but he'd kept that from his family, and his friends were still in the dark about his same-sex attractions.

Travis kept texting snippets about Voldemort from Harry Potter. It was enough to make Josh want to read the books.

He called Sara. She picked up on the first ring. "What's up?"

"Mom!" he replied. "She came to school to ask me to try coming home for the weekend."

"Whoa!"

"Yeah, what do you think I should do?"

"What do you want to do?"

"No offense to your floor, but I miss my bed," Josh said. "And BART every morning is getting old."

"I'll go with you. It can't hurt to try. You can text me even during dinner if she's driving you crazy. It'll be a test."

"Would you go to church with me or them on Sunday?"

"Whatever you want, Joshy," she replied.

He had the best sister, ever.

"Me, please. Dash from GSA goes there. The youth group is going to march in the Pride parade in San Francisco."

"OMG! Really?" she practically shouted.

He nodded and said, "Yeah."

"Oh, Josh. I'm happy for you. Can I come?"

"To the parade?"

"Yeah, if they allow straight allies."

Josh's mind spun and his heart soared. His sister wanted to be a straight ally. He didn't even know that she knew the term.

"Yeah," he replied. "They do."

"I'm so down for that. Dad might be, too!"

"You think so?"

"By the end of June?" she said. "Maybe even Mom will be."

They both laughed and said, "Nah!" in unison.

TWENTY-NINE
FRIDAY, MAY 7, 2004

Jenn

The phone rang as Jenn was arriving home. *Steve at work* showed on the screen.

"Josh called," Steve said. "I wish you'd talked to me first."

Annoyed, Jenn shot back, "I can't ask my son to come home without your consent?"

"You don't need my permission. I just want us to be on the same page."

"*Now* you want us to be on the same page?" Jenn retorted, starting to get angry.

"That's not fair, Jenn."

Humbled, she sighed, "I'm sorry. You're right. I should have called you first, but after my talk with Rinda, I was desperate... and totally clear. The only things that matter are that Josh knows I love him and that he belongs with us."

Jenn told Steve about her conversation with Rinda and about David's suicide.

After she finished, Steve replied, "Wow. That's sobering."

"We can't risk Josh's physical life."

Steve probed gently, "Can you let him be? Just as he is?"

"It'll be hard," Jenn admitted, "but I'll keep my hopes to myself. I'll pray for his transformation, but I won't ask anything of him. I know I can do that. I even told him he can go to any church he likes."

"Really?" Steve sounded pleased but skeptical.

"Yes. I'm serious. We need him home whatever the circumstances. Did he sound like he wanted to return?"

"I couldn't tell for certain. He asked me if I could drive him to Berkeley to get his stuff. It's a good sign that he's making a plan."

"Why didn't you tell me that?" Jenn got excited. "We can all go tonight. Maybe eat dinner out there."

"Don't jump the gun, Jenn, but yes, that's a good plan, if he agrees."

Jenn replied, "Call me if he gets in touch."

"You, too."

The minutes crept by. Jenn was desperate to hear from Josh, but she knew she had to wait for him to make the next contact. It took all her self-control not to reach out to him. Just before five her phone vibrated.

It was a text from Josh:

OK. I'll try.

Jenn squealed before she texted back:

great :)

Just after she hit send, the phone rang.

Steve's voice came through on her cell. "He wants to get his stuff tonight."

"He called you?" Jenn asked, knowing she sounded jealous and immature. She regretted her tone as the words came out of her mouth.

"Yes. Sorry, Jenn."

"Well, he texted me," she reassured herself. "That's something. And he's coming home. That's all that matters. Right? Did you make a plan?"

"I'll pick him up after track and then swing by for you and Rach. We'll go to Sara's, grab his stuff, and then eat out. He wants to go to the Smoked Cows or something like that."

"Anywhere is fine with me, so long as we're there as a family. Thank you, Lord Jesus," Jenn squealed.

"God is good," Steve agreed.

As soon as they hung up, Jenn went to the garage. She retrieved the cardboard tube from the corner and brought it up to Josh's room. Carefully she pulled out his posters and unrolled them. Her breath caught when she saw the image of Half Dome on the top. Jenn had missed it, too.

She left the posters rolled out on the bed, giving Josh the chance to make his own decisions about what to have on his walls.

She ran outside the moment she heard Steve pull up. When Josh climbed out of the driver's seat, her heart leaped at the sight of him. Without holding anything back, she rushed to give him a huge hug. After their embrace ended, she reached up to cup his face with both of her hands, and studied him, looking for changes. But there weren't any on the outside. She patted his cheek and then covered it with kisses, like when he was young. He scrunched his face and squirmed away, but she saw the smile on his face.

"I'm *so* glad you're home!" she exclaimed.

"Me too, Mom." Josh smiled at her.

. . .

Usually, Jenn hated being in Berkeley. The rules of the road were incomprehensible as far as she was concerned. The streets had too many bicyclists, were too narrow, and seemed to come and go randomly. Obviously, the city planning was haphazard. But today she was thrilled to be in Berkeley, like a child on Christmas morning, excited to get the best gift ever.

Steve was behind the wheel as they drove up Telegraph Ave. Rachel and Josh were in the back seat. She played it cool and didn't "make it weird" by turning around to talk to them. She stared out the window at the bustling street.

Clumps of grungy people sat on the sidewalk, leaning against buildings. It was nearly as bad as San Francisco. Sara was right: a lot of these homeless people were Josh's age. It was sad to imagine what circumstances brought them to this place in life. In the past she'd assumed they were from bad homes, but now she understood that some of them might be in Josh's situation or something similar. Jenn said a quick prayer for God to watch over them and keep them safe, and she thanked Lord Jesus that Josh wasn't one of them.

When Steve turned right on Durant, it suddenly looked like a college town. A swarm of young adults carrying backpacks and messenger bags hurried along the sidewalk like busy ants. As usual there wasn't a parking spot in front of Sara's dorm. Steve turned the corner onto College Ave and double-parked.

"I'll circle around while you get the stuff, okay?" he suggested to the kids.

"Sure," Josh said. He and Rachel opened their doors. "Are you coming, Mom?"

Jenn had imagined staying in the car, but if Josh wanted her, she would go with them. She smiled at Steve and squeezed his arm in affection.

They stood in front of Freeborn Hall, waiting for Sara to come down to let them in. Before she arrived, a student held the door open for them. Jenn had mixed feelings about that. It was polite but dangerous to let strangers into the building. She held back, but Josh didn't hesitate to enter and went straight to the elevator, knowing exactly where to go. Everything had seemed normal in the car. Now Jenn was reminded Josh had been living here for nearly two weeks.

He texted Sara while they rode up in the elevator. It was dirty, but thankfully it didn't smell like beer. Freeborn was Cal's substance-free residence hall. Jenn was grateful that Sara had chosen a "clean" environment, if not an entirely sanitary one.

Getting off the elevator, Josh turned right and led them through Sara's door. The room was empty. Sara must be looking for them. A minute later she popped in through the entryway.

"Mom! You haven't been here since you dropped me off in August," she said when she saw Jenn.

"That's not true. I've picked you up once or twice since then."

"You've never come up. Normally you just wait in the car."

Jenn thought about it. Her daughter was right. She hadn't realized Sara would track something like that. "Well, I'm glad to see your room now."

She looked around at the pictures and sayings on the wall. There were some she'd never seen before.

"I love this one," Jenn told her daughter, pointing to a sign she had just read. "Promise me you'll always remember: 'You're braver than you believe, and stronger than you seem, and smarter than you think.'—A. A. Milne."

"Maya gave it to me," Sara explained. "It's from *Winnie-the-Pooh*."

It hit Jenn that she'd only met Maya on the day she dropped Sara off at Cal. "You two are pretty close, huh?"

Sara nodded. "She's a great roommate. She was so chill with Josh staying with us. You know we put in to room together next year."

Jenn realized she owed a debt to Maya, too. "You got lucky."

"I like to think God was watching out for both of us."

Jenn smiled at her daughter.

"Let's go," Josh said.

"Smokehouse, here we come!" Sara said.

"Does Maya want to join us?" Jenn offered.

"Nah. She left for dinner already. Besides, we need some family time. In fact, group hug before we leave."

Sara spread her arms wide and beckoned with her hands. Rachel fell into place under Sara's right arm. Josh got a look on his face that said, "I'll humor you, sister," and put his arm over Sara's left shoulder. He lifted his left arm, and Jenn slipped under it, wrapping her arms around Josh and Rachel. She hugged her three kids close.

Sara spoke. "Lord, we thank You for this time together. Thank You for opening our hearts that we may receive Your love, Your truth, and Your will. Amen."

"Amen," echoed from Josh and Rachel. Jenn's throat was too full to speak, so she mouthed the word.

The Smokehouse was so old it didn't have a bathroom, but being in Berkeley, it did have veggie burgers. It was like something out of a 1950s movie. It couldn't even be called a restaurant—more like a hamburger stand with pseudo tin walls and a cement floor. It felt like you were outside even when you were under the metal roof. Half the tables were in the open air next to a patch of grass. It was sort of like the old McDonald's restaurants that were still around when Jenn was a child.

"Can we sit outside?" Sara asked.

The rest of the family nodded and pushed their way through the glass door. They settled on a picnic table with benches. Josh and Sara sat on one side, and Rachel squeezed in between Jenn and Steve. The table was shiny with new brown paint, but Jenn saw carvings in the wood. She ran her finger across some of the letters.

"Penny from heaven!" Josh said, pointing to the ground.

Jenn saw a shiny coin under the next table.

Rachel said, "Pick it up, Josh."

Josh shook his head. "Nah, God left that one for Mom."

Jenn smiled and picked up the penny. It was from 1988— the year Josh was born. She showed it to him.

"Best year ever!" Josh said.

"Uh-uh," Rachel and Sara disagreed in unison when they saw the date. Steve and Jenn laughed.

Three kids were running around on the grass. One of them ran up to the nearby adults and said something too quietly for Jenn to hear. The man nodded. The child said, "Hooray!" and jumped up and down in delight. She ran back to the grass and told the other kids the good news.

The adults lined up on the grass with two of the kids. The "mother" stood on the other side of the lawn.

She said, "Nico, you may take three jumps forward."

"Mother, may I?"

"No, you may not!" The girl laughed.

Nico growled at her.

"Just kidding. Yes, you may."

The boy named Nico bent his knees and took one big jump. Then he steadied himself and took another big jump. He was making the most of his three jumps. On the third jump, he lost his balance and put his right foot out so he wouldn't fall down. The "mother" gave him a scolding look. He brought his legs back together and stood at attention. She scrunched her face, giving something careful thought, and then looked away from him and back to the line of those waiting.

The "mother" said, "Julia, you may take two giant leaps forward."

Rachel leaned against Jenn. "I used to love Mother, May I!"

"That was a lifetime ago, huh?" Jenn said. She looked at Josh watching the kids. "You were more of a Red Light, Green Light guy, weren't you?"

"I was awesome. Best on the block, if I do say so myself." He grinned at her.

Jenn realized how right this felt. After weeks, months, of struggle, it felt normal to be together. She took Steve's hand, kissed the top of Rachel's head, and smiled over at Josh.

Sara got up and walked inside. Jenn saw her head over to a tall counter but couldn't tell what she was doing. She returned in a minute with napkins, straws, and ketchup.

"Food's up," Sara told Steve. They went inside to get it.

Jenn was struck by her oldest child's maturity. It made her proud and sad all at once. She enjoyed sitting here and letting her daughter take care of things, but it felt bittersweet. It was trite but true: her kids were growing up too fast.

At her core Jenn was still afraid for Josh, but she was going to keep her worries to herself. Jenn wasn't assured that homosexuality and salvation were compatible, but Rinda had convinced Jenn that she needed to be much more patient and loving. Taking a hard line with Josh would only drive him away. Jenn held the penny tight and vowed to keep praying for his salvation and transformation. She hadn't given up faith but was going to be gracious and indirect. That was the most righteous path to walk in this complex, heartbreaking situation.

THIRTY

SATURDAY, MAY 8, 2004

Jenn

Josh let Jenn drive to the meet on Saturday morning. He came home in a good mood because he'd done well. Rachel needed some attention, so Jenn made her favorite for dinner: tacos. She sang as she cooked. Everything felt right now that her family was together again. She was proud of herself for not asking him about how the SAT went last week. He'd only perceive it as intrusive.

Over dinner they made plans for Sunday. Jenn was jerked back to the reality of her situation when Josh said, "Sara and I are going to my church, but we can meet you for lunch after."

All four of them looked at her, anticipating her negative response. Jenn took a deep breath to steady her nerves. This was a test. Not trusting herself to speak, she gave a little smile and nodded. He'd said "my" like he belonged at First Congregational. One visit and it was suddenly his church.

"We can take your car, right, Dad?" Sara said.

Jenn literally bit her tongue. She glanced at Steve. He gave a small nod. Did he already know about this plan? He didn't look surprised or upset.

"That's fine," Jenn squeaked out, though in her heart it was anything but. *Josh is home. That's what matters most.*

"Can I go with them, too, Mom?" Rachel looked excited. "I've never been to any other church. I want to see what it's like. Please?"

Once again, all eyes gazed at her. Jenn closed her lids and nodded slowly. She slid her chair back and quietly said, "I'll be right back."

She walked into the bathroom, and as soon as the door closed, she burst into tears. She bit her hand so they couldn't hear her, the tears coming hard and fast. Somehow this day had lulled her into thinking she had her life back. The idea of walking into church on Sunday with none of her children was utterly humiliating. It would be one of the biggest disappointments of her life... and she had to pretend with her family that she didn't care at all.

When she stopped crying, she washed her face, wiped the mascara from under her eyes, and went back out—acting as if she was carefree. She appreciated her family pretending she was just fine, though they all knew the truth.

Jenn felt ill as she got ready on Sunday morning, but she hid it. She prepared breakfast for everyone and made appropriate small talk over the meal. They agreed to meet at noon at the Copper Skillet for lunch. She hugged each of her kids goodbye before they left for church without her.

Steve gave her a wordless embrace. He kissed the top of her head and said, "You're doing good. I know it's hard, but you're doing it. Ready?"

She grabbed her purse and let him drive her to church. She dreaded walking into the sanctuary and hoped they could avoid the people they knew best, but just as they pulled up, Lindsay and her family were getting out of their car.

"Just you two this morning?" Lindsay inquired.

Jenn's mind raced to find a response that was a slanted truth. When she found it, she replied as casually as she could muster, "The kids decided to worship elsewhere today. They're taking an interest in broadening their understanding of Christ."

"Oh, I'm sorry, honey," Lindsay said, taking in the news. She looked visibly shaken and full of empathy. "We would never allow that."

Jenn forced a tight smile and walked away. She thought to herself, *Yeah. That's what I used to think, too. Well, sometimes your kids stop letting you decide everything. I can't wait until it happens to you.*

Jenn knew she was being immature, but it felt good. She held her head high as she and Steve entered the sanctuary.

Sunday night Sara took BART back to Berkeley. Jenn must have passed the test, because Josh didn't go with her. She opened a bottle of white wine for a personal celebration, but she kept her joy to herself, acting as if it were perfectly normal to have Josh in the house. And she knew *much* better than to bring up treatment, but internally she vowed to continue praying for Josh's complete recovery.

"Mom, Pastor James is on the phone for you," Rachel yelled from the family room.

Jenn sighed as she picked up the extension. Before she greeted him, she took a deep breath to calm her nerves. She didn't want to have this conversation.

The pastor started talking as soon as she spoke. "We've noticed that Josh is no longer attending church or youth group. We're so worried about him."

"Thank you for calling, Pastor. I've been meaning to make

an appointment with you. I just—well, it's been so hard. As you know, Josh is struggling with a big issue." Jenn attempted to find the right words. "He, um, feels as if our congregation isn't right for him at this point in his life."

Jenn waited for a reply. The line was silent.

"Are you there?" she asked.

Pastor James cleared his throat and asked, "You and Steve support his decision?"

Jenn chose her words carefully. "*Support* is too strong of a word. We've prayed on this, a lot. *Accept* is more like it."

"You've given up on his salvation?" Pastor James questioned.

"No." Jenn shook her head. "Not at all. I pray for his full recovery every night and every morning. It's just, well, we've learned that many teens in his situation succeed in committing suicide. We don't want to put too much pressure on him."

"Do you understand that spiritual suicide is eternal?" he asked.

Jenn stammered, "I... We've decided that what's most important is that Josh feels loved and supported by his family."

"Don't you know that's how you got into this situation?"

"Excuse me?" Jenn felt attacked.

"You showered him with too much maternal affection," the pastor lectured. "That's why he has these homosexual feelings. You read the materials I gave you, didn't you?"

Jenn felt heat rise in her face. "Yes. I read everything," she said, in a voice that came out calmer than she felt. "We followed your recommendations. You know he went to camp. We appreciate your support—we do—and I pray Josh will return to treatment again. But for now... Well, I've come to accept that this is the best we can do for the time being. He's home, and he's safe. That's enough for me."

"It doesn't matter what's enough for you, Jennifer... It only matters what's enough for God."

Jenn was at a loss for words. She wanted to be respectful to her pastor, but he wasn't a parent, and he couldn't understand the situation. If she'd learned nothing else from this, she had learned that she couldn't control her children. But rather than argue with Pastor James or defend their decision, she replied, "I'll keep that in mind. Thank you for your concern and your support. I'll let Josh know you asked about him. I'm sure that will mean a lot to him. I'll see you at the welcome-team meeting on Thursday."

"I'm glad you raised that," Pastor James replied. "We've decided to go in a different direction with the team and won't be needing your leadership any longer. Why don't you plan on this meeting being your last. Okay?"

Jenn's stomach lurched. "What? You don't need me to be the chair?"

"We want to make room for new energy, so we won't need you on the team at all. But thank you for your service," the pastor informed her matter-of-factly.

"You're pushing me out... because of Josh?" Jenn asked, anger and indignation coming through in her voice.

"Jenn, there's no need to overreact," he admonished her. "It's just not the right ministry for you anymore. I hope you understand."

"No, I don't understand." Jenn had a sickening thought. "Are you asking our family to leave the church?"

"My goodness, Jenn, no!" Pastor James sounded shocked. "You are taking this too far. I am not asking you to resign your membership in the church—only your leadership on the welcome team. My deepest desire is that you and your whole family will be back in the right relationship with our Lord and Savior before too long."

Somehow Jenn managed to get off the phone. She was so stunned by the end of the conversation that it all became a blur. She'd never imagined her pastor would reject her leadership, but then she wouldn't have believed before this that Lindsay would end their friendship, either.

Betrayals from the people she trusted to love and support her cut deep, but she realized she was getting just a small taste of what Josh was experiencing. After the conversation with Pastor James, she was absolutely certain she'd made the right choice to bring Josh home—to not be one of the people rejecting him. She would stay steadfast by his side, even if she didn't agree with his choice to give up on his salvation.

Jenn found Josh in the family room working at the computer. Tenderness filled her throat.

He turned around. "What?"

"Josh." Jenn cleared her throat. "I'm sorry that I did anything to make you feel that I didn't love you."

Casually, he replied, "It's okay, Mom."

"No, Josh, it isn't. I was just so scared... am so scared. But that doesn't excuse my behavior. I am sorry." Her eyeballs started to burn. She blinked to calm them. "And I promise I'll do better."

"Thanks." Josh offered a tender smile and turned back to the machine.

Jenn hoped her words were a small consolation for the past few months, but she had a lot to make up for.

Blessedly, the family fell back into a comfortable rhythm. Sara moved back home full-time after her last final on May 21. She found a babysitting job nearby to earn spending money for the year and registered for a class in the late-summer session so the family could go on their annual family trip to Southern California in July.

Over dinner they made plans. Excited, Jenn shared an idea: "I was thinking of getting two-day park-hopper tickets. There's just too much there now to do Disneyland in one day."

"Yes!" Rachel exclaimed. "California Adventure, here we come."

"And Manhattan Beach," Josh chimed in.

"Are we doing the split thing? Half at Nana and Poppy's and half at Grandpa and Grandma's?" Sara asked.

Jenn's chest squeezed tight. She looked at Steve. He took a big breath. "Well... we aren't going to stay at Grandma and Grandpa's on this trip."

"Why?" Rachel asked.

Steve stuttered, "I haven't wanted... It's hard. I can't believe it, but they don't..." He looked at Jenn, obviously afraid to go on.

"They're old," Jenn said carefully. "They're set in their ways. It's harder for them to accept Josh..."

Jenn saw Josh's head drop to his chest, and he squeezed his eyes shut tight. Her heart hurt for him.

"That is so messed up!" Rachel said.

"Well, I never liked staying there," Sara declared. "Sorry, Dad. No offense."

Steve replied, "None taken."

"You can see them without me," Josh said quietly.

"No." Steve shook his head. "I'm not giving them that. All of us or none of us."

"They're being stupid, Josh," Rachel said.

"Rachel!" Jenn admonished. "They're still your grand-parents."

"Well, they are," she insisted.

Sara chimed in. "It's their loss!"

"It sure is," Jenn agreed.

Jenn no longer avoided being alone with Josh, so she drove for the last track meets of the year. She felt protective of her son but didn't see anyone treating him rudely; maybe they didn't know about him. Or they knew and didn't care. Either way, she was glad to be around the banter and energy of the boys again.

For the last meet of the year, Steve left work early to cheer him on at Skyline High in Oakland. Sitting on the bleachers on a warm May day, Jenn pulled out her camera. She focused on Josh. He burst out laughing, and then threw an orange peel at Grant. She clicked the shutter and then looked at the image on the screen. She showed it to Steve.

"He looks happy, doesn't he?" Jenn asked. "Like before he was..." It was still hard to say the word homosexual out loud. Then Jenn corrected herself, "I mean, before we... knew." Jenn shrugged and looked at her husband.

Steve rubbed her back and smiled. "He does look good."

"It's for the best that we know, isn't it?" she asked.

Steve agreed. "The secret was killing him. He was afraid he'd lose everything."

"I'm glad we know. Truly I am." Then she said tentatively, "*And* I still pray for his recovery."

"I know you do. Thank you for doing it, and for not letting Josh know."

Jenn asked, "Do you still pray for him?"

"Of course."

"That he's cured?"

The track coach interrupted them.

"Hi, Jenn," he greeted her, then asked Steve, "Are you Josh's dad?" The slight man with brown hair reached his hand out. "I'm Coach Bell."

"Steve Henderson." Her husband shook his hand.

"Josh is a great team member. He's very encouraging of the freshmen, which I can't say about all the juniors. I'm glad to have him for another year."

"Thanks," Jenn and Steve said in unison.

"I know he had a rough patch last month. I was glad to hear that he's back at home."

Jenn's heart beat hard and fast. The coach knew Josh had left home? What else did he know? She dug her nails into her palm, but kept quiet until they stopped talking about the team and the coach walked away.

"Does everyone know?!"

"The teachers and staff at Dublin High have been a great support to him. I know it's hard to hear, but we should be grateful."

Jenn sighed. "It's so humiliating to know people are talking about us."

She leaned against her husband. Steve kissed the top of her head. She *was* grateful. Grateful Josh was alive and enjoying himself on this beautiful day, and grateful that she and Steve seemed to have made it through this crisis. She just wanted to stop blundering into uncomfortable situations that caused bubbles of shame to burst in her.

God grant me serenity.

The last few weeks of Dublin High were filled with papers, and finals for Josh and Rachel. Ordinary life was a blessing after those hard and divisive months. Slowly Jenn grew to trust the new equilibrium in their family.

Then two days into summer break Steve pulled her into their room.

"What?" Jenn asked suspiciously. Dread bubbled up.

"Sit. You're not going to like this," he told her.

Jenn sat. "What now?"

"Josh asked me to march with him in the pride parade in SF."

Jenn stared hard at him. She wanted to scream. Instead of doing it out loud, she closed her eyes and yelled inside her own head. It actually helped.

Lord, give me patience, she prayed silently. Then out loud she calmly said, "What did you say?"

"I told him, 'Thanks for the invitation. I need to think about it.'"

"He didn't ask your permission, did he? He just told you he was doing it."

Steve nodded.

"Don't you think he *needs* our permission to do this?" she challenged Steve.

"Jenn, I don't think that's what's actually at issue here."

"What *is* at issue?" she demanded.

"He wants our love and support."

"He has my love. I don't support his homosexuality," Jenn whispered as loud as she could. "It's all I can do to keep quiet about it. And now he wants us to literally march in a parade. He's asking for too much." Jenn looked at Steve. "You're going to say no, right?" she asked.

"I haven't decided."

Jenn bit her lip. She didn't want to say something she would later regret. Her brain pulsed with white noise. Finally, she said, "I hope we can agree that marching in a parade is beyond what we're willing to do to accommodate him. Far beyond." She felt good about her calm demeanor.

"The girls are planning to march with him," Steve told her.

"What!" Jenn shrieked before she could stop herself. "He asked them, too? And they said yes?"

Steve nodded. Jenn rubbed her eyes. "Aren't we going to forbid that? Rachel's a child."

Steve replied, "I certainly don't want Rachel going without a parent."

Jenn was incredulous. "You are seriously considering going to that parade and taking your fourteen-year-old daughter? I don't know you."

"Do you want to know me? Or do you want to be so certain you're right that you lose all of us?" Steve shouted at Jenn. "He's my son! He's their brother! I would take a bullet for Josh. I'd cut off my arm for him. I'd do anything for him. So why not this?"

Steve stormed out. Jenn was left alone, stunned and hurt. She would take a bullet for Josh, too. Didn't Steve know that? That was why she was fighting this hard for his soul.

The Monday before the parade, Jenn found an envelope with her name on the kitchen table when she went to make breakfast. Her fingers shook as she opened it.

June 21

Mom,
I guess you know about the pride parade on Sunday. We're gonna leave at nine and march with the PFLAG (Parents and Friends of Lesbians and Gays) and the church. You can come if you want, but no pressure, okay?

Love,
Josh

No pressure. What a joke. She flipped on Fox News. While she cooked, she stewed inside. Obviously, *we* meant her whole family. They were going to this parade without her. Jenn had already bent as far as she possibly could. She was being tolerant and respectful and giving Josh so much leeway, but she couldn't celebrate in public.

She decided to write back rather than speak to him. She considered *Have fun without me* or *Are you crazy?* or *I have other plans* or *Thanks, but no, thanks.* She finally settled on.

Josh,

Thanks for the invitation. It's not for me.

Love,
Mom

    She crossed out her name on the envelope, wrote Josh's instead, and slipped it under his bedroom door. She took a shower and used the opportunity to have a good cry.

THIRTY-ONE

SUNDAY, JUNE 27, 2004

Jenn

The day of the parade, Jenn forced herself to get up and make breakfast. She prepared everyone's favorites: eggs for Steve, smoothies for Sara and Josh, and white toast with jam for Rachel. She was too nauseated to eat, so she didn't make anything for herself.

They came down dressed in shorts, T-shirts, and hoodies. The weather report said it would be a rare warm day in San Francisco, so she didn't send them back upstairs to put on long pants. They all sat down, and Josh reached out his hand for a prayer. Jenn's breath caught. She held Sara's hand on the right and Rachel's on the left.

"Dear God, in the name of Jesus, our Lord and Savior, we pray. Holy Spirit, fill us with love, light, and protection as we journey on this day. God, please watch over my mother"—Josh's voice caught— "and protect her heart. Amen."

Jenn felt small squeezes on her hands. "Amen" came in a chorus from her family. They released hands. Jenn gave Josh a small sad smile. She appreciated his care, but it also felt patronizing.

Rachel asked, "Is there any more smoothie?"

"You want some?" Jenn was surprised.

"It's going to be a long day. I need protein," Rachel explained.

"Protein gives you energy," Jenn agreed with a tight smile. "Smoothie coming right up."

They ate quickly and then rushed out the door. Jenn mustered the grace to hug them each goodbye.

Steve whispered in her ear, "I know this is very hard for you. I love you."

"I love you, too," Jenn whispered back. "I keep telling myself it could be worse. He could be dead."

Steve hugged her tight and then left.

Jenn washed the dishes and walked out to the garage to go to church. She sat in the car surrounded by so many things: outgrown bicycles, scooters, helmets, sports equipment. They hadn't needed some of this stuff for years. She rested her head back and closed her eyes, imagining her family getting on the BART train, joining a sea of humanity without her.

She turned the ignition on and pressed the garage door opener. The bright light stung her eyes. Jenn couldn't face the morning. She pushed the button to shut out the world, and then turned off the ignition and reclined her seat. Utterly exhausted, she didn't even have the energy to go back in the house. She'd rest right here in the dark, quiet garage.

She dozed off. When she woke up in the car, she was sweaty and disoriented. Then it all came rushing in. Her mind reeled, and she felt stuck. She longed for the comfort of prayer, though it had been hard to hear God's voice lately.

"God," Jenn said, welling up with emotion, "help me know what to do to protect my family. You know they're going to San Francisco and why. Show me what You want me to do. Holy Spirit, bind up any distractions so that I may hear Your will clearly. In Jesus's name I pray."

And then she listened. She focused on the question *What is Your will for me?* again and again. She slowed her breathing and kept her mind open. She listened carefully with all of her being for the voice of God. Clear as a bell, she heard, *Love My children.* Her heart filled with those words. A chill ran down her back. She felt full and tingling all over.

Love My children! Jenn was stunned. God had told her those exact same words last February. *His* message hadn't changed, but today she heard it entirely differently.

God had been sending her this clear and simple insight for months, but she'd been too stubborn to listen. She'd ignored all the markers He'd put in her way because she'd been certain she already knew His plan.

Maya, Kyle, Sara, Josh—they'd all been telling her God loved Josh. She knew Lord Jesus wanted more love in the world. Rather than judge, she was meant to love her son.

Jenn felt energy from the Holy Spirit surge through her body. She basked in the warm tingle. Then an overwhelming and intense need to be with her family overcame her. She was bursting to share her new understanding with Josh right now. She had to tell *all* of them that she had finally got the message: God loves Josh, just as he is!

"Thank you, God, for Your guidance today and all days. In the name of Jesus Christ, I pray."

Jenn turned on the ignition, opened the garage door, and drove into the bright morning. Everything had changed. She was going to show the depth of her transformation somewhere that she never expected. At the BART station she got a round-trip ticket to Powell. Jenn had no idea where her family was, but she needed to find them because she belonged with them.

After she was seated on the train, she texted Josh, Steve, and Sara:

I'm coming. Where r u?

She imagined their surprise and joy when they saw her message. Their faces would light up.

The car was nearly empty in Dublin, but at each stop people got on. She watched them out of the corner of her eyes, not wanting to be rude. Most were decked out in something festive. Mardi Gras beads, colorful hats, and rainbow paraphernalia were everywhere. People looked like they were going to a festival. Many of the women and some of the men wore sparkly fabric. Some couples had matching T-shirts. As they pulled out of the San Leandro station, a young man dressed in tight gold lamé shorts and a rainbow tank loomed over her from the aisle. He caught her glancing at his getup. She blushed and gave him a tight smile.

"It's okay," he said with a huge grin. Swishing his hips from side to side and waving his arms, he said, "Look all you want. I'm here to be seen today."

She was suddenly self-conscious about her clothes. She sure didn't look like she belonged here. Jenn was dressed for church, in a lavender linen shift and white patent-leather flats, not for a parade. Especially not *this* parade.

Leaning in close, the man said, "Love your necklace."

Jenn put her hand to the cross at her neck. Heat rose in her cheeks. He was making fun of her! She wanted to hide, but there was nowhere to go.

He put his hand under his shirt and pulled out a simple silver cross. "My Grammy gave it to me when I graduated high school. She told me to keep Jesus close wherever I go. Her wise words have steered me well over the years. Not everybody understands."

He nodded toward the crowd on the train, shrugged with a smile, tucked the cross back under his shirt, and then turned around to chat with his friends and other revelers on the train.

Touched by the interaction, Jenn reeled. Rather than taunting her, he was showing her that they shared something in common. He was bold as well as sweet and innocent. God had given her a sign that she was on the right path. Jenn smiled to herself—and checked her cell phone again. Nothing from her family.

By the time the train left West Oakland, the car was packed tight. Jenn felt a little panicky but took deep, slow breaths to calm her nerves. She reminded herself that, in a few minutes, she'd be off the train and away from the crowd. And that she was safe right there in her seat.

She checked her phone: still no reply. Many people got off at Embarcadero, but even more got on. Finally, they reached Powell. The crowd pushed toward the door. Nearly everyone wanted to get off here. She waited until the car was almost empty, and then she stood up. As she exited the train, she was shaky but determined.

After she stepped off the escalator on Market Street she was carried along by a mass of people. She'd never, ever been in a crowd like this. She'd had no idea so many people came to this parade. Forcing her way to the edge, she stepped out of the stream of people to stand in front of a drugstore. Jenn looked around, afraid and uncertain where to go. How would she find her family?

"Are you lost, honey?"

A very tall person with dark skin, shimmering clothes, and a lot of makeup was looking at Jenn with concern. Jenn suspected it was a man under that tall wig.

She blinked back tears. "I'm trying to find my family."

"Oh, bless your heart. I feel so bad for the tourists who don't know what they're getting themselves into today."

"I'm not a tourist," Jenn explained. "I'm here for the parade."

Dramatically arched eyebrows and pursed lips showed astonishment on the stranger's face. "You are?"

"My family is marching... with PFLAG and a church. They left without me. Well... I didn't go with them, but suddenly I didn't want to be left out. So here I am. And they don't know I'm here," Jenn explained, surprised to be blurting this out to a stranger.

"Want to use my cell, honey?"

Jenn pulled out her phone and said quietly, "No one replied."

"Services gets overwhelmed here with so many people and such tall buildings. Well, then we just have to get you to the front so you can jump right in with them when they get here. "On this day I'm all Oh-Rinda." She stuck out a large hand.

"I'm Jenn. Thank you." Gratitude for the help overrode her surprise that she was grabbing the hand of this transvestite.

"I'm here to serve," Oh-Rinda declared.

Oh-Rinda kept Jenn's hand, walked down the sidewalk for a few yards, and then pushed her way into the crowd. It was two or three people deep, but somehow Oh-Rinda got them to the curb, close to a corner.

"Here you are, dear," she said. "This is a great view. You won't miss 'em. They'll be coming from down there." She pointed east.

"Thanks." Jenn responded, grateful and bewildered by this rescue.

"Who's your family marching for?" Oh-Rinda asked.

"My son, Josh." Jenn welled up. "He's... Josh..." Jenn's throat was tight. Then she blurted out, "Josh is homosexual."

"Your son?" Oh-Rinda looked surprised. "You don't look hardly old enough to have a grown son!"

"Josh is sixteen."

"Oh, bless his heart! It takes a lot of courage to come out that young. Good for you for raising him right—strong and proud. Bless you all, dear."

"God bless you," Jenn replied back.

"He already has!" Oh-Rinda said over her shoulder as she disappeared back into the crowd.

Raised him right? Because he was brave enough to be homosexual? That was a totally foreign idea—and yet a wonderful thing to hear, even from an unconventional stranger.

Jenn took in the scene. Marchers filled Market Street. The road and sidewalk were packed with people as far as the eye could see. Jenn looked west, but she couldn't see the front of the parade. It must have been going on for a while. Maybe her family had already passed by, and she'd missed her chance to join them.

"Excuse me," she said to the tall man standing next to her. "Has PFLAG gone past yet?"

"Nope." He shook his bald head, which was covered in rainbow sparkles.

Good. She hadn't missed them. She looked at her phone again. Nothing.

When she looked up from her cell a break in the parade left the road empty. Jenn got a good look at the people across from her. The other side of the street was lined with women with strollers interspersed between. One stroller had a sign that said *I Love My Two Mommies.* Another was decked out with a sign that said *I Was Hatched by a Couple of Chicks.* The children looked at their parents and pointed to make sure they were seeing the same thing. It reminded Jenn of being at the electric light parade at Disneyland. There was such love and connection in the simple act of witnessing together. She wished she had her camera to capture the simple and complicated beauty of these unique human faces.

"Did you get it?" Jenn heard the man next to her ask. She

turned her head. He was talking to a boy who was maybe ten. The boy, accompanied by another man, held up three glow-in-the-dark necklaces with a big grin. They ripped open the packages and put the glowing tubes around their necks.

Love My children. Clear as a bell, Jenn heard God speak to her. *All My children.* She felt the Holy Spirit burst into her heart and move in her spine. *I have set My rainbow in the clouds, and it will be the sign of the covenant between Me and the earth.* Tears sprang to her eyes. She knew. Suddenly she just knew that all these people—each and every one of them in this crowd, the old and the young, the homosexual and the heterosexual, the whole human family—were God's children. God loved them, and Jesus died for them. All of them. At last, her soul surrendered completely to this truth.

All these months she'd been sure it was Josh who needed to be transformed by the Holy Spirit, but she'd been the one being tone-deaf to God's calling.

Jenn heard the crowd down the street cheer. The man nudged her and pointed. Half a block away, a large PFLAG banner rose up high above the parade.

"Why is everyone cheering?" Jenn asked.

"PFLAG! It means so much..." he said, his voice cracking. He cleared his throat. "It means so much to have your family with you in this. It's, you know... what we all dream of... our parents being proud of us."

Jenn nodded wordlessly and smiled. As the banner came closer and closer, tears streamed down her face. She searched for her family, quickly scanning each face. There were so many people, and the street was very wide. She didn't see them. Then she saw a flash of purple. Jenn got on her tiptoes. Yes! Rachel's purple hoodie. Her family was right here, and she belonged with them.

Thank you, God, for this gift of transformation. She breathed in the Holy Spirit and stepped out into the stream of life.

THIRTY-TWO

MONDAY, AUGUST 22, 2005 – FOURTEEN MONTHS LATER

Jenn

Jenn woke up early to make breakfast. It wasn't Saturday, but she was making Grandma Mary Alice's pancakes because it would be four months before the five of them would eat them together again. Teary but not fighting it, she didn't flip on the news because she didn't want a distraction. It was only right to be emotional when your beloved child was leaving home.

She yelled up the stairs, "Breakfast!"

After everyone was seated, Rachel asked, "Can I say the prayer?"

Jenn nodded.

"Dear God, in Your name we pray. Thank You for this food and all Your gifts that sustain our lives. Watch over my brother, Josh, as he makes his way to the big, bad city."

"Rachel!" Steve said.

Rachel laughed. "Just kidding, God, watch over Josh in New York City. Keep him safe in his travels and give him a great roommate. In Jesus's name we pray. Amen."

"Amen," they all repeated.

. . .

Before Jenn knew it, they were outside security at SFO. Since 9/11 they couldn't go to the gate without a ticket, so they said their goodbyes to Josh right here. This was his first time flying alone. Jenn was scared for him—and excited, too. Their son was ready for this challenge.

"Go right to the gate. Don't rush, but you want to be there when they start boarding. Make sure it says JFK," Steve instructed.

"I'll be fine," Josh assured them. "I can always text if I have any problems."

Josh hugged Rachel, Sara, and Steve. Finally, it was Jenn's turn to say goodbye to her precious son. They wrapped their arms around each other and squeezed tight. Josh blinked as he pulled away.

He walked up to the TSA agent with his driver's license and boarding pass in hand. He made it through the checkpoint and got into the long, twisting line. Steve put his arm around Jenn. She reached for Rachel. Sara joined on at the end. They stood in a row watching as Josh's head moved in and out of sight. Jenn saw him put his bag on the conveyor belt. He stopped before the scanner and then disappeared. Jenn got on her toes. She couldn't find him.

She scanned the crowd. Out of the corner of her eye, she saw Sara wave. Jenn followed Sara's gaze. There he was, looking at them with his bag on his shoulder and his shoes on his feet. He'd made it through without her. Josh waved at them. She waved back. Then he turned away and melted into the crowd, his brown hair bobbing amongst those around him like a leaf floating away down a river.

They stood there in silence, none of them wanting this to be over. But eventually Rachel broke away. They started to walk back to the car.

"Should we stay until his plane takes off? Just in case," Sara asked.

"Sure," Steve said. "We can wait at Peet's."

Sitting at the café, Jenn sent Josh a text:

Text me when u land

Will do

A few minutes later, Jenn's phone vibrated again.

I love u

I know.

Proud of you.

I know.

A LETTER FROM THE AUTHOR

Dear Readers,

Thank you for reading my story about the Henderson family. It's been a joy and challenge to revisit them nearly 10 years after I first wrote about them in the novel *Living Right*. This revised version includes Sara and Josh as point-of-view characters—something I considered doing from the start. I'm grateful for the opportunity to put their experiences more firmly in the heart of the story.

If you'd like to join other readers in keeping in touch, here are two options. Stay in the loop with my new releases by clicking on the link below. Or sign up to my personal email newsletter at my website. The link is below. I'd be delighted if you choose to sign up to either—or both! There won't be many emails.

If you were gripped by *After the Rain* and you'd like to stay in touch to hear more about my new releases with Storm, you can click on the link here:

www.stormpublishing.co/laila-ibrahim

If you enjoyed *After the Rain* and could spare a few moments to leave a review that would be hugely appreciated. Even a short review can make all the difference in encouraging a reader to discover my books for the first time. Thank you so much!

I was inspired to write this book after seeing protesters at a marriage equality rally in the late 1990s. I was struck by the group of teens and parents taking the time to stand up for their highest values. I'm imagined they were there in service of saving lives. Ironically I was also there with my wife and children, on the opposite side, standing up for my highest values, wanting to save lives emotionally and physically.

At that rally in San Francisco I didn't want to argue with anyone, but I did wish I had a way to open their minds and hearts to the possible harm they were doing. I'd wished I had a piece of paper that said, "What if you are condemning your own brother, cousin, nephew, or child? We are all gifts from God. Gay teens are four times more likely to attempt suicide than their straight peers."

In 2014 when I was considering a second novel, I remembered that moment and this story unfolded. I appreciated the opportunity to consider this issue from an entirely different point of view than my own. It allowed me to broaden my mind and grow respect for a culture that I had been taught to disrespect. I had to do for Jenn and her family the exact same thing I want someone like her to do for me.

Before I wrote this novel I believed conversion therapy was something that was done to teens and young adults by their parents. In my mind the teens were the victims of ignorant and bigoted parents. I hadn't considered the emotional and spiritual damage that was being done to parents by their very own churches, the institution they rely on for moral leadership.

Since then I've learned:

- Many of the leaders of the conversion therapy movement were and are LGBT people pretending they had been cured because they were so desperate for that to be true.

- Some parents are/were being told by their ministers —trusted authorities in their lives—that it's their fault their children have same-sex attractions.
- Many of the teens go to conversion therapy voluntarily, desperately believing in and praying for a cure.

Like most things there's a range of feeling depending on the situation. I had expected only to hear stories of anger towards parents. There certainly are many people who have just walked away from a relation with parents altogether.

I hadn't expected to talk to people who felt protective of their parents, but it makes sense. Many of the people I've talked to about it have very complex and convoluted feelings about their adolescent coming out experiences. Their parents did very hurtful things to them, when they were in a very vulnerable place, but they understand that their parents were doing it out of love. If they've worked through the issues and the parents have come to a place of acceptance, the parents feel very guilty. The LGBT person wants to both be honest about the pain, while being reassuring and connected to their parents now. It's an emotionally complicated situation.

There's a scene in my novel where Jenn explains that Josh, her son, is depressed because he has same-sex attractions. She is adamant that his depression will go away once he's been transformed. Since transformation requires faith, she can't allow herself to doubt. In her mind, her son's life depends on her faith. It's not my theology, but she fully believes it in that moment. The challenge for me as a writer was to take this character on an honest emotional and spiritual journey from that belief to a place where she could listen to God for herself and put love over "law".

Updating this book in 2024 has been an interesting process. Queer rights have come so far and yet are still up for debate in too many places. Like all of my novels I have to carefully consider the language I use to write authentic and honest stories about systemic oppression without being insensitive. For this one I thought long and hard about using the f-word and the word *transvestite*.

I chose to use the f-word because it was terribly common at that time, and it was particularly heartbreaking that Jenn is entirely unaware that she was hurting her son with her ignorance. Likewise I describe Oh-Rinda as a transvestite, a word Jenn would use, even though now I would use the term Drag Queen—but that is not a term Jenn would use in 2004. And perhaps it is a word that will not be used in ten years. Language evolves.

Many people have told me they "just don't like Jenn," including some dear friends. I try not to take it too personally. I don't know if they realize that Jenn and I are very, very similar— it's just that her certainty is about values I don't share. She loves her children deeply and has built her life around them. She's scared she is losing them as they march toward adulthood and don't need her like they used to. At the start of the novel she has a very narrow view of what it means to be a good mother. I find it impressive she could make such a huge shift in her core values in only five months, though she is infuriating along the way.

We live in a time of deep polarization and disrespect. I hope this story does something to open hearts and minds so that we may have more compassion and grace for ourselves and one another.

I appreciate hearing from readers, so please reach out through my website, Facebook or Instagram if you have a reaction or feedback you would like to share with me.

Best wishes

Laila

KEEP IN TOUCH WITH THE AUTHOR

www.lailaibrahim.com

📘 facebook.com/lailaibrahim.author
📷 instagram.com/ldibrahim

ACKNOWLEDGMENTS

Everyone at Storm Publishing for bringing this story into the world: Claire Bord, Alexandra Holmes, Anna McKerrow, Oliver Rhodes, Naomi Knox, Elke Desanghere, and Chris Lucraft, the copyeditor Amanda Rutter and proofreader Maureen Cox.

My agent Annelise Robey at Jane Rotrosen Agency.

The wonderful people who read early drafts and helped me know where I was missing, and hitting, the mark: Sheri Prud'homme, Rinda Bartley, Darlanne Hoctor Mulmat, Andrea Goss, Em Kianka, Linda Hodges, Skot Davis, Dan Goss, Kathy Post, Carmen Tomaš, Lauren Poole, Candace Kearns Read, Katrina Ford, Sandy Grayson, Gogi Hodder, Margie Biblin, Cathy Barton, Emma Delp, Anne Delp, Heather MacCleod, Susi Jensen, Lori Freedman, Hannah Freedman Tsveli, Wendy Davis, Karen Scott, Cile Beatty, Jeffrey Dickemann, Rachel Ibrahim, Sarah Prud'homme, Kateri Carmola, Aria Killebrew-Bruehl, Melissa Levine, and Sophia Killebrew-Bruehl.

The coming-of-agers at UU Oakland who challenged me to put their ideas in the story: Aria Killebrew-Bruehl (pigeon), Ella Jeffries (penny), Eliana Thompson (LEGO), Lydia Macy (sperm whale), Sara Leyser (spelling), Sophia Killebrew-Bruehl (dragonfly), and Wynnie Savageford (dog).

Deborah Cuny for sharing some of her painful and hopeful story with me.

Ori Tsveli for advice about medical issues.

Lorie Strelo for information about Dublin history.

Chris Williams for track and field information.

Catherine Shore and Andrew Shore for the NALT video.

Howie Severson and Diana Rosinus for the original cover.

Brian Brackney for years of friendship.

Kelly Kist for her dedication to my novels.

Tiffany Yates Martin for kind, insightful, and honest professional feedback.

Joel (I wish I knew your last name) for awesome editing.

Jennifer (I wish I knew your last name) for awesome editing AND letting me know you liked this manuscript.

Hannah Eller-Isaacs, Ottilia Schafer, Marcus Liefert, and Sasha Hood for historic technology info.

Sam Ames for work to end conversion therapy.

Skot Davis, Dana Forsberg, and Sheri Prud'homme for writing retreats.

Terry Goodman for taking my work to a whole other level.

The amazing family when I first wrote Living Right: Maya, Kalin, and Rinda. Down to the ground and up to the sky.

And my growing family that now includes Remy, Mitch, Maggie, Wynnie and Hazel.

AFTER THE RAIN DISCUSSION QUESTIONS

1. Has there been any situation that challenged your core beliefs? How did you respond?
2. Is there anything you care so much about that you might join a protest or write a letter to the editor?
3. Did you identify more with Jenn, Josh, Sara, or some other character? Why?
4. Who was your favorite character?
5. Did your feelings about Jenn change throughout the story? In what ways?
6. Jenn's physical location changes in the story, starting from her home and ending on a public street. What are other examples of that change, and how does the physical location add to the story?
7. Does this story parallel your life in any way? What did it feel like to read about this situation?
8. *After the Rain* explores a major controversy in our society. In what ways does this book expand your understanding of the issues?
9. In *After the Rain* Laila Ibrahim explores the theme of children growing up to be different than their

parents expected. Did she succeed in making this a universal story of parenting adolescents?

10. Did you find yourself especially angry, sad, or hopeful in any scenes?

Printed in Great Britain
by Amazon

41541349R00172